THE DAY OF THE LORD

GLEN E. DERICKSON

WESTBOW
PRESS®
A DIVISION OF THOMAS NELSON
& ZONDERVAN

WestBow Press books may be ordered through booksellers or by contacting:

WestBow Press
A Division of Thomas Nelson & Zondervan
1663 Liberty Drive
Bloomington, IN 47403
www.westbowpress.com
1 (866) 928-1240

ISBN: 978-1-9736-3359-4 (sc)
ISBN: 978-1-9736-3358-7 (e)

Print information available on the last page.

WestBow Press rev. date: 7/20/2018

TABLE OF CONTENTS

Chapter	Title	Page
	Introduction	vii

Part One — Tribulation

Chapter	Title	Page
I	Tribulation Saints	1
II	One Hundred and Forty-four Thousand	45
III	The Seventh Seal	57
IV	First Trumpet Judgment	67
V	Second Trumpet Judgment	89
VI	Third Trumpet Judgment	104
VII	Fourth Trumpet Judgment	118
VIII	Fifth Trumpet Judgment (First Woe)	133
IX	Sixth Trumpet Judgment (Second Woe)	156
X	Seventh Trumpet Judgment (Third Woe) And Four Vial Judgments	163
XI	Three Vials of Judgment and Armageddon	167

Part Two — The Millennium

XII	Saint Robert Rayburn	175
XIII	A Family Reunion	191
XIV	The Israel Adventure	209
XV	Beulah Land	231
XVI	Return to Richmond	241
	Epilogue	257

INTRODUCTION

Jesus Christ opened the sixth seal and then raptured the church. The "Day of the Lord" immediately follows.

Eighteen year old Tim Bailey, the youngest son of John and Ellen Bailey, finds himself left on earth as his entire family disappeared in the blink of an eye when they rose to meet Jesus in the air.

Tim will experience the remaining years of the tribulation in all the horror and challenges following the opening of the seventh seal, and the outpouring of God's judgments and wrath upon the world. He will join up with the Mercer family whom his family had met several months ago in a cave system in Powell County, southeast of his home in Breton, Kentucky.

Many will come to know Jesus Christ as savior. Many of these new Christians shall become martyrs for their Lord's sake. Evil will run rampant on the earth even as God's wrath is poured out. Most of the people who survive year after year will remain defiant toward God until there are none left who will seek God's salvation.

Life on earth will become progressively worse when the seventh seal is opened and the judgments continue until God decides, "Enough." "Vengeance is mine, I will repay," saith the Lord."

The somewhat isolated people in Eastern Kentucky

strive for some semblance of a normal life while other pockets of humanity around the world do the same.

The hub and wheel of world activities centers on the European continent and spreads out into Asia Minor, and the Middle East. Almost ignored during the great war; after the first few days, the tiny nation of Israel remains the center and focus of God's attention as He works His will in punishment and restoration of His chosen people.

Satan, working through the self-proclaimed world leader (anti-Christ), also has Israel as the center and focus of his attention with the intent of the total destruction of God's chosen people.

The World Leader and his minions continue their efforts in bringing the entire world under subjection and stamping out all vestiges of the worship of Almighty God, not knowing the futility of their efforts. Much of the world, such as the North and South American continents, Far East, and Pacific nations, are somewhat ignored, initially, as the anti-Christ attempts to gain control.

God and satan will play out the great struggles between good and evil, primarily in the countries that were prominent in Old Testament times and through the Middle Ages. However, no enemy of God anywhere on the face of the earth escapes His wrath.

In the beginning, the Spirit of God hovered over the earth as He brought His creation into being. During the centuries which followed, God made His presence known to man, and intervened from time to time either to rescue or punish as He saw fit. God sent his son, Jesus, to die for the sins of man as a supreme act of love and sacrifice.

Undoubtedly, the Spirit of God continues to hover

over the earth as He pours out His divine wrath on those whom He will, and rescues and saves those whom He will. Refinement is underway as God removes the dross and moves to restore the world.

Satan, the one who challenged God's authority and rule, loses the great battle waged in heaven as he fights Michael, the arch angel, and will lose again as he attempts to destroy Israel and the Jews. Simultaneously, God deals with Jew and Gentile alike as he pours out His wrath and judgment against sinful, rebellious, and evil people, and shows mercy still to those who would seek Him.

This story will end during the first decade of the millennial reign of Jesus Christ, The Lion of Judah, who will rule with a rod of iron and bring order and peace.

Tim will show great faith and courage as he meets challenge after challenge leading up to the battle of Armageddon and the end of the age. During the first part of the millennium, he and his young family will join multitudes of new Christians as they work under the authority of Jesus Christ and the priesthood of believers in the restoration of Israel and the world.

PART ONE

TRIBULATION

CHAPTER I
TRIBULATION SAINTS

Revelation 6:12-17: "And I beheld when he had opened the sixth seal, and, lo, there was a great earthquake; and the sun became black as sackcloth of hair, and the moon became as blood; And the stars of heaven fell unto the earth, even as a fig tree casteth her untimely figs, when she is shaken of a mighty wind. And the heavens departed as a scroll when it is rolled together, and every mountain and island were moved out of their places.

And the kings of the earth, and the great men, and the rich men, and the chief captains, and the mighty men, and every bondsman, and every free man, hid themselves in the dens and in the rocks of the mountains; And said to the mountains and rocks, Fall on us, and hide us from the face of him that sitteth on the throne, and from the wrath of the Lamb: For the great day of his wrath is come; and who shall be able to stand?"

Revelation 7:9-14 "After this I beheld, and lo, a great multitude, which no man could number, of all nations, and kindreds, and people, and tongues, stood before the throne, and before the Lamb, clothed with white robes, and palms in their hands; And cried with a loud voice, saying, Salvation to

1

our God which sitteth upon the throne, and unto the Lamb. And all the angels stood round about the throne, and about the elders and the four beasts, and fell before the throne on their faces, and worshipped God, Saying, Amen; Blessing and glory, and wisdom, and thanksgiving, and honour, and power, and might, be unto our God for ever and ever, Amen.

And one of the elders answered, saying unto me, What are these which are arrayed in white robes? And whence came they? And I said unto him, Sir, thou knowest. And he said to me, These are they which came out of great tribulation, and have washed their robes, and made them white in the blood of the Lamb."

A week after returning from Richmond, John and Ellen Bailey walked out of the house at 8:00 a.m. holding hands, to take a stroll around the front yard. They often did this early in the morning just for the pleasure of quiet time in each other's company.

Helen asked, "John, what's different? Look at the sky. Look at the billowing white clouds. Look at the sun and the surrounding atmosphere. It's absolutely beautiful! It's surreal!"

John remarked, "Helen, wait right here. I'm going to get the rest of the family out here so they can enjoy the view."

Soon, John had the rest of the family out in the yard to enjoy the scene. Looking to the east, they could see a dove sitting on top of a statue of Jesus Christ in the Breton Memorial cemetery.

The earth began to tremble. The trembling soon became a shake. As the shaking increased, a rumbling noise could be heard and increasing as the shaking increased.

Ruth pointed to the west. "The moon is turning red."

Jesse exclaimed. "Look at the sun. It is getting dark and it seems twilight is coming back!"

As they watched, the moon became more blood red and the sun became darker and darker. The quaking of the earth became more violent. Terror began to steal upon them.

John spoke loudly to be heard above the increasing noise. "Let's all get in a circle and hold hands and pray." John prayed and gave thanks to God for the glory of God, the providence of God, and God's love for all his family, and for sending Jesus Christ down to be their savior, and for saving them all from the horrors that had come upon the earth in the past few months.

They all stood in a circle, holding hands, with heads bowed. John told them, "Look up and watch for Jesus!" They all looked up.

Suddenly, Jesus Christ appeared in the billowing clouds in all His glory. The sky lit up in Shekinah Glory. All the surrounding earth stood out in brilliant relief.

The blood red moon and the black sun could still be seen, but had no effect on the surrounding light. The quaking and the noise subsided.

As they stood, holding hands and looking up, they heard the trumpet pealing out. They saw Jesus Christ coming down from the clouds closer to the earth in power and great glory! Looking to the east, they saw hundreds of transformed bodies rising from the graves and ascending into the sky in the twinkling of an eye.

They immediately felt the change as their bodies transformed from corruptible to incorruptible, and they rose in the twinkling of an eye and met Jesus Christ in the air!

Tim had been holding hands with the rest of the family

as they stood in a circle. He saw the billowing clouds, the red moon, and the darkened sun. He saw an image of a person in the clouds; he heard mutterings as of someone speaking.

Suddenly, Tim stood alone in his front yard and all of his family had disappeared. He was absolutely terrified. He looked about frantically for his family. They were not to be seen. Trixie, standing at Tim's side, looked up at him and whimpered. The sky again darkened, and the red moon shone eerily as the sun became darker. The earth began to shake more violently, and cracking and rumbling noises became louder.

Tim suddenly realized what had happened. He had missed the mark. He had not surrendered his heart and life to the Lord; had never been born again, and as a result, had missed heaven. Tim immediately fell to his knees in full repentance, petitioned God for mercy and salvation, and became one of the first of the Tribulation Saints who would occupy the earth during the remainder of the tribulation and beyond, if he survived.

There was great rejoicing in heaven as Tim was born again!

Tim had mixed feelings. He missed his family, but at the same time, he rejoiced, knowing they were in heaven. He also rejoiced that he had surrendered his life to God and would someday join his family in heaven. As all these thoughts and emotions coursed through his mind and body, he also experienced the rising tumult of the earth around him. Tim had no way of knowing it, but the shaking of the earth and the upheaval in the sun, the moon, and the stars, encompassed the entire earth. The terrifying shaking, booming, and cracking noises, darkness, and flashings across the sky, would have been overwhelming if not for the fact that he knew he was now a child of God and totally within His care.

Old fault lines, which had lain dormant for centuries, suddenly began to crack and open up. South of Tim, the fault line that ran from Western Kentucky, through Eastern Kentucky, and into West Virginia, cracked and opened in several places. In Powell County, the fault line opened a gaping slash just north of Furnace, on Furnace Mountain. A significant split continued, passing just south of Natural Bridge State Park, and on across the Red River Gorge, crossing Swift's Camp Creek just south of Rock Bridge.

The New Madrid fault line affecting Tennessee, Missouri, and six or seven other states including Kentucky, became intensely active resulting in massive upheavals, trembling, and shaking the hills and mountains, all of which directly affected the earth around Tim.

Along the Pacific coast, the San Andreas Fault began mighty upheavals causing a section of the west coast, beginning at San Francisco and moving north, to slide away and disappear into the depths of the Pacific Ocean. Mount Saint Helens exploded and spewed smoke, ashes and lava; more intense than the 1980 eruption.

Alaska, which normally felt more than ten thousand earthquakes annually, suddenly quaked and shook almost continually, with several massive upheavals taking place. Dozens of the more than 100 volcanoes became active. The Pavlov volcano which had erupted in 2016, suddenly spewed forth lava and ashes, obscuring the skies for hundreds of square miles.

The opening of old fault lines was occurring all around

the world; and in some cases, opened cracks to great depths, allowing lava to spill forth.

The caldera under Yellowstone National Park became active, and spewed forth from several areas besides the existing geysers and pools. A full eruption would be catastrophic.

Volcanic eruptions around the world threatened to pollute the atmosphere to the point of bringing on another artificial winter.

Truly, nothing of this magnitude had occurred since the outpouring of God's wrath at the time of the flood. Mankind trembled and quaked, as the earth trembled and quaked. Many people died from fear and quaking and failing hearts. Mankind finally acknowledged, "Truly, this is the Wrath of God!"

Alone, and scared by all the events happening around him, Tim prayed to God for strength and courage to see him through it all.

Night would soon be coming on and Tim was afraid to stay in the house because of the earthquakes and upheavals. He went inside and quickly collected bedding and some food and water. Trixie kept at Tim's heels as he carried the bedding and other materials to his campsite in the middle of the yard. He was afraid to camp under the trees for some of them were still whipping and swaying in an alarming way. Tim slept little that night.

Throughout the world, entire mountain chains were going through upheaval with rocks breaking away and tumbling down the mountainsides. Mountains and caves were not a good place to hide as caves collapsed and rocks rolled and bounded and crashed against other rocks. After twenty-four hours, the turmoil in the heavenly elements began to subside, and, consequently, the earthquakes, roaring, rumbling, and shaking, became less frequent and less intense.

Although still apprehensive and stressed, Tim began to breathe easier. As a relative degree of calmness returned, he began giving thought to returning to the house. However, waves of tremors and shaking continued on through the day and into the night. Although the activities were less severe, Tim decided to stay outside one more night.

By mid afternoon of the second day, Tim made the decision and moved back into the house. Although still tired and still stressed from all the nerve wracking experiences of the last three days, he first sought out his father's Bible. He thought, *Never again will I be so careless and thoughtless to the teachings of God's word.*

The people of the earth were beginning to figure things out. Perhaps they could explain away all the wars, starvation, pestilence and persecution of Christians as either man-made or nature related, or something else explainable. However, they had to face the reality that what was now happening was the pure, unadulterated wrath of the Almighty God!

All over the world, millions of people who were "almost persuaded" when the Holy Spirit of God had wooed their spirit in times past, suddenly were again convicted of their rebellion and sins against God and their rejection of Jesus Christ as savior.

During and immediately after the cataclysmic events which occurred after the opening of the sixth seal, millions of those convicted souls surrendered their lives to Jesus Christ as their Lord and Savior and to God the Father. Millions joined the growing number of the Tribulation Saints. Sadly, many millions more who came under conviction still rejected the wooing and drawing of the Holy Spirit.

Sadly, millions more, who would have been saved if they had lived through the events of the past two or three years, lost their lives to the nuclear war, starvation, and pestilence, and the upheavals of the past two days. SAD! So many were lost and gone to hell because they waited too long.

Tim, restless, wandered aimlessly around the house, and then went into the shelter and looked around. Finding nothing of great interest, he went back to the house and began working with the radios to see if he could get them to function and find out anything. Finally, he gave up on that and just sat down and stopped.

I need to pull myself together and do some planning, he thought. He dug out a sheet of paper and a pen and began jotting down notes: (1) Try to get some of the radios to work and see what's happening in the rest of the world. (2) Check on food and water supplies and think about survival needs. (3) Do some long range planning. Stay here? Go to Richmond? Go to Cave City? Go to the Mercers? Go someplace else?

Tim finally got the radios powered up and spent about an hour tuning the receivers to different frequencies but never picked up any meaningful transmissions. Some of them were intelligible but were mostly meaningless chatter. Some of them were in foreign languages and un-intelligible to him.

Tim finally gave up on the radios for the time being and went back outside and started checking the two vehicles in the driveway. Neither had a key left in them. He went back inside the house and searched, but didn't find them. Tim then went to the vicinity where the family had disappeared. He found the two sets of keys in the trouser pockets of Bob and his dad. Tim gathered up all the family's clothing and took them in the house.

Tim went back outside and opened the door of his dad's pickup for Trixie to jump in. He got settled in the driver's seat, placed the key in the ignition, and then started the truck. It seemed to run just fine. The gas tank registered three fourths full. He drove the truck down the lane, turned onto the road, and drove two miles toward Breton. He turned the truck around and then drove back home. Getting out of the truck, Tim began looking around and finally found six five gallon gas cans. All of them were full.

Seeing that his immediate need for transportation was available, Tim decided to see if he could locate the Mercers. He had no way of knowing if they had been raptured or not. However, in thinking back, he didn't recall any conversations pertaining to church or any other subjects related to Christianity when they had visited the Mercers a few months ago. Tim's impression of the family was that they were very nice people, but he had no way of knowing if they had been Christian or not. He pondered the rest of that day on just what to do next.

As Tim spent more time reflecting on the trip he and his brothers had made, he began to get more excited as he recalled his interaction with Pamela, Alvin and Paula Mercer's daughter. The decision then became easy. He would visit the Mercers!

Over the next few hours, he collected food, cans of gasoline, clothing, a rifle, a pistol, extra ammunition, and everything else he thought he might need for the trip. He also took the Geiger counter. Tim was limited in what he could take, and knew that if he decided to move permanently, he would need to come back and salvage what he could. He took his father's Bible, a few pictures and other family items, that were precious to his memories, in the event he never came back.

Finally, with everything packed, he secured the shelter, disguised the entrance, and then went to spend the night in the house. Trixie had followed Tim faithfully throughout the day sensing something unusual was about to happen. Trixie had been an outside dog, but tonight she was invited in and curled up on the carpet at the foot of Tim's bed.

The trip from home to the top of Morris Mountain was uneventful, although somewhat spooky. The lack of human or animal life except for insects, occasional segments of broken pavement, accumulations of trash along roadways, and occasional animal skeletons was enough to give a person the creeps. The loneliness was overwhelming.

Tim stopped off in Stanton and looked around. The town was deathly still and silent. He drove around the court house square and then up Maple street. At one place to the left, there was an abandoned pizza place. Across the street from it was a bare lot where a house and old garage once sat. It formerly had a nice looking paw paw tree on the corner, which was now missing.

Trixie stood on the seat with forepaws on the dash most of the trip. Tim was glad to have Trixie with him on the otherwise dismal journey.

Finally, after wending and winding, and sometimes backtracking to get around obstacles, they arrived at the top of Morris Mountain. After parking in the most secluded place he could find, Tim dismounted and began collecting food, water, the rifle, and other items, needed for the trip to the cave. "Come on Trixie, let's go."

Trixie trotted on ahead, seeming to know the way. They weren't challenged until they were quite close to the cave system. "Halt!"

Tim replied, "It's me, Tim Bailey. Are you one of the Mercers?"

"Yes it is," James replied. "Come on over."

Tim walked down the trail until he met up with James. He laid the rifle down and then shook his hand.

James asked, "What brings you up here Tim?"

Tim replied, "My family all disappeared at the time of all the earthquakes and the other things going on in the sky with the moon and the sun. I'm sure that they were taken up to heaven by the Lord and I was left down here all by myself."

"We lost two of our family the same way," James replied. "I'm sure it was what they called the rapture, where Jesus came down from the sky to take all Christians to heaven. Some of us just weren't ready at the time."

James continued, "Come on and let's go on down to our home and meet the rest of the family. I'm sure they'll all like to see you and get some information from the rest of the world."

They wended their way down the trail and shortly arrived at the entrance to the cave system. Tim spoke up, "James, Trixie is an outside dog and I wonder if there's somewhere she can stay?"

James replied, "Sure thing, Tim. We'll fix her a bed in our wood shed for the time being." They took Trixie over to the shed and got her settled in.

James led Tim over to the cave entrance. They worked

their way on back through the different passages and entered the living area.

"Tim, things have changed quite a bit since you were here last. Alvin, Rhonda and their family don't live here anymore. They moved into a farm house about a mile from here down close to a creek. My family is staying here in the caves so we can protect it and also have it available if we need to take shelter again. I have a detection system set up so we can monitor all the trails coming in and we don't have to stay out there on guard all the time."

James continued, "We had a pretty scary time during all the earthquakes. Part of our cave system collapsed. Fortunately, it wasn't in the living area."

James asked Tim, "What can you tell us about what's going on in the rest of the world?"

Tim replied, "Practically nothing. I had absolutely no contact except with family and with the few people at Cave City and Richmond. After the family left, I tried to get information from the radios but really didn't learn anything. Whatever you can tell will be that much more than I know."

"I'll fill you in as much as I can," James replied. "We still have radio contact with several sources in this country and around the world. There's a station in Switzerland that seems to have some pretty reliable sources. They give out what seems to be the most accurate and believable information. We're also able to pick up broadcasts from a few news stations in this country. How much of the information is factual and true is anybody's guess.

"From sorting through all the reports, it seems the United States suffered by far, the greatest damage from the nuclear war than any other nation on earth. When push came to shove, all the hype and bluster from our government about rebuilding our military, renovating and increasing our nuclear capability, and becoming again the most fearsome nation on the face of the earth was just that, hype and bluster. Although we had one president who really tried and had significant success, he couldn't overcome the decades of decline and decay of the nation militarily, morally and materially, since Reagan.

"We have had reports of a national government and demands that we move to assembly locations, but so far we haven't seen any evidence or heard any news that indicates there's any substance to it. This country has, apparently, been so badly damaged that the rising One World Government centered in the old world nations isn't paying much attention to this part of the world. That has its good points.

"Just as some order was being restored in some parts of the country and skies were beginning to clear from all the dust and fallout from the nuclear war, we were hit by the tremendous earthquakes, volcanoes erupting, ash, smoke, and such, and now we're living in perpetual haze again. Although it does seem to be clearing up, I'm beginning to wonder if we'll ever be able to raise crops and food.

"Reports coming out of Europe and the Middle East indicate a much more advanced recovery and a very strict dictatorial government set out to rule the entire world."

Tim spoke up. "Dad was absolutely sure we're at the end times. The disappearing of all Christians pretty well bears that out. I've started studying the Bible to see if there's any way we can predict what may be coming next."

James replied, "The way I see it, about all we can do is try to survive. Food is going to be our primary concern. So far, we haven't seen any signs of outside interference. We're staying as vigilant and prepared as we can. We haven't had any way to check for radioactivity, but we assume it must be OK by now."

Tim replied, "I brought my Geiger counter and everything I've checked looks good."

James continued, "Tim, after you and your brothers were here last time, Alvin and I and our families talked quite a bit about the idea of getting your family to join ours. We were all 100 percent in agreement and excited about the possibility. On the basis of that, I can say that you are welcome to stay here and cast your lot with us. We have no way of knowing what the future holds, but you being here would be a great help to us and, hopefully, to you also."

Tim replied with emotion, "Thanks a lot James. I appreciate your thoughts and your kindness. I've been lonesome and depressed since I lost my family and have been thinking about the possibility of joining with you and Alvin and your families. I will accept that offer."

James reached over and shook Tim's hand. "Come on Tim. We'll go tell the rest of the family."

They went into the room where James' family was gathered and he announced, "I invited Tim to move in with us, and he's accepted."

James' wife, Paula, David, Tiffany, and Ron, got up and gathered around Tim. They held his hands, placed their arms around him, and let him know without doubt he was welcome.

After a time, Tim approached James and broached the subject of all the material and equipment back at his home in

Breton. They tentatively agreed they needed to make a trip within the next few days to salvage what they could.

"Tim, before we make the trip back to Breton, I'd like to bring you up to date on all that's going on around us that has a bearing on how we're living now and how we will probably live in the future. We'll get together with Alvin and his family and give you some idea of our thinking. We have some pretty sound information that quite a few settlements are developing throughout the United States. Some of them are located in former city suburbs. Some are in small towns that weren't destroyed; some are small colonies or clusters of people that have just sprung up and banded together for mutual protection, survival, support, and association."

James continued, "Just don't expect to find millions of people in this country. It's more likely tens or hundreds of thousands. We have no way of knowing."

James went on to explain, "There was a lot of anarchy and mayhem during and immediately following the war, but these settlements have formed their own governments and elected their own law enforcement. The anarchists and outlaws have been depleted to where they aren't as much of a threat as they were. Most of them have died off because of the exposure to radiation, starvation, and disease."

Tim replied, "That sounds encouraging, knowing there are more people out there. There where I lived, we were completely isolated. We had to travel to places like Richmond and Cave City to see very many people."

"We are actually quite isolated here," James replied. "This is one of the things we'll need to consider in our future plans. We'll have to decide whether to stay here or move to a location where there are more people. I'll really hate to leave here, for we have quite a few assets we would have to leave behind."

James continued, "It's been over two years now since the war started, and we're just now beginning to see our way clear for possible survival if something else doesn't happen. We'll be interacting with a lot of individuals and settlements in the future. Much of our supplies will be obtained by bartering instead of using money. You'll be surprised to find out how much we have going for us. In the morning, I'll take you on a tour."

The Mercer family went about their routine activities for the remainder of the day. Following the evening meal, they spread out, and were soon reading books, working puzzles, or working on other projects they had going.

James went to their communications room to contact Alvin. Part of their communication setup included a UHF base station with six hand held transceivers. The system could communicate up to twenty miles as long as it was line of sight. The hand held units were equipped with rechargeable batteries. In addition to the batteries in the units, they had six spares that were rechargeable, either from a 120 volt ac charger or from an adapter attached to a 12 volt dc source.

Alvin powered up the UHF transmitter, keyed the mike, and spoke: "Station two, do you read me?'

About thirty seconds later, Pamela, Rhonda and Alvin's youngest daughter, replied, "I read you loud and clear, over."

James continued, "Pamela, let everybody know we have company. Tim Bailey came last night and will be staying with us for the foreseeable future. Is Alvin or Rhonda handy?"

Pamela replied, "Mom and dad are right here and have heard you. Go ahead."

"Alvin, if it's alright with you and Rhonda, we'll all come down and visit for awhile and bring Tim with us."

Rhonda replied, ""Let me talk to Paula. We may want to go ahead and have lunch together. In fact, we may want to do supper also."

Paula, who had heard James in the other room and walked in to listen in on the conversation, replied, "Sounds good to me, Rhonda. What would you like for me to bring?"

James and Alvin signed off and left their wives on the radio planning lunch.

Next morning, James' family got ready to go down the hill. David, Tiffany, and Ron asked their mom if they could ride their bicycles.

Paula replied, "Not today. I have things for each of you to carry, and I don't want our lunch and supper scattered all over the hillside. Anyhow, you know you have to push them all the way back up again."

"Aw mom!" was their disappointed response.

"Tim, I would like for you to carry a rifle," James requested. "We never go anywhere without guns." James and Tim went back to the armory. James handed Tim a rifle, donned a pistol belt with holster, an automatic, and two pouches of ammunition. He picked up another rifle and led the way to the trail.

They started down the hill. After a quarter mile on the dirt and rock road, they came to an opening in the trees that led into a fairly level field of about four acres. The field, on the south side of Morris Mountain, faced east where it got the early morning sun.

James spoke up. "Paula, take the kids on down to the

farm. I'm going to stop here with Tim and show him what we have at this location."

The road entering the field was a single lane but wide enough for trucks, cars, and farm equipment to travel. It went across, approximately through the middle, and then started downhill back into the woods.

A chicken house with a fenced-in enclosure was located just to the left as they entered the field. It had an eight foot high, welded wire fence all the way around with welded wire fabric over the top. Six inches out from the bottom of the fence and eight inches high, a single wire was fastened to insulators on a pipe extended out from each post.

"Don't touch that wire!" Jim cautioned. "That's an electric fence. We were fortunate enough to find several solar powered fence chargers and miles of electric fence wire at one of the abandoned farm supply stores. Without this we would never be able to keep out the 'coons, foxes, coyotes, and other predators. Fortunately, we found all sorts of other fencing material as well."

Jim pointed out the water supply. "This pipe comes from a spring not too far from the cave. There's a thousand gallon concrete tank up there where it comes out of the spring. We have piping that runs from there, down past all of our barns, pens, etc, and then to the farm house. It's really good spring water."

Just inside the chicken enclosure was a watering trough. A two inch plastic pipe, coming down the hill and out of the woods, attached to the trough and ended at a valve. A piece of pipe attached to the valve connected to a float valve on the side of the trough.

"We have a lot of fun in the winter time, draining pipes,

etc at the right time to keep everything from freezing up. Freezing the water lines would be a disaster. With all the tanks filled up, we can go several days with the pipes empty." He continued.

To one side of the chicken house and chicken yard was a shed that housed a half-dozen metal garbage cans that contained the chicken feed. Down on the far end of the field, on the left (east) side of the road, was the pig pen. The pig pen was sturdily constructed with a pig house on the south side. The pen itself was constructed of wire panels connected together between sturdy posts. The building had a door on the south side for entry for feeding, and the storing of feed and equipment.

A water pipe ran along the south side of the field, went under the road, and then over to supply the hog area.

Another solar powered electric fence charger was used to power electric fencing at the bottom outer perimeter of the pen and also across the top of the fence itself. Predators would definitely have to work to get access to the hogs.

"Let's go on down to the farm." James said. "You'll be surprised at what we've done and have accumulated. Fortunately, we're very isolated and so far, haven't had any problem with prowlers. We have had a few people show up, but none of them have caused any trouble."

James led off, and soon, they came back out of the woods into an open field. The road ran past a good sized barn and then toward the farm house. The road went to the left of the farm house, back into some more woods, and out of sight. "We'll go to the house now and I'll show you the barn and all the other surroundings later," James said.

Going into the house, it took only a few minutes of

exchanging greetings until Pamela singled out Tim. They found an unoccupied corner of the room and began bringing each other up to date on their lives since they had last met. Tim had some difficulty controlling his emotions as he explained to Pamela the disappearance of his family and his subsequent surrender to the Lord Jesus Christ.

Pamela was very moved by Tim's story. "Tim, as soon as we have time, I would like for you to read the Bible with me and help me understand about God and Christianity and becoming a Christian. I've heard some about it but really don't understand."

Tim replied, "Pamela, I'm ashamed to admit I never paid too much attention to what I had been taught at home and in church. After my family disappeared, I suddenly woke up to the truth. I'm not that knowledgeable as to what the Bible teaches, but we can study together. Maybe others in your families can help us."

Tim and Pamela spent the rest of the morning together. They left the house and Pamela took Tim on a grand tour about the place and showed him everything except the barn area.

"Tim, I don't know all that much about what is going on at the barn, so I'll let dad or Uncle James explain it all to you. I'll take you now and show you the orchard. We have a good selection of apple, pear, cherry, pawpaw, and grapes. Most of them were already here when we moved in. It's a good thing, for newly planted trees take years sometimes before they start bearing," Pamela explained.

They heard the ringing of the bell at the house. "It's lunch time!" Pamela exclaimed and led off at a more rapid pace toward the house.

Following lunch, James and Alvin, accompanied by Tim, David, and Herbert, went out to the barn. The area in front of the barn was open. The barn was two stories high and double doors opened into the loft area. At ground level, other double doors opened into the barn.

To the left side of the barn was the corral. One end of it was attached to the barn, with a door giving access to the stall area. The corral was 50X70 feet with two gates. One gate opened into the open area in front of the barn, and the other gate opened into a pasture east of the barn. Horses and cattle grazed in the pasture.

Tim exclaimed, "Wow! I had no idea you would have this many animals!"

Alvin commented, "We started out with just a few but we worked hard the past two years to grow our herds."

To the right of the barn there was a lean–to shed with six tractors and two buggies sitting in a row. They all looked fairly new. Behind the barn was another lean-to shed with a row of twelve fuel tanks setting on concrete block supports. Alvin explained. "We figured out early on that gasoline would disappear quickly, and we got the bright idea that there might be enough diesel fuel being left behind so we could collect it for farming and that a few small tractors might be useful for small, local hauls. Here again, they may be useful for barter."

Alvin responded, "At first we didn't have anything except a few chickens and pigs. Over time though, we've scoured the countryside, collecting everything we could find in the way of animals, equipment and supplies. In the beginning, fuel was fairly plentiful, and we were able to tow a trailer and pick up quite a bit. Just wait until you see inside the barn!"

The barn was full of quite an assortment of materials

and equipment. "I won't try to tell you all that we have in here, but it's a lot. We also have food stashed in different locations. Most of it is in the cave system," James explained.

In one end of the barn there were at least thirty bicycles. Piled in the corner was an assortment of spare bicycle wheels, tires, and other parts. "Why do you have so many bicycles?" Tim asked.

"Bartering materials," Alvin responded. "As time goes by, transportation will become more and more of a problem."

One Amish buggy and one farm wagon were also just inside the double doors.

"We also have one other barn not far from here. It's down just past the creek. It contains two farm wagons, two more Amish buggies, and a few farm implements. We won't try to make it down there today." Alvin stated. "We'll come back down here tomorrow and I'll show you the rest of the place."

"Well, now that you've seen our barn area, we'll go back to the house, visit some more, and call it a day." Alvin said, and led the way back to the house.

Tim paired off with Pamela, and they found an unoccupied area where they could spend time together and become better acquainted. Anybody who was paying attention could see they were quite interested in each other.

Suppertime came, and they all gathered around the table. Paula and Rhonda, with the help of Rachael and Pamela, had prepared the meal, set the table, poured drinks, and had everything ready. Once they were all around the table, Alvin spoke up. "Tim, none of us grew up around people who claimed to be Christian and up to now we can't say we are Christians, but from what we're learning, we're looking in that direction. Having said all of that; would you mind saying grace?"

Tim, somewhat flustered and confused, replied, "Sure, I'll be glad to. Dad always asked the blessing at our house, but I heard it enough times; I think I can do it."

They all bowed their heads, and Tim prayed, "God, will you bless this food and help us all to learn more about you. Amen." They all began eating, and for a few minutes all were subdued and silent. Soon, they were all back to normal, finished their meals, and then began preparing to settle down for the evening.

A half hour before dark James called out to his family, "Time to head back up the hill before it gets too dark." Tim said his goodbye to Pamela, and soon they were all walking briskly up the hill and toward the cave.

After arriving back at the cave, they all sat around and talked. Tim and James discussed their plans for the next day, their trip back to Tim's place, and some potential activities in the following days and weeks.

At 9:00 p.m. James announced: "Bed time."

All activities immediately began winding down, and at 9:15 all were in bed, with the lights out.

At 6:00 a.m. the next morning the lights came back on. Following thirty minutes of activities, all the Mercers were settling down and waiting for the next momentous event: the call to breakfast. Following breakfast, each of them set out on their scheduled activities for the day.

"Tim, let's go back to our armory and pick up some weapons and equipment and then I'll take you on a grand tour of our place and some of the surrounding countryside." James went to the back corner of the cave with Tim following.

They each belted on a holster with a pistol and extra ammunition in pockets on the belt. James picked up a satchel containing extra ammunition, binoculars, and first aid kit. James handed Tim a semi-automatic long gun and picked up another one for himself. He handed Tim a satchel with two loaded clips and two extra boxes of ammunition, one box for the automatic sidearm, and one box for the long gun.

They went back through the kitchen, filled their canteens, and picked up a lunch that had been prepared for them and left on the table.

As they went out the door, James spoke. "Tim, let's grab a bicycle for this trip. By the time we get back, we will have traveled about five or six miles."

They got on the bicycles and headed over the hill. Four hundred yards down the hill, they turned down a path to the left and then angled back up toward the cliff line. They entered a relatively flat, grassy area and stopped next to a concrete tank imbedded on a slight slope just below a flowing spring. Flowers had been planted in and around the open area, giving it a really beautiful appearance.

"We made this into our flower garden, James remarked. "It's too shady to grow vegetables. The flowers here and around Alvin and Rhonda's house are Pamela's project."

James explained to Tim the spring and tank setup, with all the associated piping. A 2,000 gallon tank was imbedded in the earth with the upper wall level barely above ground. The bottom of the tank at the lower end was slightly below the surface. A four inch pipe stuck out of the tank six inches above the bottom of the tank. A four inch shutoff valve was next to the tank and a four inch excess flow valve was just downstream of that. Piping out of that valve turned down and went underground. Blanketing and insulation were available in a waterproof drum, when needed.

James got back on his bike, and with Tim following, went back to the main trail and down the hill toward the farm. Going to the farm house, they met Alvin out front. After greetings were exchanged, Alvin got on his bicycle and the three of them went to the barn.

Alvin led them across the corral and through the barn door that opened into the stall area. "Tim, here is where we keep the saddles, bridles, and all the other tack and harness we need for the horses, wagons and buggies."

"Tim, have you ever ridden horses?" James asked.

"Not really," replied Tim. "Father put me up on one at as neighbor's house once, but I've never ridden."

James replied, "You need to come down here and get one of our older children to help you learn. Three of our horses are gentle and broken to the saddle. The horses come in handy when we're trying to move cattle, check on cattle out in the pastures, and so forth."

"We are trying to get all the family involved in every aspect of tending to animals, growing gardens, tending bees, etc. It gives us a lot more flexibility in what we can do," Alvin explained.

"I'm more than willing to do whatever there is to be done," Tim replied.

"James, I'm going to let you and Tim go on to the other barn, the creek, etc and I'm going back to the house. There are a few things I need to be doing," Alvin advised.

James laughed and responded. "I'll go ahead and give Tim the grand tour."

James and Tim rode their bicycles back to the house and

got on the road that went to the other barn. James showed Tim the other two Amish buggies, two more farm wagons, and some farm implements. This barn also had quite an assortment of materials and equipment stored inside. In addition to the barn, there were two other roofed shelters with rolls of hay stored underneath.

"James, I notice you have quite a bit of hay, sacks of feed, salt blocks, and other materials for feeding animals. How long will that sort of stuff keep without spoiling? Will you ever run out of feed and minerals to feed them?" Tim asked.

"Tim, you have just asked the question of a lifetime. We're doing a lot of planning and work toward being able to grow hay, corn and other crops for the animals. Right now, we're pretty limited in what we can do. We still have enough to get by for a few more months, but it won't last. Animal feed can become critical. We made an extra effort to collect salt. In addition to all the salt blocks we have for animals, we have quite a bit of other salt stored away."

James continued, "We still need some more select animals. Following the war and all the radiation fallout, it was doubtful if there would be any animals left, either wild or domestic. As time passes we're learning of more and more animals. The ones we need badly are horses and mules as beasts of burden; or to pull plows for farming or gardening."

James explained, "Tim, one of our big concerns is feed and hay for the animals. Mowing the hay is the biggest challenge. We must eventually locate some horse-drawn mowers.

"Right now, our plan is to use a disc mower drawn by a diesel tractor to do the mowing. We have a supply of diesel stashed here on the farm, but it will eventually run out. Using it will buy us some more time for finding other mowers."

"Once the hay is cut, we can flip it by hand with pitch forks to help it dry. After that, we can either make haystacks or toss it into hay lofts in barns the old fashioned way.

"Without fuel, much of the farming is going to be a challenge."

James walked inside the barn to the north end. "Let me show you what we have here. I may have already told you that before the war Alvin ran an electrical and electronic business in Mt Sterling. When all this began to happen, he picked up some steel mast sections and windmill apparatus and brought them out here. We haven't had the time or an urgent need to set it up yet. It could be used for charging batteries, or even providing some lighting.

"He also has enough solar panels and equipment stashed to set up a solar system. The need for it hasn't become great enough to set it up."

James and Tim got on their bicycles, and Tim followed James as they rode around the farm and went a short distance down the path to a small branch which led on toward the south.

James spoke, "It's time for us to turn around and head back. This gives you a pretty good sense of our layout."

As they came back to the farm, Tim asked, "Would you mind if I stopped off and visited here before I came back up to the cave?"

James laughed, "Go ahead, Tim, I'm sure you will find someone there who'll be interested in seeing you."

Tim blushed but didn't reply.

In other parts of the world, activities were many and varied. Over two years ago, shortly after the nuclear war and the establishment of a world government, the New World

Leader and his government, the New World Order, made a seven year peace treaty with Israel.

Israel quickly took advantage of the extended good will and began reconstruction of the war damage. Since Tel Aviv was totally destroyed, that city was abandoned, and the rest of Israel's government moved to their capital, Jerusalem.

They also began rebuilding the temple. Fortunately, much of the materials and furnishings were already available, and the building of the temple progressed rapidly.

Somehow,the Dome of the Rock and Al Aqsa mosque were both utterly destroyed during the nuclear war, but not by nukes. The Dome of the Rock housed the location on Mt. Moriah where Muslims claim Abraham offered Isaac as a sacrifice. Muslims and Arabs screamed bloody murder when the New World Government sanctioned and encouraged the rebuilding of the temple on the original temple mount.

During the war, the Wailing Wall was not destroyed. At the signing of the seven year peace treaty, two men took up residence there and immediately began to preach, prophesy, and witness to the eminent return of the Lord and Savior, Jesus Christ; the Messiah; the Lion of Judah.

The two witnesses were immediately attacked by a group of Palestinians who were summarily incinerated by fire coming from the mouth of the two witnesses. After a few more attacks with similar results, they were left alone.

Although a number of Christians lived in Israel before the war started, it was mostly a secular state with a significant number of Orthodox Jews still practicing the Jewish religion. An uneasy stability pervaded the land, with "uneasy" being the operative word.

Tens of thousands of Jews, many of them in Israel and

many of them scattered across Europe and the rest of the world, had a feeling, a premonition, a tugging force which later proved to be from God. The very atmosphere seemed to be electrically charged and ready to burst.

After the war, electrical power grids and communications were a top priority in the countries and regions being re-established and governed by the new world government. (The New World Order). Food was absolutely the most critical and sought after commodity throughout the new world.

Taking census, and then categorizing and marking people with identification, became another top priority, which was made easier by the overwhelming need for food. No ID. No food.

Christians, who again became quite numerous following the earthquakes, volcanic eruptions, and other earth-shaking events, refused to be marked and immediately became outlaws and fugitives, making their survival ten times harder. For these Christians in the controlled areas of the world government, discovery many times became deadly.

In the other parts of the world, such as the United States, control had not yet been established, and their concerns were not as great. The population had been so badly decimated and infrastructure of cities, roads, and bridges so badly destroyed, that the United States was non-existent as a part of the New World Order.

In the New World Government nations, television, radio, and telephone communication was all closely controlled by the new government. Access to electricity was severely limited. Mostly the elite and government officials had it, and even they were limited to lights and refrigerators unless they were really high up.

Assembly centers throughout the countries were established where people could meet at certain times during the week and be brought up to date on all the latest news (propaganda). As people met, there was a distinct lack of friendship. Suspicion and distrust was carefully nurtured by the ruling authorities. Practically every person considered every other person a spy. The new government officials loved it: the more divided, the easier to control.

Transportation was extremely limited due to the shortage of gasoline. Gasoline which had been produced before the war was now close to three years old. Most of it had either been consumed or was now so old it was becoming useless. Work was being done in parts of the world to bring gasoline production back on line, but it was still months away.

People sought after horses. However, most horses had died during and after the war from radiation and starvation. Many of those that did survive were eaten. The new world government had confiscated and acquired enough of those that were left that they were able to breed them and raise enough for future transportation uses. They were still very limited.

In South America, Australia, and a few other parts of the world, horses as well as other animals were more plentiful. Over time, if sea going traffic expanded, they would find their way to needier parts of the world.

Bicycles became very prominent as a means of transportation. Bicycles and bicycle parts were a highly sought commodity in the barter market. Human propelled handcarts were also becoming quite numerous. "Shanks Mare" (walking) was the most prevalent, although not the most popular.

Ships at sea were becoming more numerous, and smaller boats were plying the inland rivers and waterways. Work was being done on some of the world's ports and waterways, but almost three years would elapse following the war before there would be substantial sea traffic between the old world and the new world. Work was being done on the waterways to allow access to the Mississippi River.

Ocean going vessels were being armed and carried contingents of soldiers and government handlers, either for protection or for coercion of people they discovered, whichever might be needed. As time passed, the possibility of interference and danger from outside sources became more possible to the remnants of the population living in the United States.

The use of aircraft was extremely rare and limited. It was also becoming more and more dangerous as the aviation fuel became older. Although efforts were underway in several parts of the world to get oil production and refineries restarted, much of the equipment technology and human expertise was lost during the war and following.

Alvin and James had tentatively agreed that Alvin would hold and protect their house and surroundings, and James would do most of the travelling, reaching out, and coordinating their activities. They also agreed that Tim would accompany and assist James in his travels.

Alvin and Rhonda's children were old enough now to be significant workers in the joint endeavor for survival. Rachael, their oldest was now almost twenty-one. Herbert, Alvin and Rhonda's oldest son, now 19, paired off with David, now 15, the oldest son of James and Paula. Of course, Tim, now almost 19, paired off with Pamela who would soon be 18.

Although they had developed a reliable alarm system throughout their area, they still did some patrolling and guard duty. Rhonda and Paula would pair off from time to time with their husbands, mostly to break the monotony of doing only the household chores. Tiffany, 13, and Ron, 11, James and Paula's other two children, had their assigned chores as well. The combined families worked smoothly as a team to insure their survival.

The entire family participated in the harvesting of black walnuts, hazelnuts, possum grapes, paw paws, and other products of the wild. They also all participated in preparing the soil, planting and caring for the crops, taking care of the chickens and hogs, and helping hunt and trap rabbits, squirrels, raccoons, and other edible wild animals

James and Alvin decided that it was time for James to make an exploratory and bartering run to see what they could get for their products and learn more about their surrounding area. Not knowing what was out there could prove to be dangerous, if not deadly. They already knew the Lexington area had been utterly destroyed, and they would not venture any farther west than Winchester. From Winchester, they would go south to Richmond, then to Irvine, east to Beattyville and then to Booneville. From there, they would go over to Jackson, then to Hazard and Harlan, Prestonsburg and Paintsville. Heading back west, they would visit Grayson and Morehead, then swing down by Cave Run Lake, go on to Mt Sterling, and then back home.

They should be able to learn quite a bit about the potential for trading and also the makeup of the population in the surrounding area and in the eastern part of Kentucky.

One valuable commodity they placed in the truck was

quarts of honey. Honey bees not only survived the radiation fallout from the war, but also appeared to have thrived. One question they could now answer was the amount of radioactivity that might be in the honey, if any. Tim Bailey's hand-held monitor could be used to test it.

The Mercers had found and relocated some active bee hives, housed in brood boxes and with supers, plus materials for making more. The bee hives were more than two miles away from their new home so relocating them was not a problem. Bee hive materials would be another item they would look for as they traveled.

Fortunately, the Mercers had saved and collected quite a few fruit jars. One of the articles they had stored in advance of the war was a bountiful supply of new jar lids. In their bartering expeditions, getting replacement jars as they sold the full ones, would be a given.

They also had a good supply of walnuts for bartering. They took several sacks of hulled walnuts and a few pints of shelled walnuts. Before they headed out, they double checked to make sure they had enough bedding, food, water, firearms, and ammunition for the trip.

As they traveled, they crossed over Red River, went through Stanton, which appeared to have been quickly abandoned after the war, and went west toward Winchester. Any survivors from Stanton probably joined up with a larger group for better protection. As they traveled, they observed and took notes on potentials for future crops, salvageable materials, and anything else that might be of interest.

Winchester, being relatively close to Lexington, appeared to have been significantly damaged during the war. The city seemed to be totally abandoned. Traveling south toward

Richmond, they spotted one farm that showed signs of recent activity. They decided to stop by and see if they could make contact. Visits to places like this could be tricky and dangerous. They needed to be very careful.

They stopped 200 yards from the house, blew their horn, stepped out of the truck, and moved a few feet away from the truck door. James yelled. "Hello the house!"

A man came to the front door and stepped out, holding a rifle. "What do you want?"

James replied, "We're out looking to trade some honey and walnuts for something; preferably for food or something else we can use."

"Come on over," the man replied. "Just be careful where you put your hands."

"I'm James Mercer and this is Tim Bailey. We're on our way to Richmond to do some trading and saw that someone lived here so we thought we'd make a stop."

"My name is George Stephens. My wife and I live here with our child. Most of our family died from radiation and sickness during and after the war."

James expressed his regrets and then waited for George to continue.

"The honey sounds good. We don't have much but we do have some corn. You should be able to use some of it for seed also if you need some to plant. It isn't a hybrid."

James and George concluded their transaction.

"What do we look for when we get to Richmond," James asked.

"Go to the south side of Richmond. The settlement includes the Eastern Kentucky University campus and the surrounding area. It's a pretty nice setup with a local government, law enforcement, stores, markets, and a church. You'll like it. The old downtown section and surrounding area was pretty much destroyed during the war."

"We were here in the Richmond area once before, over a year ago. It was after the war and before the earthquakes. I'll bet it's grown quite a bit since then," James replied.

"Yes, I was here too," Tim added.

"George, what do you know about the security in the area around Richmond. Do you think it would be relatively safe?" James asked.

"Yes." George replied. It has grown quite a bit and the people moving in seem to be good citizens. However, you need to see Mike Linden, the sheriff, or George Braddock, the mayor. They will be able to give you more detail."

George ended up with a quart of honey and some walnuts, and hazelnuts. In return, Tim and James left with a sack of corn, some beans, and a half gallon of kerosene, which was a much sought after article.

They went to Richmond and located the active business center, which was very small by normal pre-war standards. There were places where they could barter for hardware, clothing, guns, ammunition, jewelry, candles, food, knives, bows and arrows, animal traps, and any number of other items that could be imagined.

Before doing any shopping, their first order of business was to locate the Mayor and/or sheriff. They found Mayor George Braddock at his home.

They knocked and the mayor came to the door. James introduced himself. "Good morning, Mayor, I'm James Mercer and this is Tim Bailey. We're just passing through and would like to get some information on Richmond and the surrounding area. We live northeast of here in an isolated area and are considering locating where there are more people. We're interested in learning about potential opportunities and also about the security and safety."

Mayor Braddock replied. "Well James and Tim, it's good meeting you. We're always looking for more solid citizens to join us. Come on in to my office and have a seat."

Once inside, the Mayor continued, "We have somewhere between 500 and 600 people living here in Richmond and in the surrounding area. Most of them came here after the war and the devastation which came with it. Following the war, the anarchy, radiation poisoning, starvation, diseases and other pestilences practically wiped this place out. Richmond was left almost a ghost town. Survivors in the surrounding area, and from elsewhere, recognized this as a place they could assemble for mutual protection, grow food, and survive. It continues to grow.

"From a security standpoint, we have possibly three or four dozen men and women who could be considered potential troublemakers. However, we know who they are and each of them have been contacted by our sheriff, Mike Linden, and cautioned. Mike explained to them that we're living in different times and there shall be zero tolerance for stealing or crime of any other fashion.

"For punishment of serious crimes or repetitive smaller crimes, incarceration is not an option. Since each individual in the area are dependent on the whole population for food and other means for survival, dealing with crime or other serious problems will need to be swift and final. So far, we've had only a few minor incidents which the sheriff has handled.

Since drugs and alcohol are now practically non-existent, that problem has solved itself."

James and Tim thanked the mayor for his information and then went back to the business district.

One place of business that they gravitated to and really liked was run by two young Jewish men who introduced themselves as Asher Caslari and Meir Janner, both twenty-five years old. They were fitting in quite well with the current population and had begun attending the new church that had started in that area. Being Jews, they were skeptical, but very attentive, and were both studying their Bibles.

As yet, the church had no permanent pastor. Until recently, they had leaders who would take turns getting up and expounding on the teachings of the Bible and telling of their experiences and their belief in God and Jesus Christ. A month ago, they had heard of a young man by the name of Thomas Allen Daley, who had attended the Southern Baptist Theological Seminary in Louisville, Kentucky. After meeting with him, they asked him to come and be their interim pastor, and he accepted.

The church had no official membership, just a gathering. They had unanimously decided to call it "The Lord's Church." They would take up an offering each Sunday and use that to either meet the few needs of the facility or mete it out to some needy person or persons.

The objects offered were many and varied. Food items were popular, especially canned foods. Inedible offerings could be bartered at one of the local markets.

After depleting most of their barter materials, James and Tim got in the truck and drove down to Irvine where they turned on Hwy 52 and went east toward Beattyville.

They saw occasional signs of life as they drove along but saw no farm animals along the way. If many or any existed, they were probably kept well hidden.

Their journey took them through Beattyville, through Booneville, and then to Jackson. There had been a small settlement in Irvine, one in Beattyville, and one in Jackson. So far there had been no indications of a significant population. Each populated area had their guards posted. James and Tim were stopped frequently and questioned. Some of the encounters were touchy until mutual trust could be established. A few of the characters at the check points were scary.

Jackson and Hazard both had small settlements. Prestonsburg and Paintsville had combined into one settlement at Paintsville. They traveled back west through Grayson, which had a small settlement; then on to Morehead where a group had gathered. The next settlement they found was at Cave Run Lake. They speculated that most of the people within the area they had circled probably lived in remote and secret locations; fearful of their existence and whereabouts becoming known.

The security provided by settlements and the social nature of humans to gather were drawing more and more survivors out of isolation and into the settlements. The gathering of the people could be a good thing or a bad thing, depending on what the future held in store.

They found another settlement as they passed through Mt Sterling. This rounded out their exploration, and they went back toward their home, south of Morris Mountain.

Following the exploration, they soon made a trip to Tim's old home. They recovered and salvaged as much as they could, including the extra batteries for the Geiger Counter. The Geiger Counter was still working with the old batteries, but probably not for long. They brought all the food, including quite a bit of long term storage supplies, which consisted of freeze dried foods, vacuum stored grains, and a host of other supplies that would serve them well.

They also found a significant supply of long term storage non hybrid seeds which they would be able to plant in the spring and expand their food sources. They would be able to judiciously sell and barter away some of the seeds to other people. After the first year of harvest, seed supply needs would become less critical.

Tim and Pamela paired off quite frequently and worked at gardening, collecting firewood, picking greens, and collecting anything else that might be usable or eatable. Their duties also included acting as guards when they were scheduled. Tim sometimes served guard duty by himself, but certainly enjoyed it when Pamela volunteered to help.

On rare occasions, when strangers would approach their area, they would be asked to either go back the way they came or go around. Usually, names would be exchanged, and the Mercers were able to collect useful information on who was in the general area.

Skies continued to clear and they became more optimistic about growing food. Their big dilemma was tilling enough soil to grow a significant crop. Alvin remembered an increasingly popular growing technique called no till. Some farmers had obtained a machine called a No-Till drill which they pulled behind tractors. The drill would cut a groove in the soil, just wide and deep enough to inject the seed, and then cover it up. However, that method should be preceded by spraying weed killer. Once the plants were sprouted, they should be sprayed again with week killer. The weed killer method required a specially treated seed.

In order to use the no till technique, they would have to come up with another method of controlling the grass and weeds. They could possibly use leaves, bark, etc. for mulching. By taking care of their growing sites, perhaps over time they could get the weed problem under control.

James sat down with Alvin, and Tim. "I've been studying and evaluating our circumstances on locations and different options for the future. I think it's time we did some old fashioned brainstorming about what we need to do."

Alvin and Tim both agreed so they called together the entire family. For once, they didn't leave anybody on patrol.

James started out. "Since Tim and I took our trip, I've been feeling unsettled about our location and our situation. This cave system in a remote area was great for survival through the war, and all that followed, but it's becoming unhandy for future living. The floor is open to discussion and comment."

A flurry of voices began speaking. "Hold up a minute," James asked. "Try it one at a time. Let's hear from the women. Rhonda, you speak first."

Rhonda spoke up. "I agree that we probably need to do something. We are really limited in what we can do here in the way of trying to socialize with other people. We have grown children that someday need to meet others of their age and possibly get married and have children and families of their own."

Paula spoke up. "Amen to that. As the months have gone by, I've begun to feel claustrophobic in these surroundings."

Rachael added, "I'm about to go crazy out here away from everybody and everything. It would be nice just to sit down and talk to other people."

"Alvin, what are your thoughts," asked James.

"I've been feeling much the same way. While we were in apparent danger, this place was great. Now that the world seems to have settled down, hopefully it's safe enough for us to get out and mix with other people. We're very limited with what crops we can grow in this location, and before long we're going to run out of food. Being so far out, we're also limited in our transportation and travel options. I believe it may be time for a move."

"Tim, what are your thoughts?" James asked.

Tim replied. "I have no problem with moving if that's what you all decide to do. I also have no problem with staying here. I look at what you have here, and I can see so much in the way of the work and time you have invested. However, I certainly understand the potential for more safety in the numbers of people we would have around us."

"Pamela?" James asked.

Pamela responded, "I agree that it's time to move. It's lonesome out here."

All the members of the households were allowed their opportunities to speak their mind and it was unanimous that the right thing to do was move.

Alvin spoke up. "Well, James, do you have any suggestions where we should go, based on what you saw on the trip?"

James replied, "Considering social opportunities, somewhere in the vicinity of Richmond seems to be the best we've seen. What do you think Tim?"

Tim replied. "That's the most likely place we saw. There

were some nice looking abandoned houses around Stanton, Clay City, Irvine, and Richmond. Stanton and Clay City seems to be a little far out though."

"Alvin, since you and I have the families, why don't we take off over that way and look around. We could leave Tim here and take Rhonda and Paula with us."

Paula spoke up. "I think that's a great idea. We can make that trip in about three or four days and hopefully, everybody will be safe during that time."

Rachael, Tim, Herbert and Pamela sat down and worked up schedules for guard duty, cooking, chores, feeding, and general activities. They were well prepared when the older Mercers left on their trip. Although they were somewhat apprehensive at the responsibility, they faced up to it quite well.

All went well, and the Mercers located two abandoned farms about five miles south of Richmond and selected them as their new homes. The two farms were two miles apart by road, but only a half mile across country. They got permission from the owner of the farm in between to make themselves a shortcut.

Changing locations was not easy. It took close to six months before they were completely settled. Moving their stored farm equipment, including two of the tractors, wagons, buggies, etc. took a lot of innovative thinking. Fortunately, they had a lot of barn space at the two farms, and the farmer between them offered his barn, if needed.

When some of the people in Richmond found out about their new neighbors, they pitched in, provided vehicles, and assisted in getting them moved. Although the people who helped were reluctant to be paid, the Mercers were careful to be fair and to reward them the best they could from what they had. When all was said and done, all involved seemed satisfied with the outcome.

James and Paula's new location had a spring with adequate water, but Alvin and Rhonda had to dig a well. A lack of electricity and water was a tremendous setback from their former way of life.

Tim took up residence with James and Paula and their family. Although they were on separate farms, Pamela and Tim were almost inseparable as they worked, studied, and played together. It appeared almost a given that this relationship would not only grow stronger, but eventually become permanent. It would be just a matter of time.

While all of this was taking place, world events were in motion, with satan, the anti-Christ, and the false prophet moving forward to do their worst in the way of evil. Christians were their primary targets. They were plotting against the Jews, even though, at the same time, they were helping them. God was simultaneously moving His "Day of the Lord" activities forward in Jerusalem, as the New World Government worked closely with the Jews to rebuild the temple and also rebuild the infrastructure of the city.

The two witnesses who had suddenly appeared upon the scene at the time of the signing of the 7 year peace treaty had now been active for almost three and a half years.

As this period of more than three years passed, the temple was completed.

Orthodox Jews carried on business as usual. All of them were pleased that the World Government leaders were leaving them alone and observing the peace treaty which had been made almost three and a half years ago.

There continued to be quite a bit of military activity in the countries surrounding Israel as armament was being moved about, and more troops deployed on their borders. Many of the people became uneasy.

The Jews were living in a guaranteed peace with no reason to believe the peace would not continue.

A few of the Jews in the country had accepted Jesus Christ as savior following the rapture, but in relatively small numbers. These Christians came under immediate persecution by the secular and Orthodox Jews at the behest of the World Government representatives.

A large number of Jews in Israel and around the world were being wooed by the Holy Spirit of God and convicted of their sins and lost condition. A momentous supernatural event was eminent as God's plan evolved.

The World Government was making its own plans related to Israel. Many of the subordinates of the World Leader were laying out plans and a timetable for finally and forever dealing with the so-called "The Jewish Problem."

CHAPTER II
ONE HUNDRED AND FORTY-FOUR THOUSAND

Revelation 7:1-4, "And after these things I saw four angels standing on the four corners of the earth, holding the four winds of the earth, that the wind should not blow on the earth, nor on the sea, nor on any tree.

And I saw another angel ascending from the east, having the seal of the living God: and he cried with a loud voice to the four angels, to whom was given to hurt the earth and the sea, Saying, Hurt not the earth, neither the sea, nor the trees, till we have sealed the servants of our God in their foreheads.

And I heard the number of them which were sealed; and there were sealed an hundred and forty and four thousand of all the tribes of the children of Israel."

Even before the first bomb fell and well before God called them out for service, the 144,000 were more than likely being supernaturally protected, with the Holy Spirit working within their hearts, preparing them for their future service.

Following the tremendous upheavals in the heavens

involving the sun, the moon, and the stars; and the horrendous earthquakes, volcanic eruptions, and shakings following the rapture, an awesome silence and calm suddenly fell upon the entire earth. The Holy Spirit of God fell upon the Jews in Israel and in other parts of the world and began the work of calling out the one hundred and forty-four thousand. The one hundred and forty four thousand joined the ranks of the Tribulation Saints as they became saved Christians and immediately began the work of witnessing to a lost world, beginning first with the Jews. God worked through them to seek and to save that which was lost. Satan worked through the anti-Christ and false prophet to destroy.

In Israel, Europe, and the old world, spontaneous revivals broke out across the land as members of the 144,000 Christian Jews began witnessing, first to other Jews and then to the Gentiles.

The leader of the World Government, the anti-Christ, immediately began mobilizing forces to counter this sudden rebellion against their anti-Christian laws.

Armed cadres were dispatched to ferret out the witnesses and the new Christians to either imprison or destroy them. Those who were unfortunate enough to encounter one of the 144,000, dropped dead in their tracks.

The 144,000 who had been sealed by God were supernaturally protected and impervious to capture or harm. Locations of witness-held revivals were not to be found regardless of the intensity of the searches.

The secular and orthodox Jews were suspected and soon became targets of reprisal raids. Israel, and especially Jerusalem, was a very dangerous place for any Jew.

After six months of frustrated attempts to quell what

appeared to be a rebellion of the Jews, the world leader, the anti-Christ, retaliated by declaring martial law in all of Israel. He cancelled the seven year peace treaty exactly three and one half years after its signing. The anti-Christ immediately moved his headquarters to the temple, declared himself god, and mandated that all people worship him.

Immediately after declaring himself god, he sent soldiers to kill the two witnesses. The two dead witnesses were left lying where they fell and remained there for three and a half days. At the end of that time they rose up, alive, and ascended into heaven.

For the next several months, forces were mobilized in Europe, the Middle East, Asia, the Far East, and in other parts of the world. They began taking up positions around and all through Israel and Jerusalem. Once this stranglehold was established, local Jews were recruited to supervise and closely control and monitor all the inhabitants of Israel. Christians, when found, were captured, and immediately sent before a tribunal. They were given one opportunity to renounce Jesus Christ, take the Mark, pledge allegiance to the World Leader, and vow to worship him. Those who refused were moved immediately to the execution chambers and beheaded.

Members of the 144,000, still supernaturally protected, continued their witnessing.

Meanwhile, back in Richmond, Kentucky, Tim and the Mercers were getting settled into their new homes. They decided to work as a team to manage both farms.

Once the basic functions of furnishing the homes and establishing the routines of cooking, eating, sleeping, and normal living had been settled, they immediately started planning and executing the business side of their farming, as well as other ventures.

Alvin, 39, and James, 37, had done some pre-planning and called the entire family together to discuss their future activities. Alvin assumed the spokesman role and addressed the group. "James and I have done some pre-planning, and we've come up with a preliminary list of the major areas of concern and possible future endeavors that we may wish to undertake. I emphasize, this list is preliminary. Items can be added to, or items taken away as our planning evolves."

Alvin continued, "I realize that some of you are adults and may decide to branch out on your own. Due to the very nature of our circumstances and the times we live in, I'm assuming all of you will want to remain close for mutual support, protection, and security. Until you tell us otherwise, we'll plan accordingly."

Alvin picked up some papers off the table. "I have only four handwritten lists. You can look at them and then pass them around. Someday soon, I hope we can put together a generator, computer, and printer to simplify this process. There should be lots of printer paper, and, hopefully, cartridges, around."

The list contained the items: (1) Employees, (2) Transportation and Vehicles. (3) Fuel, (4) Farm crops, (5) Honeybees, (6) Farm animals, (7) Barter materials – coming in and going out, (8) Carpentering, (9) Security and Surveillance.

Alvin stated,: "This gives you some idea of some of our major concerns. Look over the list, think about it, and add to it if you think of something else. From time to time, we'll get together and work on it." Alvin continued, "James, give us your ideas on employees."

James spoke up, "I believe we should plan to do more than just try to survive. We could zero in on just our survival needs and probably get by, but there are hundreds of other people in and around Richmond that could benefit from our doing more. One way would be to involve a few people in our work and let them benefit from the results. My idea would be to start out with just two or three helpers. Since we don't have money, we would have to pay them in barter goods or produce from our farm."

"Where would they come from, and how would they get here?" Asked Rachael, Alvin and Rhonda's 20-year old daughter.

James responded, "Depending on where they live, if it's close enough, we could let them use one of our bicycles; or if necessary, I guess we could plan to build a bunk house."

Tim, now 20, and David, 15, the son of James and Paula, were assigned the task of obtaining fuel. There wasn't a lot of gasoline still available, at least, not in the near vicinity. However, they hoped they might find some diesel fuel either in tanks at service stations or in tanks on farms. Searching for fuel required fuel unless they traveled by bicycle or horseback. Burning what fuel they had left to search for more fuel seemed to be risky,

The Mercers were getting dangerously low on gasoline. The move from the cave in Montgomery County had taken a heavy toll on their supply. The shopping center and local government offices were five miles from their farms. The church was also located in that area and the Mercers had a strong desire to attend whenever possible. They all looked forward to making their weekly visit to the town.

Fortunately, they had the three buggies and a few horses. That, plus the bicycles, appeared to be their best hope for future traveling. For the time being they would use the pickup.

The church in Richmond had been quite popular for the young men and women, especially the teenagers and the ones in their early twenties. I guess there could be some question as to whether the sermon was the biggest attraction, or something else.

Counting Tim, there were eleven of the Mercers. Leaving at least one of them at each farm as a guard still left ten people to pack into the pickup truck. On their trip to town, they would also do what shopping they could. Since the primary shopping day was Saturday, the church service was held from 10:00 a.m. to 12:00 a.m. on Saturday: the Sabbath.

For security, Tim stayed at James and Paula's farm and Herbert stayed at Alvin and Rhonda's. Both of them were fully armed with semi-automatic pistols and rifles. Each also had a twelve gauge double barrel shotgun with buckshot rounds, and field glasses so they could spot any potential intruders early on. So far, there had been no reports of security problems in the Richmond area, but it was probably just a matter of time until something happened.

Alvin and Rhonda, with Rachael, and Pamela, left at 7:00 a.m. and drove over to pick up the rest of the Mercers. They all headed out for Richmond to go to church and do some shopping. Five were packed into the cab with the other five in the truck bed with all their bartering goods. The truck was well loaded.

Arriving in Richmond, they scattered and began looking and shopping. They planned to meet at the church at 10:00 a.m.

By 9:45, people began entering the church and filling up the seats. As they arrived they were met at the door and greeted warmly by the interim pastor, Thomas Allen Daley.

Thomas was a handsome young man, 25 years old, 5 foot, 11 inches tall, and weighed 150 pounds. He looked slim and wore a gray suit, blue tie, and black, polished, dress shoes. He projected an air of friendliness, maturity, and confidence.

Thomas had been on the verge of graduating from the Southern Baptist Theological Seminary in Louisville, Kentucky when the bombs came down.

Later, when the rapture occurred, it became immediately apparent that he had missed the mark and had not been born again. As so many others had done, Thomas turned his heart and life over to God and became one of the numberless Tribulation Saints.

The Mercers arrived at the church a few minutes before ten and greeted Thomas as they came in.

Rachael's heart fluttered as she shook his hand. "I'm Rachael Mercer," she greeted in an un-characteristically soft voice.

"I'm Thomas Daley," he returned, losing a little of his assured composure.

By 10:00 a.m., all the seats were filled and people were lining up around the walls. There was soon an overflow crowd.

Promptly at ten, Thomas went to the podium and began to speak. "Good morning. For those of you who don't know me, I'm Thomas Allen Daley, pastor of this church which is known as 'The Lord's Church'. Most people call me Thomas or Brother Thomas." He chuckled. "Some folks used to call me Tad, but that's not my preference."

He continued, "We've just about grown too big for this building, and we're looking into a larger facility just down the road at the old Eastern Kentucky University campus. We'll keep you informed as we learn more about it.

"Following our normal opening worship service, we'll have two special speakers today. During the night, God laid a burden on my heart to have Asher Caslari and Meir Jenner to come and speak. I anticipate a great blessing from God."

The worship service then continued with prayer and song, followed by a prayer and then an offering.

Thomas went to the pulpit and began to introduce the speakers. "Most of you already know Asher and Meir from doing business with them and seeing them here at church and in town. I'm asking them at this time to come forward and speak as God gives them utterance."

A hush fell over the sanctuary as the two men came to the front.

Asher spoke first. "I wish to quote a Scripture to you from the Holy Word of God. This is taken from the book of Revelation, chapter 7, verses 1 through 4. 'And after these things, I saw four angels standing on the four corners of the earth, holding the four winds of the earth, that the wind should not blow on the earth, nor on the sea, nor on any tree. And I saw another angel ascending from the east, having the seal of the living God and he cried with a loud voice to the four angels, to whom was given to hurt the earth and the sea. Saying, Hurt not the earth, neither the sea, nor the trees, till we have sealed the servants of our God in their foreheads.

And I heard the number of them which were sealed; and there were sealed an hundred and forty-four thousand of all the tribes of the children of Israel.'"

Asher continued, "Meir and I are two of the 144,000 who have been called out and sealed. We are to be witnesses for our God, Jehova, and our Messiah, our Lord and Savior Jesus Christ.

Most of you already know we're living in the end times. God has come to judge the people of the world and to bring recompense to those to whom recompense is due. God is a merciful God, and even at this late hour, He is not willing that any should perish but come to eternal life through Jesus Christ, our Messiah and Lord.

"Pray to God for forgiveness; cry out to him for salvation. The bible teaches in 2 Corinthians 6:2 'For he saith, I have heard thee in a time accepted, and in the day of salvation have I succored thee: behold, now is the accepted time, behold, now is the day of salvation.'"

Asher stepped back, and Meir stepped forward and began to speak. "Read your Bible. Read and heed what the Scriptures say in the Gospels. Repent, and confess your sins, or be damned! Read and heed the teachings in the book of Revelation. Read chapter 7 and heed that the judgments are falling! They will fall faster and faster. They will soon reach the end and the last opportunity to receive God's mercy and grace shall be gone! Don't wait!"

Meir continued: "God's judgments are falling faster and faster upon the earth. They are all supernatural events. Satan and his followers are seeking to destroy all they can before God binds Satan and destroys his followers.

"Know this: Meir and I are supernaturally protected by Almighty God. You are not. Again I say, don't wait!"

Asher and Meir stepped down, walked to the back, and left the church. Their faces and foreheads, which had begun to glow as they spoke, resumed their normal color as they left.

Following the exit of the two Christian Jewish witnesses, an absolute revival took place in the church as dozens fell upon their knees, confessing their sins and begging for forgiveness and salvation. Several people left the church, not feeling the need to repent.

Thomas regained order and then worked with the new converts individually and allowed each to confess their repentance and their surrender to God and Jesus Christ before the others in the congregation.

All of the Mercers, parents and children, accepted Jesus Christ as their Lord and Savior.

Lunch was completely forgotten as Thomas continued to answer questions about baptism: the meaning, the need, and the baptism itself. Because of the urgency of the time, most were feeling the need to be baptized as soon as possible.

They discovered that not too far down Lancaster Road there was a creek with a hole deep enough for baptizing. After several more minutes of planning and discussion, it was mutually agreed that the baptisms would take place on the following day at 2:00 p.m. That would allow everybody plenty of time to make preparation by gathering up clothing, towels, and anything else they might need. It would also be much warmer by that time of day.

Needless to say, a large number of people left the church on that day literally transformed. Another group left the church in various moods, from "almost persuaded", to intensely angry.

Four of the men who attended the service were not happy. They stomped out before the service was over, highly incensed, and outraged that two Jews, of all people, were allowed to get up in a church in the United States of America and speak! The very idea, that they could tell them they were doomed to hell without repentance!

After leaving, they located a half-dozen of their buddies and worked themselves into a frenzy over a jug of moonshine, loudly venting their rage. About an hour later, they collectively decided they needed to do something about it.

As they headed toward the market, they picked up clubs, stones, pieces of brick, and other weapons to use to "teach those Jews a lesson." They would show them!

A dozen customers were in Asher and Meir's shop as the would-be attackers entered and went straight toward the two Witnesses. Asher and Meir were caught totally by surprise and didn't have a chance to react. As the attackers drew back to throw their objects, or otherwise menace Asher and Meir, they dropped to the floor like stones. Customers were frozen in shock and amazement. There were no marks on the bodies of the would-be attackers. It was as if their life and soul had departed their bodies in the twinkling of an eye.

As word of the event spread throughout their area, another sensation was occurring in other parts of the world just as spectacular as the church service where so many had accepted Jesus Christ as Savior and Lord.

Worldwide, pairs of the 144,000 Jews, marked in their forehead by Almighty God and supernaturally protected, began their witnessing across America, Europe, Asia, Israel,

Africa, Japan, China, and every other part of the world where these called-out Jews resided.

The newly saved, the Tribulation Saints that no man could number, flocked to Jesus Christ as Satan's film of deceit was removed from their minds and hearts, and they could finally discern the truth. As this great revival spanned the earth, fewer and fewer people remained whose heart could be penetrated and softened by the "Good News."

The evil people remaining upon the earth would terrify, kill, torture and do as much damage as they could, before the fast approaching end. As they spread their evil, God's wrath became more and more severe, and the judgments became more and more frequent.

"The message remained as ever: Time is running out. Soon, there will be no more time for repentance."

CHAPTER III
THE SEVENTH SEAL

Revelation 8:1-6 "And when he had opened the seventh seal, there was silence in heaven about the space of half an hour. And I saw the seven angels which stood before God, and to them were given seven trumpets. And another angel came and stood at the alter, having a golden censer, and there was given unto him much incense, that he should offer it with the prayers of all saints upon the golden alter which was before the throne. And the smoke of the incense, which came with the prayers of the saints, ascended up before God out of the angel's hand. And the angel took the censer, and filled it with the fire of the alter, and cast it into the earth; and there were voices, and thundering, and lightening, and an earthquake. And the seven angels which had the seven trumpets prepared themselves to sound."

A revival swept the earth as a supernatural calm descended upon the heavens and the earth.

For the next several months, Asher Caslari, Meir Jenner and the rest of the 144,000 sealed Christian Jews, would travel from community to community in the United States and other countries of the world, witnessing to those who still had "ears to hear". In Richmond, Thomas Daley worked with the people, arranging for the baptisms on Sunday afternoon.

The Mercers finished their shopping, loaded back into their pickup truck, and headed toward home. James went by and dropped off Alvin, Rhonda, Rachael and Pamela at their farm, turned around, and drove back out to the road.

When they got home, Tim was there to greet them. "I was beginning to get worried."

James replied, "Tim, you'll never believe what I have to tell you about what happened to us today. We went to church, met the new pastor, heard the two Christian Jews, Asher and Meir, speak, and all of us in Alvin's and my family, accepted Jesus Christ as savior."

Tim was flabbergasted. "Wow! Unbelievable! Praise the Lord! I've been concerned about all of you but just didn't know what to say to help you understand. All I could tell you was what happened to me." Tim exclaimed, "I just can't wait to see Pamela."

Paula spoke up, "It's been a very exciting day and a long one. We're all tired, so let's go in the house, have some supper, and rest."

It took some time for everybody to wind down and finally get ready for bed. They had another long and busy day ahead of them tomorrow, as they would be going back to town for the baptisms.

Sunday morning, everybody was up early and busy. James called Tim over. "Tim, how would you like to hitch up one of the buggies and drive over to Alvin's and see if three of them could go with you later today in the buggy?"

"I'll be glad to," Tim replied. "I'll wait until I get back to get dressed."

"What about breakfast?" Paula asked.

"I'll either have some breakfast over there or eat something here when I get back," Tim answered.

As soon as Tim got to the other farm, he was greeted enthusiastically by all, especially Pamela.

"Tim come on in and get a plate. We just ate and there's plenty more." Rhonda invited. "Pamela, help him find all he needs."

Pamela ran over, grabbed Tim by the hand, and excitedly led him into the house. Although they had seen each other the day before, she acted as if it had been weeks.

As Tim followed Pamela through the door, her enthusiasm and excitement touched Tim in such a way, he closed the door behind him, locked it, and grabbed her in a fierce embrace. He kissed her in a lingering kiss, and then kissed her again.

Breathless, Pamela gasped, "Tim! What has got into you?"

Taken aback, Tim stuttered, "P-Pamela are you mad at me?"

Pamela tittered as she hugged him in a convincing way, "No, silly. I'm not mad. I'm surprised, that's all, and I'm just happy."

"Pamela, you know I really do love you." Tim said.

Pamela replied softly, "I dearly love you, too, Tim."

Somebody tried the door. "Who locked the door? What's going on in there?" Rhonda called out.

Tim unlocked the door and let her in.

Rhonda stopped, looked at Pamela for a few seconds, and then looked at Tim. "Don't tell me - - -" she said, as she smiled. "Eat your breakfast Tim."

Pamela sat close to Tim as he ate. "Tim, I'm so happy that I'm a Christian now. I feel more free and secure than I've ever felt in my life."

Tim smiled and replied. "We have a busy day with the baptisms and all. Just as soon as things settle down around here, I'd like for us to start getting together more. We have a lot to talk about. I really miss you when we're apart."

Pamela replied, "Tim, I'd really like that. When you aren't around, I just don't feel complete."

Tim jumped up from the table. "I need to get out of here and back home. I don't have a lot of time to get dressed and back here. I'll see you later." He grabbed Pamela, gave her a quick kiss, and headed out the door.

Sunday afternoon at 3:00 p.m. more than 300 people gathered at Taylor Fork Creek for the baptisms. Sixty four people, including Tim and Pamela, lined up and walked confidently forward to be baptized. Thomas Daley, their pastor, led them one by one into the baptismal waters until they were waist deep.

Thomas held his right hand to heaven and prayed for the individual and proclaimed, I baptize you, (their name) my (brother or sister), in the name of the Father, the Son, and the Holy Ghost. He then immersed them completely, raised them back up, and then led them to a helper who helped them back out of the water.

Alvin, Rhonda, Pamela and Rachael had spent the evening before explaining salvation to Herbert, who had been on guard duty the day that Asher Caslari and Meir Jenner had witnessed to the church. Following the witnessing of his family, Herbert professed his faith in God and Jesus Christ. He was also baptized at the same time as the rest of his family. Following these exciting days, the Mercers went back to work on their farms.

By mutual consent of all the Mercers, Pamela and Tim were designated the beekeepers. Later, when they got the beekeeping under control, they would also take on the chicken enterprise.

The bees were kept on the south side of Alvin and Rhonda's farm, on a south facing, gentle slope leading down to a small brook. It was about two hundred yards from the path they used when crossing through their neighbor's farm to get to James and Paula's farm.

Bicycles were their primary mode of transportation. With the help of some of the others, they were building a shed to house their tools and equipment. At present, they had a total of twelve hives with the patented brood boxes and supers. Each hive had at least one super installed, and they had a few spares that would be stored in the shed.

The week following their baptism, Tim and Pamela met at their bee farm to continue their work. Pamela had packed a lunch which they placed in a cool and shady spot at the edge of the creek. They had been looking around, wandering aimlessly, and then, as if by mutual consent, they approached each other, embraced, and kissed.

Tim went down on one knee in front of Pamela and grasped both of her hands in his. "Pamela, I am so in love with you. Will you honor me by marrying me and becoming my wife?"

Pamela replied softly, "Yes I will, Tim." She continued, "Oh Tim, I love you so. I would be honored to be your wife and spend the rest of my life with you."

Tim rose to his feet, held Pamela in a long, caressing

embrace, kissed her gently and then fervently. "Pamela, I'm really not in the mood for working right now. Let's find us a place in private where we can just talk. We need to understand each other better and see where we need to go from here."

"Tim, I agree," she replied. "We live in uncertain times and we shouldn't waste any of it. I so want to stay close to you all the time."

They walked down to the creek to their favorite spot and spent the next two hours talking about their thoughts, their dreams, and their love for each other.

"Pamela, I don't know how you feel about it, but I think we should go ahead and get married and spend the rest of our lives together."

"Tim, where would we live? What would we live on? We can't just go off on our own and be able to survive."

Pamela, my thoughts are that we would build a small house right next to James and Paula's house if they will allow it. I'd like to build a house and live out here but I don't think it would be safe on our own."

"Tim, should we go ahead and tell everybody about our plans to get married and then just go ahead and do it?" Pamela asked, anxiously.

Tim put his arms around her and held her. "Pamela, let's go right now to your folks' house, and I'll ask your dad for your hand. If he has no objection, we'll go tell James and Paula, and then we'll ask Paula, Rhonda and Rachael to help plan it and make it happen."

That pretty well took care of the work for the day. Pamela and Tim got on their bicycles and headed out for Pamela's home.

When they got to the farm, Tim went in with Pamela and asked Rhonda where he might find Alvin.

"He's out at the barn, Tim." Rhonda advised.

Tim went out to the barn, located Alvin, and nervously asked, "Alvin, could I talk to you for just a minute?"

Alvin replied, "Sure thing, Tim. What do you have on your mind?"

Tim grinned and answered in one word. "Pamela."

Alvin replied, "Oh. I see."

Tim, becoming more serious, explained to Alvin, "Alvin, Pamela and I love each other and we'd like to get married. We'd like to spend the rest of our lives together."

Alvin pondered for several moments before he spoke. "Tim, you know we're living in very uncertain times. In fact, from what we're learning through studying the Bible, we're probably living during the time of the seven year tribulation the Bible talks about. The next three or four years could be uncertain. Have you and Pamela thought about what that might mean?"

Tim replied. "We've had some discussion on that, but we've decided that, regardless, we want to spend the rest of our lives together."

Alvin responded, "Tim, I'm telling you now, I think you're a wonderful young man, and I'll be proud to have you for a son in law. Having said that, let's go back to the house and sit down with Pamela and Rhonda and just talk."

Arriving back at the house, Tim went to Pamela and put his arm around her waist.

Rhonda spoke up. "Let's all go to the living room where we can get comfortable."

They settled down with Pamela and Tim very close together, holding hands.

Rhonda spoke first. "Pamela, this may be embarrassing to you and Tim, but, have you thought about children? Without doctors, modern medicine, and all the conveniences, there are more possibilities of complications. Also, I hope you've given thought to the kind of world they would be born into."

Pamela answered, "Mom, we understand the potential risk. It's no more than the generations before us dealt with. We'll just trust in the Lord and deal with circumstances as they arise."

Alvin spoke up, "Tim, have you thought of where you'll live?"

Tim replied, "Yes. I haven't talked to Paula or James yet but my thinking is that we could build a house over next to James and Paula's house, if Pamela and everybody else agrees."

Alvin responded, "Yes, I think that it would be good for you to live close to them or close to us. Living out somewhere separate probably wouldn't be safe."

"Rachael is in her room doing some sewing. Let's call her out here and tell her the news," Rhonda suggested.

Pamela exclaimed, "I'll do it!" She jumped up and walked quickly into the hall and down to Rachael's room. Rachael was excited when she heard the news.

They went back into the living room, and Rachael listened as they told her more about their plans to get married.

Rachael, blushing, spoke up. "Thomas is coming over to see me tonight. The last time we were at the church, he asked me if he could come calling, and I said yes. Would you like for me to mention to him that you're getting married and his services might be needed?"

Time looked over at Pamela. "Is that alright with you?"

She replied in a soft voice, "Yes, Tim, that's just fine with me. Now that we've decided to get married, I think the sooner we do so, the better it'll be."

"Pamela, would you like to go with me back over to James and Paula's and tell them what's taking place and see what we can come up with in deciding on a place to live?" Tim asked.

Tim and Pamela got on their bicycles. Using the shortcut through the farms, they were soon back at James and Paula's house.

Excitement prevailed as all aspects were discussed, and an agreement was reached on where they would build their house.

With fall coming on and harvesting to be done, in addition to building the house, the Mercers and Tim had their work cut out for them. Thomas Daley, who had good carpentering skills, volunteered to help. He moved into the bunk house with Tim and spent most of the next month helping build the house. Rachael came over each day and worked with him as a carpenter's helper, harvesting crops, and anything else she could do to help.

Paula also came over to help on the house. It turned out she was good with hammer and saw and other carpentry tools.

Part of their task included dismantling an abandoned house in Richmond and then hauling the materials to the farm.

Roofing was a concern until they found several bundles of shingles in an abandoned warehouse behind a hardware store. They found roofing tar and roofing nails in the same location.

Tim and Pamela also built a storage building behind the house. They put in a doggie door in one end of it, and just inside in the right rear corner, they built a room for Trixie. They also put in a window on the side of the dog room so there could be air circulation in the summer. They used an abundance of insulation on the sides and above the ceiling to help keep it warm in the winter.

Thomas and Rachael were very attracted to each other, and it was obvious another dwelling would soon be needed.

On Saturdays, Church and Bible study took priority. Shopping was done in the afternoons, and stores laid in for the coming week.

Since the baptisms and the incident with the attack on Meir and Asher, a great calm had fallen over the land.

By the middle of October the house for Tim and Pamela had been built and the crops were in. Their wedding took place at the church Saturday afternoon, November third.

In Europe and the Middle East, at mid-morning on November fourth, a supernatural fire fell from the heavens and encompassed the land. There were voices, thunder, and lightning, and an earthquake.

Waves of fire, voices, thunder, and lightning rolled westward, and circled the earth. The Mercer families were awakened by a distant shaking and rumbling. They saw flashes in the sky which somewhat resembled the aurora borealis.

The silence had ended.

CHAPTER IV
FIRST TRUMPET
JUDGMENT

Revelation 8:7 "And the seven angels which had the seven trumpets prepared themselves to sound. The first angel sounded, and there followed hail and fire mingled with blood, and they were cast upon the earth; and the third part of trees was burnt up, and all green grass was burnt up."

Relative calm had prevailed in the one world government domain for several weeks. The world leader, the anti-Christ, working through his ten regional leaders and local subordinates, continued tightening his grip over the people of the land.

Concentration camps had been established in the ten regions. They were used to house dissidents, primarily Christians, who would not take the mark of the beast and/or would not renounce God and Jesus Christ. Each contained its own death house with facilities for beheading. Each facility had plenty of volunteers for performing the executions.

The cities adjacent to each concentration camp were occupied by guards, executioners, and administrators of the facility. All other occupants of the city had been thoroughly vetted to insure their loyalty to and worship of their World Leader, who proclaimed himself as their god.

Most of the dissidents (Christians) had been rounded up by this time. The detention centers, where the initial processing had taken place, were either closed, or scaled way back.

Many groups of Christians were still at large, in hiding, and in constant grave danger.

Death from starvation and disease was prevalent throughout the area controlled by the New World Government. There were two great societal distinctions: The elite and the masses. Essentially, the elite ate and had health care while the half starved masses succumbed frequently to disease and illness.

Death wagons traveled the streets each day, picking up those who had died overnight. They never came back empty.

The great majority of the masses cursed God. The greater majority of the elite cursed God. However, God, even in this time of the wrath of His judgment, still offered salvation to those who would seek His face.

In their attempt to normalize conditions, the ruling powers had upgraded the transportation facilities significantly. They had repaired some of the oil fields and refinement facilities in the Middle East, and fuel was available for aircraft as well as ground vehicles. Diesel fuel was also being produced. Some trains were back in service, and trucks were seen on the highways more often, especially in the Middle East and some places in Europe.

Roadways between cities had been reopened. Many that had been severed, however, would never be repaired.

Some of them were severed during the war and some by the horrendous earthquakes at the time of the rapture.

In addition to ground transportation, airline flights between major cities had also been re-established in their new world. Airline flights were still relatively short, due to lack of refueling facilities at more distant locations. Airline use was still restricted to government officials and the elite.

The New World Government continued to enlarge its area of consolidated control. So far, Scandanavia, Europe, Asia Minor, The Middle East, and North Africa, were included. They were working on Russia. Since Russia still had a significant (and unknown) number of nukes, they were taking it slow.

They had influenced Russia to adopt similar policies related to population identification and control, such as the mark, and similar practices toward Christians.

At mid morning on the fourth of November, God cast a supernatural fire from the heavens upon His enemies in the land. There were voices, thunder, lightning and an earthquake.

The flash illuminated the land, much brighter than the mid morning light. The noise was horrific. Immediately following, God cast hail, fire, and blood from the heavens and wreaked havoc on His enemies throughout Scandanavia, Europe, Asia Minor, Middle East, Russia, and North Africa, and other parts of the world. 'Vengeance is mine, I will repay, saith the Lord.

Millions were on the streets within the area under siege by God as the hail and fire fell. Millions died immediately from the crushing hail and the intense heat from the fire.

Gobs of blood, reminiscent of the plagues of Egypt,

rained down and splashed off buildings and splattered on the ground.

Many trees burst into flames and all the grass was immediately consumed by the searing flames and heat.

The cities in the vicinity of the concentration camps were utterly destroyed. The people living in these cities had been spooked by the initial earthquake and lightning and had rushed outside in time to get the full brunt of the falling hail, and fire, and blood.

The concentration camps were unharmed by the earthquakes. The prisoners remained inside behind locked doors, but the guards and operations personnel rushed outside to see what was happening. Too bad.

When the tempest had passed, and all became quiet and calm, the prisoners, who were mostly Christians, discovered that all the locks were open. They made their escape without any sign of pursuit.

The World Leader (the beast. a.k.a. the anti-Christ), and the false prophet were not harmed. Their mansions and the surrounding compounds were spared during the earthquake. Many of the servants and minions within the compound had rushed outside when they heard the initial noise. Most were caught in the onslaught and perished. Needless to say, the events of the day would be a significant setback to their plans.

The land of Israel had areas of minimal damage and areas of significant destruction. Many of the 144,000 protected Christian Jews lived in Israel. In their immediate vicinity, no harm was done.

God's enemies in Israel, Jewish and non-Jewish, did not fare well.

Alvin Mercer had set up his short wave radio equipment

soon after they moved to the Richmond area. They were able to use the receiver and get outside news without too much power drain by using batteries, which he recharged when absolutely necessary. He did the monitoring in the evening when radio signals were at their strongest as they reflected off the different Ionosphere layers.

The evening after the shaking, rumbling, and flashing lights in the sky, he tuned in to some of the more dependable frequencies to see if he could get some news. Unfortunately, all he got was heavy static and noise due to the atmospheric disturbances.

"Well, I'll try again tomorrow night and see if conditions are any better," Alvin told Rhonda, who had followed him into the room.

The following morning, Tim approached James. "Pamela and I are going over to work with the bees today. Following that, we'll bike over to Alvin and Rhonda's and visit for a couple hours. We should be back by dark."

The morning was cool and they both dressed with long sleeves. Pamela wore blue jeans and pulled on a toboggan hat.

Tim laughed. "Pamela! That toboggan looks like overkill."

Pamela came right back at Tim, "My head, my hair. I'm not taking chances on getting my ears cold. Plus, the cap keeps my hair from getting terribly tangled."

Tim laughed. "Let's go."

A short time later, they were at their bee farm and started the cleaning of the area and securing the hives for the winter. They also removed the extra brood boxes and supers from the storage area and began scraping and cleaning the insides.

They collected all the wax scrapings and pieces of wax

they had gathered from the hives and placed them in buckets, which they would haul back to the house. The wax would be used for making starter comb for the honey racks. Any extra wax would be made into candles, or used as barter material.

Following the work with the hives, they biked over to Pamela's parents' house. Pamela hurriedly parked her bike, rushed into the house, and grabbed her mother in a passionate embrace.

Rhonda laughed. "What a surprise! You almost knocked me over."

"Mom, I've really missed you all. It's really strange living away from my family. I know we're not very far away but it's so different." She paused, blushing, and then continuing as she looked at Tim, "but it's a REALLY good difference!" They all laughed.

Rhonda commented, "Thomas is here to see Rachael. They walked out to the wooded area at the back of the farm."

Tim and Pamela looked at each other, and Tim spoke up. "When's the wedding?"

Rhonda laughed, "If there's been a proposal, I haven't heard of it yet. I wouldn't be surprised if it happens soon."

Tim asked, "Where's Alvin?"

Rhonda replied. "Alvin went to town about three hours ago. He should be back soon."

Rhonda continued, "I see Alvin coming down the lane right now."

The horse and buggy came on down the lane and pulled up to the porch. Alvin stepped down, walked over, and gripped Tim's hand. At the same time, he got a big hug from Pamela.

Following the greeting, Alvin got their attention. "I heard

some news today which indicates that disturbing events took place in Europe, the Middle East, and in other areas being dominated by the World Government." He continued, "We got an inkling of it with the light in the sky and the shaking and rumbling. Hopefully we'll be able to pick up some news tonight on the radio."

Tim asked, "Do you need for James to come over tonight and see what's going on?"

Alvin replied, "Tim, tell James I'll monitor the radio tonight and come over there in the morning to tell him what I know. I also have some information on happenings here in Kentucky and in other parts of the United States. I had a long talk with our local law enforcement and learned a lot."

Thomas and Rachael walked up to the group, who were still standing outside. Tim shook hands with Thomas, and Rachael hugged Pamela.

"Tim, I'm planning on having a Bible study each Saturday afternoon, starting this coming Saturday. It will begin at 2:30 p.m. and last one and a half hours. I'm hoping you and Pamela can come." Thomas explained.

Tim replied, "I wouldn't miss it for anything."

The following morning, Alvin arrived at James and Paula's house at 8:00 a.m. He was accompanied by Rhonda and Rachael. They had bicycled over.

Tim and Pamela heard them arrive and walked over from their house to join the rest in the living room.

After the normal greetings and chatter, James spoke up. "Alvin, what can you tell us this morning?"

Alvin replied, "Quite a bit. Atmospheric conditions were still pretty bad last night, but I was able to get some idea of what might be happening in the world. I'm not sure of all the area affected, but it sounds like all the countries controlled by the New World Government, plus Russia and other parts of Africa, were hit hard by a deluge from the sky consisting of large hail, flaming fire, and big gobs of blood. It was deadly and nasty, and from the reports, millions, if not tens of millions, were killed."

He continued, "I would say this has been a big setback for the New World Government. Their concentration camps were somehow liberated, and it seems the Christians and the other dissidents were able to just walk out and escape. They lost most of their infrastructure and personnel that controlled the prisoners. It will take months, or years for them to recover."

"What about the World Leader and his inner circle?" James asked.

Alvin replied, "It seems that they were somehow protected during the event." He continued: "I also got a sketchy report that other parts of the world may have been affected as well. It usually takes a few days for information to filter in after something happens in the Far East, South Pacific, Australia, India, and other distant places. Atmospheric conditions around the world are iffy right now."

"Tim said you had some local and state news from our local law enforcement. Did you talk to Mike Lindon?" James asked.

Alvin replied, "Yes. Mike was there, and he had a deputy with him by the name of Russell Grose. They've developed quite a network of communication and co-operation with other locations here in Kentucky and also in other states. We need to meet with them on a regular basis and share information."

"How do they communicate?" asked Paula.

Alvin replied, "They communicate mostly by radio. They have generators, gasoline and diesel fuel available which allows them to communicate at pre-set times. They supplement that by using regularly scheduled messengers to deliver information back and forth. Kinda like the old Pony Express."

"Saturday should be interesting." Alvin added. "In addition to the regular church services, Thomas will be teaching a Bible class in the afternoon. I'm pretty sure it will be from the book of Revelation and the end time prophecies."

"We're living in some strange times," commented Rhonda.

"I can say amen to that." Rachael agreed.

Routine work continued on both farms, and Thursday afternoon, Alvin sent Herbert over to James and Paula's house to invite all of them over for the evening. He informed them that Thomas would be there, as well. Their intent was to catch up on all the latest news.

Although it would be after dark and fairly chilly, Tim, Ron, and David decided to ride bicycles. James, Paula, Pamela, and Tiffany would go in the buggy.

Following an enjoyable meal and an hour of gossip, kidding of Rachael and Thomas, and some fellowship, they all gathered around the short wave radio as Alvin began tuning in on one of his favorite news channels. It was the one in Switzerland and came on at 8:00 p.m.

Atmospheric conditions were not the best at this time, but, hopefully, they would learn something.

Tim paired off with Pamela and found a dark corner. Thomas paired off with Rachael and found a dark corner.

The newly-weds and the not quite newly-weds held hands while listening attentively as the news came through.

The events that had occurred on Sunday, November fourth, had encompassed the entire world. Population centers seemed to have been primary targets. Tens of millions died. Major disruption of normal living was manifest all over the earth. Recovery, if possible, would be slow and painful.

Following the broadcast, Alvin called Tim, Thomas, James, and Herbert, off to one side. "What would you guys think about my going to town tomorrow to see if I can set up a meeting with Mike Linden for Sunday, or whenever they have time to meet with us? We need to see if we can all pool and share the information that's available."

They all discussed the matter and concluded that a meeting would be a good idea.

Friday morning, Alvin took the buggy and headed for Richmond. In addition to trying to set up a meeting with Mike Linden, he would also do some bartering and shopping. He loaded some jars of honey, eggs, pumpkins, potatoes, canned beans, and corn into the buggy. They had harvested several bushels of potatoes, which were turning out to be a very popular product.

Back before the Mercers moved to Richmond, the lack of currency had become a problem as the bartering system became more and more awkward. Bartering was fine, up to a point. When someone went to the market to purchase small items, such as a dozen eggs or a few vegetables, it became more difficult.

Several of the local residents and merchants had been talking about the problem for a few months. Finally, they approached the Mayor and City Council and asked them if they could look into it and see if they could come up with a solution.

The City Council studied the problem and agreed to approach a former banker in Richmond by the name of Toby Little. They asked him to help them pick a committee to work with him to come up with a solution. Four well known and respected local residents were selected to become a part of the committee. They all agreed.

Toby and his committee held meetings until they came up with a plan which they thought might be viable. They submitted their proposal to the City Council.

The City Council studied the proposal, and when they were satisfied with it, called a general meeting for all interested parties in and around Richmond to come and hear the plan.

Although the Richmond area didn't have a sophisticated voting system in place, they believed they could get enough of an idea to make a decision.

Four locations were set up for handing out straws. Each person going through the line was given a long and a short straw. A short straw bucket and a long straw bucket was set up at each location. The long straw meant yes. Short straw meant no. When the straws were totaled, the plan was approved overwhelmingly.

The same voting method was used to approve or disapprove of the hiring of Toby Little and his committee to set up and operate the new banking system. The vote was overwhelming to approve. Toby would work with different members of the committee, as needed, to get the job done.

As the first order of business, Toby named the bank The First Bank of Richmond.

The new wealth system was initially established as a credit system. One credit would be approximately equivalent to the old dollar bill.

During the establishment period, the bank owned no assets. Property owners were allowed to come by the bank and set up an account, and borrow credits. They secured the credits by signing a lien against their property or other assets. Property or assets could be a farm, cattle, horses buggies, etc. Then they were issued certificates of credit in their name. Certificates of credit would be in denominations of 100, 50, 20, and 10. For smaller amounts of change needed, goods would be exchanged.

Upon receipt of the certificates, the account holder would date each certificate for the date received. When purchasing with the certificate, they signed and dated the purchase date. In the next step of the process, the receiver of the certificate would keep it for currency in making change, or turn it in at the bank and have it deposited into their account.

Regular accounting practices at the bank would entail adding to or taking away from individual accounts.

An account holder who was depositing more than withdrawing, could eventually pay off their lien and continue building up their account balance.

The system was still rather cumbersome, but certainly less so than strictly bartering. As long as the account holders were not too numerous, the system was practical and not overly prone to counterfeiting.

After finishing his shopping and banking chores, Alvin went to the sheriff's office. Fortunately, Mike Linden and Russell Grose were both there.

Alvin walked in and grasped Mike by the hand. "Good

morning, sheriff." He then shook hands with Russell. "Good morning, deputy."

"Would you care for some coffee?" Mike asked.

"I certainly would," Alvin responded.

"Let's sit around the table," Mike suggested.

They all fixed their coffee and took seats around the table. "What do you have on your mind, Alvin?" Mike asked.

"Mike, my family, Tim Bailey, and James' family all met at my house last night to listen to world news on the short wave radio. Following that, we discussed the possibility of us sitting down with you and Russell from time to time and sharing news and information."

I think that's a great idea," Mike responded. "Did you have any particular time in mind?"

Alvin replied."We have church and Bible study on Saturday, and we could meet with you Sunday or Monday, or any other day that would be best for you."

Mike thought for a few moments. "Alvin, we have a dispatcher coming through every Tuesday and Friday. He brings current news and messages which are being passed around throughout the country. I believe Wednesday would be the best day for us to meet. That way, any news I get on Tuesday I can share with you, and any news I get from you on Wednesday, I can share with the dispatcher on Friday."

"Good." Alvin replied, and then continued: "Mike, I'm getting ready to ask you and Russell a personal question. I hope you won't take offense. I believe you'll agree we're living in a very troubling time and we don't have time to wonder if we're being insensitive. That being said; are you Christians?"

Mike smiled and replied, "I am. When possible I attend the church services where Thomas preaches."

Russell spoke up. "Alvin, I'm not yet a Christian but Mike is working on me."

Alvin replied soberly, "Don't wait too long. Times are too uncertain. None of us knows if we'll be here tomorrow."

"I know," Russell replied soberly.

Alvin continued: "Come to church Saturday if you can. Also, come Saturday afternoon. Thomas is teaching a Bible study from 2:30 until 4:00. He's teaching from the book of Revelation about the end time prophecies. It may give you some insight on what we've been going through and what may be coming in the next few years."

"I'll be there both times if I possibly can," Russell replied.

"Same here," Mike responded.

Alvin said his goodbye and made his departure. He still had quite a bit to do in the way of bartering and purchasing.

Saturday came and at 10:00 a.m. they were all in the church and seated.

Alvin looked around and sure enough, Mike and Russell were there.

Russell had a ruddy complexion and reddish hair. He stood slightly under six feet tall and looked to be in his mid to early twenties. Russell was dating a young lady in the community, but she wasn't at the service.

The sermon was evangelistic in nature, and at the end of the worship service when the invitation was given Russell and three others went forward, confessed their sins, and asked the Lord to come into their hearts and lives.

Following the service, many of the people went to the front, greeted them, and welcomed them as brothers and sisters into the family of God.

Thomas had reminded the congregation at the beginning

of the service that the Bible study would be held at the church at 2:30 p.m.

The Mercer clan accepted Thomas' invitation and used a classroom at the church to eat their lunch which they had brought from home. Rachael invited Thomas and assured him they had included him in the preparation of the food.

Following the meal, Thomas excused himself and went into his study and closed the door. He spent the remaining time before the Bible study in review, meditation, and prayer.

At 2:30 the church sanctuary was filled. Additional chairs were placed in the aisles to accommodate the overflow. At least 300 were in attendance.

The existing population in and around Richmond was predominantly non-Christian. In the non-Christian category, there were those who were ambivalent toward God. There were those who were hostile toward God. There were those who were evil, mean, dangerous, and virulently anti-God and anti-Christian.

The Mercers and their friends paid attention in Richmond and the surrounding area and remained vigilant toward potential threat and danger. It was a given that it wasn't safe to go unarmed. Practically everyone packed a weapon of some type. It was mostly open carry for convenience sake.

At the Bible study, it looked odd to see so many people with rifles held between their legs. Where multiple members of a family were present, there were usually only one or two weapons showing.

Thomas took his place behind the podium in the front of the auditorium. "I'm overwhelmed at the number of you who have come out here for the Bible study. I realize that hearing will be a problem since we don't have a sound system yet. We're working on one, but I'm not sure when it will be ready. I'll speak as loud as I can, and, hopefully, you'll all be able to hear.

"Starting next week, I'll teach two classes each week. One will be the same as today: Saturday at 2:30 p.m. until 4:00. The other one will be Tuesday, 9:00 a.m. until 10:30. The classes will be held here."

"The class on Tuesday will be focused on two primary subjects: what is Christianity and how to become a Christian. The class on Saturday will be on Bible history, prophecy, and end-time events.

"These classes will continue as long as there are enough people who are interested, or until we're providentially hindered.

"Getting closer to the subject of the day, I would like to say this: Some of you may see this as more of a sermon than a Bible study. I can't help that. The Bible in its entirety is a message to mankind from God.

"Most of you are probably familiar with the terms: Revelation, Seven Year Tribulation, Armageddon, The Church, The Day of The Lord, The Rapture, Millennium, End Times, etc. Since we're at the time in history where we're caught up in some of the actual events, I'll try to give you an overview of the way I see it. I'll approach this by working forward; after I tell you where I think we are at this time.

"In the book of Revelation – and by the way, the book of Revelation is the Revelation of Jesus Christ to the Apostle John while John was imprisoned on the Isle of Patmos; there's a lack of agreement among scholars on many parts of the book. Recent events, that we've actually experienced or heard about; and coming events, no doubt, will help us understand much of it more clearly.

"I believe we're living in the end time during 'The Day of the Lord,' well past the middle of the seven year tribulation period."

"The Day of the Lord is the time in history when God pours out His wrath, and death, on ALL His enemies living on the earth. Who are His enemies? Be sure you understand. His enemies are; regardless of how good, bad, or terrible, those who have not been born again, who have not accepted Jesus Christ as savior.

"At the end of the battle of Armageddon, which comes at the end of the seven years of tribulation, God will have killed every human above the age of accountability, who is not a Christian. In other words, if you're still alive and not a Christian when the end comes, you shall die. You shall go to hell.

"I know this sounds harsh, but that's just the way it is."

"If my understanding is correct, in just another two or three years, there won't be one living enemy of God left upon the face of the earth. The anti-Christ and false prophet will have been cast into a lake of fire, and satan will have been bound and cast into the bottomless pit for a thousand years.

"I'm going to give you a brief overview of what I suspect has taken place in the past few decades. Mind you, I don't claim to be a scholar. I don't dispute others with their beliefs or what they suspect. Knowing what little I know, you could say this is my best guess.

"I believe a milestone was passed and the clock started ticking when Israel was reborn as a nation in 1948. I believe the next major event which occurred was when Jesus Christ opened the first seal. This is found in Revelation 6:1 and describes the rider of the white horse. I believe this began a period of time when leaders of the earth tried to bring peace to the earth through the United Nations,; small wars, or "police actions," and diplomacy. Our country also used covert, and overt tactics to try to influence or overthrow governments we thought needed a change.

"When was the first seal opened? I don't know. It could have been 1948 or sometime after would be my guess.

"I believe the nuclear war was the opening of the second seal which describes the rider of the red horse, suggesting war. The third seal depicting the rider of the black horse indicated starvation, and the fourth seal, with the pale horse, predicted the horrendous death tolls caused by pestilence, starvation, and disease.

"The opening of the fifth seal speaks of the martyrs who are crying out in heaven and asking the Lord how long would it be before they were avenged.

"Up to this point, the people of the earth don't see this as the wrath of God coming upon them but as the result of the decisions of earthly rulers and nations. Another key point is that at this time, Christians are still living upon the face of the earth. God said that Christians would not be subjected to His wrath.

"Then we come to the sixth seal in Revelation 6:12-17, where it talks of the horrendous events concerning the sun, the moon, the stars, earthquakes, upheavals, and, as most of us sadly learned the hard way, the rapture.

"A big question is, where are we now in time and in history? As I told you earlier, I believe we're somewhere within the time of The Day of The Lord. I believe we've just experienced the sounding of the first trumpet talked about in Revelation 8:7. 'And the seven angels which had the seven trumpets prepared themselves to sound. The first angel sounded and there followed hail and fire mingled with blood, and they were cast upon the earth; and the third part of trees was burnt up, and all green grass was burnt up.'

"Please note: It doesn't say they fell. It says they were cast. An angry God cast them.

"If this is where we are in history, we'll soon experience six more trumpet judgments, and seven vial judgments. To reiterate, these judgments are the wrath of the Almighty God being poured out on His enemies, all non-Christians; to torture and to kill them.

"These judgments will come faster and faster until Jesus comes down and destroys the remainder of His human enemies at the time of the battle of Armageddon.

"The one big question in all our minds - - -"

Suddenly, noise from the scraping of chairs, loud cursing, and stamping of feet interrupted the class. More than a dozen people got up and stamped and cursed as they left the building.

Several of the people in the class went on the alert with their firearms, but fortunately, no shots were fired. It took about fifteen minutes for everybody to calm down and resume their seats.

Thomas went back to his position behind the podium, looked up, smiled questioningly, and remarked jokingly; "Must have been something I said?"

Everybody laughed, breaking the tension that was still apparent.

He continued, "I apologize for this happening. I could

tell we had a group of people that were getting pretty antsy, but I couldn't see how I could change what I was saying."

Thomas resumed his teaching. "Now, back where we were at the time of interruption: the big questions in our minds is: what will happen right here where we are, and what happens to us, Christians and non-Christians? What should we do?

"What is my answer to that? I don't know. My advice would be to continue on with our daily lives. Trust God. Worship God. If you aren't yet a Christian, don't wait to get right with God. Non Christians are the target of God's wrath. There is no escape.

"Back to the questions; what will happen and what should we do? My understanding at this time is that all Christians and children under the age of accountability who still survive at the end of the Day of the Lord will continue on and live during the millennium."

A lot of "ooh's" and "ahh's" could be heard as the people absorbed that bit of information.

Thomas continued, "Now mind you, I could be wrong. However, at this time in my studies, that's my understanding. If this is true, then I believe it would behoove us to structure our lives and livelihood as if we'll continue to live on through the coming decades.

"I have a word of caution. We have no way of knowing how many of us may be killed by events that take place during the wrathful judgments of God. We need to be prudent in what we do, where we go, and who we keep company with. I don't recommend hanging out where non-Christians hang out. I don't know if that matters, but who knows.

"I'm going to give you a short description of the events

following the six remaining trumpet and seven vial judgments. After that, we'll quit for the day. During our next sessions, we'll try to fill out and expand upon the coming events." Thomas continued, "Following the last of the vial judgments, Jesus Christ shall destroy the remainder of His human enemies at the battle of Armageddon. His human enemies around the world who are not at the battle of Armageddon shall also die.

"Jesus Christ then throws the anti-Christ and the false prophet into the lake of fire. He also chains satan and throws him into the bottomless pit where they will stay for a thousand years.

"Jesus Christ then rules the people remaining on the earth with a rod of iron for a thousand years. His saints rule with him.

"At the end of the thousand years, Jesus releases satan and his angels for a period of time. Satan again deceives the non-Christians in the world and leads them into a rebellion against God. Following that, Jesus Christ again destroys all of God's enemies and throws satan into a lake of fire. As far as I can tell, that is the end of sin. Period.

"At that time in history, or thereabouts, the New Jerusalem (The Holy City) descends from heaven and hovers above the earth. Some say it hovers over the old Jerusalem. I don't know. The new Jerusalem is huge. It's 1500 miles wide, 1500 miles long, and 1500 miles high. Think of the size of it! If it hovered above the United States, it would cover almost half of it! The description of it is found in Revelation 21.

"The New Jerusalem shall be 100 percent sin free. Nothing sinful shall ever enter it, ever. It will be occupied, in part, by resurrected Godly people, including the saints of the Lord's church, Old Testament saints, and the martyred tribulation saints."

Thomas concluded the Bible study with a word of prayer.

Following the class, the Mercers went to the front and said their goodbyes to Thomas.

Rachael spoke up. "Dad, wait for me. I'd like to visit with Thomas a few minutes, and then I'll be right out."

Everybody left and went home except Alvin, Rhonda and Herbert, who waited outside until Rachael joined them.

CHAPTER V
SECOND TRUMPET JUDGMENT

Revelation 8:8-9 "And the second angel sounded, and as it were a great mountain burning with fire was cast into the sea and the third part of the sea became blood. And a third part of the creatures that were in the sea, and had life, died; and the third part of the ships were destroyed."

Winter in Richmond was rough. Temperatures dropped into the single digits several times and a few times, went below zero.

Activities on the farms were reduced to a minimum. Keeping the animals fed, sheltered and watered was their primary concern. During the times of the hard freezes, keeping water available for the animals became the most difficult. At times, they stored water in the house, in tubs and used whiskey barrels, and carried it out to the animals. When their water source thawed, they would refill the tubs. At the worst times, they would take chunks of ice into the house and melt them.

Fortunately, they had laid in a good supply of firewood

and were able to stay warm. They also supplemented their wood with coal, which they had been able to barter for in Irvine.

When temperatures were above freezing, the Mercers would visit back and forth between farms and sometimes make a trip to town.

Thomas made frequent trips to Alvin and Rhonda's to visit Rachael. Thomas had proposed to Rachael and a wedding date had been set for April 15.

Alvin made occasional trips to Richmond and coordinated with Mike Linden on current events and news. Locally, everything had been quiet. Mike had been getting troublesome reports about some renegade groups. There was one around Charleston, West Virginia; one up in Eastern Kentucky; and one down in Muhlenburg County, in Western Kentucky, not far from Paradise Point on the Green River and one at Elizabethtown.

Hopefully, the ones in Western Kentucky and the one in West Virginia were far enough away they would never be a problem. The one in Eastern Kentucky could be close enough to be a threat.

Alvin remarked, "Mike, at first our families had considered going into the Harlan area. I'm glad now that we changed our mind and came here instead."

Mike replied, "Alvin, I'm glad you made the change. If we ever do have problems, I'm sure we can count on your help."

Alvin responded, "Mike, just let us know. We'll do what we can." He continued, "What are you hearing about governments: local, state, and National?"

Mike responded. "Locally, we're it. There's no county government. We had a visitor from Frankfort one day who told us that state officials in Frankfort were trying to piece a state government together. They were interested in collecting taxes, primarily. We called our local government together, met with him, and convinced him he had wasted his trip and could forget us in his planning."

Alvin laughed. "Good for you. That would be just what we need; somebody coming in to pick our pockets."

Mike continued, "He presented us with a set of rules and guidelines. You can imagine what they were like, coming from liberal politicians. We certainly would never have accepted them, not even at the point of a gun. Essentially, we told him to get lost and not come back.

"Incidentally, he traveled here on a bicycle."

Alvin stated: "Mike, on my radio, I keep getting rumblings of a national government. I believe they could have been encroaching on us by now. Apparently, this latest event that took place around the world somehow set them back. Hopefully, we won't have to worry about them."

"What about international?" Mike asked.

Alvin replied. "It seems they're still trying to recover from their last setback. The Christians and dissidents that escaped are still roaming free. Hopefully, the escaped Christians can link up with other Christians for mutual assistance and support. I'm sure though that those who don't have the mark are having a tough time trying to survive.

"From what I hear, those with the mark, unless they're part of the government or the elite, aren't faring much better. Apparently, there's an extreme famine worldwide. We're very fortunate we're in a farming area."

The middle of April rolled around, and things were looking much brighter than they were in the winter. Grass was growing, trees were blooming and leafing out, bees were working, and everybody was in much higher spirits. Winter had been tough. Tim and Pamela had lost one hive of bees. It could have been much worse.

The first of May, Tim walked in on Pamela who, apparently, was quite nauseous. "Pamela! What in the world is wrong with you?" He exclaimed.

"Tim, I'll give you three guesses and the first two don't count," Pamela replied.

Tim thought for a minute and then blurted out. "You're pregnant!"

Pamela, still shaky and pale, replied, "you guessed it."

Tim grabbed her, hugged her, and exclaimed, "Oh joy! We're going to have a baby! I'm so happy, and I so love you!"

Pamela returned the embrace and replied softly, "I'm so glad you're glad Tim, and I'm so happy."

Tim replied, "Pamela, I'm so sorry you're sick."

She replied, "Don't worry about it Tim. It should go away fairly soon. I'm probably about six weeks to two months pregnant."

Tim did some swift figuring. "This means the baby should be here sometime around the middle of November."

Tim and Pamela went back to their tiny living room and sat down on the couch, still holding hands.

"Pamela, I hope we've made the right decision, bringing a child into the world during these uncertain times. I know we've talked about it, prayed about it, talked with your parents, also James and Paula, and the pastor, about it."

Pamela replied, "Tim, pure and simple, it's a step of faith. We'll have to trust God to guide us and watch over us."

"Pamela, shall we tell everybody or wait awhile?"

"Tim, let's keep it to ourselves for now. I'm pretty sure the secret will get out soon because of the morning sickness. If not, somebody will notice when I start showing."

"Are you going to feel up to going with me to check on the bees?"

"I think I'll wait a few days and see if my system settles down," Pamela replied.

The wedding of Thomas and Rachael took place on April, 15. The church was crowded with people. Following the reception, which was held at the church, Thomas and Rachael returned to Thomas' home where they spent their honeymoon.

Thomas, with the help of some of the people at the church, had found a vacant brick house on the south side of Richmond when he first came to the area. He did a lot of cleaning, painting, and fixing, with the help of others, and ended up with a nice dwelling. The house was 1,000 square foot. It had three bedrooms, living room, kitchen, and a bath. By carrying water, he was still able to use the commode.

The house was easy to heat and had a wood and coal stove. He also used it in the wintertime for cooking. For summer cooking, he had a charcoal burning grill on the back porch. Instead of charcoal, which he didn't have, he burned wood and coal.

Rachael liked her new home. It had a small, but nice, front yard, with plenty of places to plant flowers.

For a house warming, they held an open house on May the fifteenth, a month after they got married. Dozens of people came by at random times and shared their coffee, tea, and cookies. Most of them left small gifts, and their best, and well wishes.

Rachael quickly became a help meet for Thomas in church work and other community activities. They had a food pantry at the church, and she helped with receiving and handing out food to needy people.

Rachael also called upon her mother to help and went after the house with a vengeance. They thoroughly scrubbed and sterilized the inside of the house. Thomas was somewhat skeptical of all the cleaning for he had done quite a bit himself, and from a bachelor's viewpoint, well _____ .

On Wednesday, May 28, God's angel blew the Second Trumpet, pronouncing another judgment upon God's enemies that were still living upon the face of the earth.

Select oceans and seas around the world were bombarded with fiery masses. The waters in those areas turned to blood and sea life died. The decaying sea life rose to the top, drifted to the shores, and immediately began the process of decay.

The Mediterranean sea was one of the areas God selected. Over the next several days, the pollution of those waters, horrible beyond imagination, would cause untold suffering. Humanity would suffer from the loss of food, causing more starvation. Humanity would suffer from the gagging smells and the blinding vapors floating in the air. Humanity would also suffer from diseases which would rise and drift into thousands of square miles.

The oceans and seas around the world that were polluted would never produce food again in the lifetime of God's enemies, who still survived.

The beleaguered world leader and his minions, who had never regained stability after the first Trumpet Judgment, now had another crisis on their hands.

By Friday Alvin had picked up enough news over the

radio to know that another major event had occurred. He went into town and, after visiting with Mike Linden and explaining to him what he had heard he went over to Thomas and Rachael's house.

"Hi dad," Rachael greeted. "What brings you here today?"

Alvin replied, "It seems that another one of God's judgments fell upon the earth yesterday, and I wanted to come by and let you know what's going on."

Rachael replied. "Thomas went to the church to do some work. It's almost time for lunch, so why don't you go get him and bring him home. I'd like to hear what you have to say."

Alvin got back in the buggy and had his horse trot over to the church. He went inside and located Thomas.

"Good morning, Thomas," he greeted.

"Good morning Alvin. What brings you to town today?"

Alvin briefly explained he had heard some news last night. "Thomas, Rachael suggested that I bring you home for lunch and then tell you both at once about the news."

Thomas replied, "Good idea. Why don't you go back over there, and I'll come on my bike?"

Alvin responded. "Throw your bike in the back of the buggy. No need to bike when you can ride a buggy."

When they got back to the house, Rachael had their lunch prepared.

After asking a blessing on the food, they ate, and then retired to the living room.

Alvin explained. "The picture isn't very clear at this time, but it seems that in various parts of the world, huge fireballs, slabs of fire, gobs of fire, or whatever you want to call them, fell into the oceans and seas. The waters looked bloody, and in some places, viscous. Fishes and other sea creatures were floating to the surface and drifting toward land. Wreckage of ships was also drifting to shore. About thirty-six hours after it started, the dead fish and animals were beginning to smell."

Thomas replied, "Alvin, what you've described sounds like the Second Trumpet of God's judgment. Here, I'll read it to you from the Bible. Revelation 8:8-9 " And the second angel sounded, and as it were, a great mountain burning with fire was cast into the sea and a third part of the sea became blood. And a third part of the creatures that were in the sea, and had life, died; and a third part of the ships were destroyed."

Alvin replied, "Sounds like that is what may have happened. It's hard to say what effect that may have upon the world. I suspect it will cause a lot more starvation and probably a lot more disease."

Thomas continued: "From all I can tell from the Scriptures, this was a supernatural event. Nature didn't supply the materials that fell. God provided them. The targeted areas, no doubt, were selected by God for His reasons."

Alvin responded, "Our information is still very sketchy. I would think that in another two or three weeks we'll have a better picture of all the locations that were hit."

Rachael spoke up. "Thomas, if this is the second trumpet, when will the third trumpet sound, and what will happen at that time?"

Thomas replied, "The third trumpet affects the inland waters: rivers, springs, etc. They'll be made bitter, and many people will die from it."

Rachael asked, "Will it affect our water here in Richmond?"

Thomas replied soberly, "We just won't know until it actually happens."

Alvin got up. "Thomas, I'll see you and Rachael in church Saturday, Lord willing. I'm going to head out and do a little shopping on the way."

Alvin went out and unhitched his horse and drove the buggy back downtown to the business area. Coffee was getting in short supply, and he needed to do some looking around. For some time now, they had been running their old coffee grounds through a second time. The previously used grounds were boiled and the water then used to brew the coffee, using the new grounds.

Alvin thought there could be no fast recovery from the calamity that had just befallen the world. The horrendous loss of lives, the subsequent loss of their skills, and the destruction of most of the world's civilized infrastructure placed the people of the world in a state very close to paralysis. This made the old slogan, "where there's a will there's a way," much more challenging.

The people of the world were practically back to the basic level of needs of food, clothing, shelter and survival. Sadly, most of them didn't have the knowledge, skills, or resources to cope, except at the most basic level.

Alvin drove the buggy back to his house and tied the reins off at the porch. He went inside, hugged and kissed Rhonda, and then asked, "Where's Herbert?"

She replied, "He's out in the back field working in the corn."

"Rhonda, I'm going to see if we can get all of our

family together Sunday or Monday and do some sharing of information and some planning. We need to be sure that all of us understand the best we can what's going on in the world and what can be done to prepare and cope with it, looking to the future." Alvin explained.

"I agree with you Alvin. We're surviving right now, but our livelihood and our ability to cope seems precarious," Rhonda stated.

"Rhonda, I'm going down to the cornfield and work with Herbert for awhile. We'll be back in time for supper." Alvin unhitched the horse and drove down to the corn field.

On Saturday, they went to church, and while there, set up a meeting for Monday at 10:00 a.m. They decided to meet at the church.

Thomas offered a suggestion. "What do you think of inviting Mike and Russell as well as the Mayor and City Council?"

James replied by asking a question. "What do we know about the Mayor and City Council? Are they Christian or non-Christian? Would they be supportive or non-supportive?"

Thomas replied. "Some are Christians, and some are not. I've met them all, as well as most of their families. In all of them I've met, I haven't detected any hostility, but a few are pretty stubborn and resistant to becoming Christians."

James commented, "In this meeting we're planning, we'll be talking about God and Jesus Christ. It could be a good witness. It may draw some closer to God, and it may push others farther away."

After more discussion, they unanimously agreed to invite them.

The meeting was arranged, and at 10:00 a.m. on Monday,

everyone met at the church. Rhonda, Paula, Rachael, and Pamela had prepared sandwiches and drinks.

"Oh, for the good old days, when we could run down to the store and buy a loaf of bread, sandwich meat, and a jar of spread," Rhonda offered.

"You can say that again," Paula replied. "We didn't know when we had it so good."

As everybody arrived, there was a lot of milling around, meeting and greeting. The mayor, city councilmen, and sheriff, had all brought their wives. Altogether, there were thirty-five people in the room.

After twenty minutes of getting acquainted, Alvin called the assembly to order. "Ladies and gentlemen, it's a real pleasure to be able to greet all of you. We've asked for this meeting so that we can all share information and try to come to grips with just exactly where we are in history. By doing so, I hope we can prepare for the future in such a way that we can enhance our survival."

Alvin continued: "I realize that some of us in this room are professing Christians and some aren't. Up until fairly recently, I and my family were not. However, because of what we were able to learn, we turned to God and Jesus Christ. Our intention is not to convert you."

Alvin smiled and continued, "However, if you are converted in the process, we'll certainly rejoice."

"Very briefly, I'll try to explain what I believe our situation is. I believe we're living through a time when God is judging the inhabitants of the earth and pouring out His wrath on His enemies. In addition to the loss of lives, His actions are resulting in a lot of physical destruction to many of the structures and infrastructure made by man, as well as parts of the earth, the oceans, and the seas.

"Countless lives have been lost since the war began and through everything that has followed. Countless more lives will be lost as the judgment events continue. These judgments will become worse and worse until the time of Armageddon. At that time, ALL of God's remaining enemies shall be destroyed.

"The question is, If we accept this as a given, where does this leave us and what should we do?"

Alvin looked at James, who was sitting on the first row. "James has been our scavenger and planner related to food and materials, etc. I'm going to let him continue this session."

James came to the front and stood behind the podium."As Alvin said, we believe things will get worse, not better. As far as you can see into the future, you can forget all the manufactured products. There could be some remote warehouses, storage facilities, etc. in some parts of the United States that haven't yet been scavenged, but for all practical purposes, we must assume there aren't.

"Some of the products we're missing are inconveniences. For example: Napkins, paper towels, toilet paper, tissues, etc. etc. Coffee is getting in very short supply. Many of us will miss it dearly when it's gone. Then we get into a more serious area. Salt is becoming very scarce. We brought quite a bit of salt with us when we came here, but it won't last forever. We may need to start looking for salt licks or other sources. Kentucky relied on salt licks and a salt cave in Western Kentucky in early pioneer times. I don't know if we can find any or not.

"One great disadvantage we have versus those who lived

THE DAY OF THE LORD   †

centuries ago is that we were thrown into this environment, whereas they evolved into it. It'll probably take decades for us to evolve into a situation where we're able to exist above basic survival.

"Due to these circumstances, we need to plan ahead, anticipate problems, and try to solve them before they become overwhelming. As I see it, we're reliant almost exclusively on the human ingenuity and resources we have right here in the surrounding area. We need to solve our own problems for survival.

"Now, I would like for Thomas to come forward," James concluded.

Thomas stepped up to the podium and began to speak. "I'll be brief. I believe we're in the last half of the seven year tribulation period. During this time, the earth and the people on it are subjected to the anger and wrath of God. The way I interpret the Bible, I believe we have less than two years to go until it's over."

"I don't want to hurt any feelings by what I'm about to say. However, my understanding is that, at this very time in history, God is bringing judgment and punishment on His enemies. When it's over, all His enemies will be dead. His enemies are non-Christians. Period.

"Again, if my understanding is correct, the next judgment will be the contamination of fresh water sources. Will this be everywhere? Will it affect our water? I don't know. Can we protect our water? I don't know. We'll probably do well to fill all of our water containers just in case it might help.

"In Revelation 8:10, we have the Scripture describing the star "Wormwood" as falling from heaven and turning the waters bitter. Just what does all that mean? To me, it means that God will use His supernatural power to contaminate water, turn it bitter, and many people will die as a result.

"I pose this question. Is there any record in the Bible of God turning water bitter? I don't think so. However, we have two instances where God used His supernatural powers to turn bitter water to sweet. One instance is found in Exodus 15:25 and another in 2 Kings 2:19-22.

"The one thing we know for sure is that God is punishing and killing His enemies. He's using His supernatural powers to accomplish His purposes.

"Another question is this: As God's punishment falls on His enemies, will the Christians living on earth today be protected? I've seen nothing in the Bible to indicate that Tribulation Saints will be protected in any way. There's a verse in the Bible that says the rain falls on the just and the unjust. That's all I have to say right now, Alvin," Thomas concluded.

Alvin went back to the front. "I'm going to let the Mayor speak, if he wishes."

The mayor went to the front. "My name is George Braddock. I've very recently become a Christian, along with my family. We've heard some very sobering and disturbing things here today. My wish would be that we would meet like this every two weeks so we can share information and collectively work together for future survival. Alvin, do you have any idea how long this will last?"

Alvin stood up and replied, "I'll let Thomas explain that."

Thomas stood up. "The best I understand it, in about 18 months to two years, God's judgments should end. Following that, it's my understanding that all Christians, and the children living at that time, will continue on into the thousand year reign of Jesus Christ.

"Life on earth should get better and continue to get better after that. As to whether we will ever be driving cars, flying in airplanes, eating cheerios from the supermarket, or drinking sodas, I just don't have a clue."

Thomas sat down and Alvin stood back up. "Is there anybody else in the room that would like to add anything to what has been said?" he asked.

Nobody responded, and all began to get up, walk around, visit for a few minutes and then leave.

The Mercer clan all congregated together until everybody had left.

James spoke to Thomas. "What do you think, Thomas? Do you think people should be warned of the prophecy related to the contamination of fresh waters?"

Thomas replied, "I realize there's a lot of disagreement among scholars and theologians over many of the scriptures, especially in the book of Revelation. Not being a theologian, and not being a scholar, if I erred, I'd err on the side of caution. I think we should bring it before the church. I think we should go so far as to recommend that people store, or somehow protect, a supply of drinking water if possible, for themselves and their animals."

CHAPTER VI
THIRD TRUMPET
JUDGMENT

Revelation 8:10 -11 "And the third angel sounded and, there fell a great star from heaven, burning as it were a lamp, and it fell upon a third part of the rivers, and on the fountains of waters, and the name of the star is Wormwood; and the third part of the waters became wormwood; and many men died of the waters, because they were made bitter."

The Mercer clan continued with their farming and gardening chores during the first week of June. They also rounded up all the tubs, barrels, jars, and other containers they could find to store water. Fortunately, they had several used whiskey barrels, which made great rain barrels.

Tim and Pamela went to their bee farm to work. They'd located several sheets of corrugated tin at an old garage just south of where they lived. Tim got Herbert to help him retrieve the tin and haul it to the bee farm.

Tim and Pamela picked a shady location under some trees, leveled areas for individual sheets of tin, plugged the nail holes with roofing tar, bent the ends up, and made them watertight enough to hold about an inch of water each. They fixed ten sheets that were ten feet long. Their hope was that if fresh water were contaminated, the water in their panels would remain pure enough, and their bees would survive.

Tim spoke up. "Pamela, let's hop on our bikes and see if we can bum some lunch from your mom."

Pamela replied, "Good idea, Tim. I'm tired, hot, and a little weary."

When they arrived at the farm Rhonda came to the front door and then out onto the porch.

Tim and Pamela parked their bikes and walked toward the porch.

Rhonda exclaimed, "Pamela! Stop right there!"

Pamela stopped dead in her tracks. "What's up, Mom?" she asked.

Rhonda continued: "Turn around slowly."

Pamela turned and stopped with her back to her mom.

Rhonda continued: "All the way around."

When Pamela again faced her mother, Rhonda blurted," you're pregnant!"

Pamela blushed, and grinned, "I kept all of you fooled for a long time."

Rhonda walked quickly over, placed her arms around Pamela, and replied, "You sure did honey."

Rhonda continued, "Come on into the house and I'll fix you some lunch. By the way, what are you two up to?"

Pamela replied. "I was feeling tired, and thought I'd like to come and visit awhile and get a little TLC from my momma."

Rhonda hugged Pamela again and then looked at Tim. "Tim, Alvin is down at the barn looking at his four-year old mare. She should be foaling any time now. You can go down there, or you can wait here. I expect him back in about fifteen or twenty minutes."

Tim replied. "I think I'll trot on over there. I would kinda like to see the horse." He took off at a fast trot toward the barn. He slowed down to a walk as he approached. He entered quietly and walked up to the stall where the mare was standing.

"Good afternoon Alvin," Tim greeted.

"Good afternoon, Tim. Come on over and take a look at Brownie. She looks like she could foal any time now, possibly tonight. I'm curious to see whether it will be male or female."

"Which would you prefer?" Tim asked.

"Actually, I prefer a female. Right now our most serious need is more horses. The way things are shaping up, horses could end up being our primary source of transportation and also horsepower for farming. We're going to have to do a lot of innovation and work to get to the point of self sufficiency, food wise." Alvin replied.

As they walked back up to the house, Alvin asked Tim, "What brings you up this way today?"

Tim replied, "We were working with the bees and decided we'd like to come and visit for a time. Pamela was feeling a little washed out and wanted to visit and rest awhile."

At lunch, Rhonda broke the news to Alvin about Pamela and Tim's prospective parenthood. Alvin congratulated them and commented, "Don't guess you'll be learning in advance whether it's a boy or girl, will you?"

Tim laughed. "I'd say those days of sonograms won't be around again for quite awhile, if ever. Whatever it is, I just hope it's healthy. With all the radiation and fallout during the war, we have no way of telling what effect it may have on genetics, health, and general well being."

Rhonda interjected soberly, "Tim, you're absolutely right. Since both of you were in sheltered areas for weeks after the war, I'm hoping you both missed being damaged."

"So do we all," Pamela replied, fervently.

Alvin thought, *That sure is a leap of faith on their part, having a baby at this time in all the uncertainty of the future.*

Tim asked, "Alvin, what projects are you working on right now?"

He replied, "Well, Tim, I've been doing a lot of studying and thinking about the transportation and hauling needs we have, here and in other locations. I'm concentrating on building up a horse herd and also a supply of wagons and buggies. In addition, raising food for animals and food for people is a top priority. I'm hoping we can make some forays into the countryside and other locations to find some of the materials we need."

Tim responded, "Alvin, if you ever need any help or need me to go with you, let me know."

At church on Saturday, June 7, Thomas spent a lot of the sermon time encouraging those who weren't Christian, to seek God. He spent part of the time reviewing some of the end-time prophecies. "I'd like to emphasize that I'm not too well versed in end-time prophecy Scriptures. I do believe that the remainder of the trumpet judgments and vial judgments are supernatural events executed by Almighty God. These supernatural events are on the same order as the ten plagues in Egypt at the time of Moses. They were supernatural. They can't be related to, or compared to, natural events.

"The important fact to remember is, we're living through

the times and we must cope with whatever circumstances may befall us as the days, weeks, and months, go by. If we can learn anything from the Scriptures that could help us anticipate and prepare, I think we should try.

"However, one word of encouragement; the time of tribulation and judgment from God shall not last forever. We need to be patient, trust in God, worship God, and try to help each other with whatever circumstances arise."

At altar call, eleven people went forward to meet with Thomas and expressed their belief in God and Jesus Christ, and affirmed their renouncement of sin and their desire to serve God and Jesus Christ.

Most of the congregation went forward and affirmed their joy and welcomed them into God's Kingdom.

Following the service, the Mercer clan went home to rest, meditate, visit, and prepare for their work for the coming week. Although somewhat apprehensive about potential water contamination, they knew they had prepared the best they could.

Later, on Saturday night, the third trumpet sounded. On Sunday night, Alvin turned on his short wave receiver and began to listen to his most reliable news source in Switzerland. The station, located in the Alps not too far from Zurich, monitored stations from all over the world. They filtered and sorted the news, and then re-broadcast the information that seemed the most reliable and pertinent.

Sketchy news was coming in indicating that a wide contamination of water was taking place. Fresh water sources all over the world were becoming polluted. The effects on humanity were not immediately known.

Alvin thought about sending Herbert over to the other

farm to give them the news but decided to wait until morning. He shut down the radio at 10:00 p.m. and then went outside to one of their water storage barrels and sampled it. The water looked and tasted OK. After that, he went to bed.

Alvin and Rhonda were up at 6:00 a.m. Rhonda went to the kitchen and started a pot of tea, while Alvin started the fire. While the tea was making, they went to the living room and sat down.

"Rhonda, on the news last night I picked up some information on the water contamination. It seems to be pretty widespread, but so far there's no word of the impact it may be having," Alvin explained.

Rhonda responded, "I really hope it doesn't affect us here."

Alvin continued, "After breakfast, I'm going to hitch up the buggy. I'm going by to see James and Paula, and then I'm going on into town and check in with the Sheriff to see if he's heard of any local problems. After that, I'll stop by and see Thomas and Rachael for a few minutes."

Rhonda replied, "While you're in town, how about dropping off four dozen eggs at the market. Just have them credited to our account."

Alvin hitched up the team and drove over to James' farm. As he went toward the house, Tim and Pamela came out the front door and met him on James' porch. Pamela hugged him. "Good morning, dad. I see you're out early."

Alvin replied, "I'm on my way to town and stopped by to share the latest news."

They went into the house and congregated in the living room. After exchanging greetings, Alvin told them all he'd heard on the radio. Alvin asked James, "have you checked your fresh water today to see if it's contaminated?'

James replied, "Tim, David, and I have been sampling water in the creek, the pond, the spring and in our storage, and so far, we haven't found anything wrong with any of the water. We'll keep checking it every day to make sure."

Alvin replied, "That's quite a relief, knowing the water hasn't been contaminated."

Paula asked, "Alvin would you like some tea or something else to drink?"

He replied, "No thanks. I think I'll go to town and see what I can find out. Do you have anything you need me to pick up, or send to market?"

"In fact, we do," James said. "We have some green onions, turnip greens, mustard greens, and lettuce we can send; if you can wait about an hour."

"I'll help you pick," Alvin responded.

Following their picking of the vegetables, Alvin drove into town, went by the market, and dropped off the produce. He got a receipt for the credit to James' account and then went to the sheriff's office.

"Good morning, sheriff," he greeted.

"Good morning to you, Alvin. I was hoping you'd come by. Do you have any late news?"

"I have some," Alvin responded. "The information I have on the water contamination is sketchy. It seems there's widespread contamination in other parts of the world, but, as yet, we don't have news about the impact it may be having on people's lives."

The sheriff responded, "The courier brought me one cryptic note this morning. It reported there was some water contamination east of here, but nothing specific. The note said there would be more information later."

Alvin replied, "We're all good so far at the farms. I hope it stays that way." Alvin left the sheriff's office, finished his shopping, and went back home.

Herbert, now 21, met a young lady at church. She was nineteen years old and pretty as a picture. Her name was Barbara McKnight. Barbara was quiet and reserved, as was Herbert. They gravitated toward each other, as the more outgoing young men and women gravitated toward those more like themselves.

Barbara was the only child of Bill and Helen McKnight, who owned a farm about ten miles east of Richmond.

Barbara and Herbert had progressed in their relationship to the point that their marriage was planned for the 23rd of November. The wedding was to be held at the church.

Bill and Helen had offered Herbert and Barbara a full partnership in the farm.

There was a vacant frame house in Richmond that Herbert had decided to move and rebuild on the farm. The house was fairly new and had thermal windows all around and was well insulated; both in the walls and in the attic.

Soon after Herbert and Barbara became engaged, they, with a lot of help from friends and family, had begun dismantling the house, moving it to the farm, and reassembling it. The enthusiasm and exuberance of the young adults was quite an encouragement for the entire community.

The church was used as a place for people to sleep when they didn't want to waste the time traveling back and forth to their homes.

Meanwhile, the farm work had wound down. The

Mercers picked early November as the best time to butcher the hogs. Two weeks later would probably have been better to insure the weather would remain cold after butchering. However, with the house building going on and the wedding coming up, this seemed to be the best time.

They had found a scalding vat at one of the abandoned farms and transported it to James' farm back in the summer. As time permitted, they had mounted it on large rocks made it ready for use. They also laid in a good supply of firewood.

They had four hogs to butcher. With this much work, they assembled the full Mercer clan, including Thomas and Rachael. Herbert stayed with his house building.

Once each hog was killed, it was bled out, suspended from an A frame with a block and tackle, and then lowered into the scalding water. Once the hair was sufficiently loosened, the hog was then removed, laid out on the platform, and scraped. Once that was done, it was cut into hams, roasts, shoulders, side meat, etc. and salted. It was then placed on shelves in the smoke house, and left for future use.

The hogs were quite fat. The fat was removed, and the chunks were placed in a wooden trough until they could be placed in the huge cast iron kettles for rendering into lard. Part of the lard would be retained for cooking purposes and bartering.

The remainder of the rendered fat would be mixed with lye and made into soap. The lye had been collected over the months from ashes from the wood fires which they'd been using for cooking and heating. Soap was becoming one of the more critical items as time went on. In the beginning after the war, quite a bit of soap had been salvaged, but it was now almost gone.

The processing of the hogs ended up being a four day operation.

They were now in late fall, and winter was fast approaching. In the middle of October, Pamela and Tim had winterized their bee hives and made all the other preparations for winter, Inside her body, Pamela's baby had grown considerably. She had begun to stay home and let Tim do the outside work. She could still do some of the processing of the honey and wax, and storing of the honey in jars.

Pamela went into labor on November the 13th. She had been having false labor for about two weeks.

Just at daylight, as she moved her leg to get more comfortable, her water broke.

"My water broke!" Pamela exclaimed.

"Wow!" Tim exclaimed, "They sure did! You wait right there. I'll go next door and get Paula, and then I'll get on a bike and go tell your mom."

"Tim, slow down." Pamela replied. "I think we'll have more than a few minutes. First, get me some towels. I'm a mess, and the bed is a mess. As soon as you get the towels, fix us a cup of tea. By then, Paula and James should be up."

By the time the tea was ready, Tim had calmed down to some extent. He didn't waste a lot of time drinking his tea before he took off to see James and Paula. He explained to them what he planned.

James replied. "Tim, instead of you riding a bike over there, let me hitch up my buggy and go get her. I'm sure she'll have some things to bring. This way, you can stay close to Pamela. I'm sure she'll do just fine, but we're not always that sure about new daddies."

Paula spoke up. "Tim, go home and stay with Pamela.

I'll be there in about thirty minutes. If you need me before that, come and get me."

Tim went home. Pamela had lain back in the bed and relaxed as best she could. She was having contractions about eight minutes apart.

An hour and a half later, Rhonda showed up.

Rhonda spoke to Tim. "Tim, you're free to go and do whatever you need to do today. Feel free to come by and check on Pamela anytime. Paula, Pamela and I have everything under control. If we need you, we'll holler."

"Good enough," Tim replied, and then went out and toward the barn.

At 8:45 p.m., a very tired Pamela gave birth to a girl; eighteen inches long and weighing around seven pounds. After cleanup, they wrapped the baby in a blanket and handed her to Pamela.

"Pamela, have you and Tim decided on a name?" Rhonda asked.

"Yes we have, Mom," Pamela replied. "We decided that if it was a girl, we'd name it Cathy."

"What about a middle name?" Rhonda asked.

"We haven't decided on that yet," Pamela replied.

"Welcome to our world, Cathy," Paula greeted, as she caressed Cathy's tiny arm.

Cathy was already showing signs she was hungry and looking for something to eat.

Pamela spoke up. "If you'd like to go in the other room and take a break, I'll see if I have anything to feed her."

They all left the room, and after a time, Pamela called them back. Cathy had eaten and then she had gone to sleep.

Rhonda and Paula made their plans to leave. Rhonda decided to spend the night at Paula's.

Rhonda told Pamela, "If you need anything at all tonight, send Tim."

The new baby created quite a stir. This was the first child born into the Mercer clan in the new world environment. There was a lot of wondering, without a lot of discussion, on how this all might play out as the years went by.

After a few days, life settled down, and the attention shifted back to the upcoming marriage of Herbert and Barbara.

Herbert and Barbara were married on the 23rd of November, which was a cold and blustery day. When they got to their new home, where they would spend their honeymoon, they found a nice cheery fire burning in their wood stove in the living room.

Alvin continued monitoring the news each evening. More information was coming in related to the contaminated waters. The contamination was widespread. Arid and semi-arid lands were the hardest hit.

Tens of millions died in the Middle East as their fresh water sources were contaminated. With no other fresh water available, the people had no other choice but to drink the contaminated water, and it killed them.

When China, Russia, the South Pacific, and all the other parts of the world were included; no doubt, hundreds of millions died.

Alvin spent another two hours checking stations in different parts of the United States. Some transmitters were now coming on line, powerful enough to be heard across the United States. The powerful station collected information from weaker stations and then re-broadcast to the rest of the world.

Alvin passed the news on to the rest of the Mercers and then went into Richmond to visit the sheriff and mayor.

"Good morning, Alvin," greeted Mike Linden.

"Good morning, Mike. I came by to give you the latest news. Do you think we could go and visit with the mayor and share information with him at the same time?"

"Good idea, Alvin. Let me get my hat, and we'll walk over to his office." Mike grabbed his hat and they walked down the three blocks to the mayor's office.

After greetings were exchanged, Alvin briefed Mike and George on the latest information he'd collected from around the world.

George commented soberly, "There's no doubt God is angry. It's really scary living through these times. We have no choice but to ride it out and do our best to survive. I continue to pray every day that God will have mercy on us."

"Amen to that," Mike agreed.

"OK. It's my turn now," Mike continued. "There appears to be some outlaw bands forming in different parts of Kentucky. It seems that the people who didn't take the time to dig in and plant gardens and crops are now banding together to rob those who did."

Alvin asked, "Are we in danger from those bands?"

Mike answered. "So far we haven't been bothered, but I believe it's only a matter of time. There's a band we have known about operating down around Elizabethtown. I don't know if it's the same group that was at Paradise Point or not. We've heard rumors they may be planning raids. They're relying on saddle horses and buggies for transportation mostly, but a few of them have motorcycles."

"Where in the world are they getting gasoline that's still good?" Alvin asked.

Mike responded. "Somebody must have stored a bunch of gasoline using an additive to extend its life. I wouldn't think there's a lot more of it left."

"What do we need to do to get prepared?" Alvin asked.

"We'll have to give that more thought," Mike replied. Mike then asked, "Alvin, do you have any radio contact with people here in Kentucky? If not, could you try to find one? It would be good if we had a way of being notified, if and when that band starts moving."

Alvin replied, "I'll try again. So far I haven't had much success."

Mike added, "Mayor, Alvin, I believe we need to have another town hall meeting and get input from some of our citizens to see if we can come up with a plan."

"Good idea," the Mayor responded. "When would you like to have the meeting?"

"Let's start announcing the meeting on Saturday and set it up for Tuesday afternoon at 2:00 p.m. That way, everybody can get their chores done for the day, before coming."

CHAPTER VII
FOURTH TRUMPET JUDGMENT

Revelation 8:12 "And the fourth angel sounded, and the third part of the sun was smitten, and the third part of the moon, and the third part of the stars; so as the third part of them was darkened, and the day shone not for a third part of it, and the night likewise."

On Tuesday, December 10, the town hall meeting convened. The Sheriff and the mayor addressed the 300 in attendance at the church facilities.

The Mayor spoke first and explained. "We have two plans. The Sheriff will explain the first plan which is defensive, and after that, I will explain the other one."

The Sheriff explained the plan of defense. Hopefully, the first news of a need to prepare would come by the courier from the Sheriff in Elizabethtown. For the second plan of notification, the alert would come by radio to Alvin.

Alvin had been able to contact a ham radio station in Florida, who contacted a ham radio station in Elizabethtown. The station in Florida would act as a relay station for messages. Because of frequency bandwidths, Alvin could talk to Florida and Florida to E-town, but not Alvin to E-town. Bud Warner was the contact in E-Town, and he would stay in touch with the Sheriff.

The sheriff explained, "Here is where the plan becomes more complicated. Unless the Mayor's plan works, which he'll explain later, my plan is to intercept them on the way here and ask them to turn back.

"Here's what we know about the outlaw group. There's about fifty of them, men and women, not including the children. So far in their raids, they've been selective in whom they've raided and fortunately, haven't killed anybody. However, they've beaten up and bullied both men and women.

"They've used threats, assault, and bullying to extort or blackmail people, mostly remote farmers, to get food for their families. However, they're getting more bold, and rougher. Their opportunities in that area have become limited.

"Local law enforcement is putting more pressure on them and there's a good possibility they intend to change locations. It's possible they've already sent someone here to scope us out to see if we'd be an easy target or not."

"Hopefully, they'll never come here, but if they do, our first action will be to try to communicate with them and turn them back. While attempting to communicate with them, we'll have already used our notification system to alert everybody in the area of an impending threat, and will have designated people go to the three potential entry points to our area."

"The person who meets with them to communicate will be me. There'll be five other people within sight, a half mile back, who'll be heavily armed but will observe only. If I'm killed or detained, one of our unit will head back here to warn you. The other four will try to take out the motorcycles if they try to give chase to the one coming to warn us.

"For those five, I say this: we aren't looking for any martyrs. Just slow them down and make it on back here.

"I now turn the meeting back over to the mayor." Mike concluded.

The mayor got up and spoke. "Folks, I don't even like to think about having to take lives. However, I've seen absolutely nothing in the Bible that indicates we shouldn't defend ourselves. This is a matter of survival for us and our families.

"Now, I'll explain the other plan. We're going to try to contact their leader and offer an alternative to their raiding and taking what they want by violence.

"We'll offer to help them set up their own gardens and farms, and offer them the ability to be productive and earn their own way. We'll help them only if they renounce violence and thievery. Even if we can't convince the entire group, maybe we can peel off some of the ones who're only with them out of desperation."

The entire group at the meeting applauded the mayor, and there were many yells of, "good luck!"

The meeting broke up, and everybody scattered and headed for their homes.

Alvin approached the sheriff and mayor. "Let us know what you need."

Work went on apace at the farms as preparations continued: preparing for winter and possible threats from the outside.

Tim decided it was time to harvest sassafras roots. The

sap was down and it was a sunny and calm day, although chilly. He and James had gone a few months ago and located four trees that would be suitable. For the amount of sassafras they intended to harvest, they wanted enough trees so the root loss wouldn't be harmful to an individual tree.

He approached Tiffany and Ron, James and Paula's children, and asked them if they'd like to go on the sassafras root gathering trip with him. Both agreed that they'd like it very much.

They took their usual assortment of firearms. For tools, they took a grubbing hoe (mattock), a hand saw, and five burlap bags.

Although Tiffany and Ron were still fairly young at sixteen and fourteen, they were both willing and hard workers. They dug and sawed until lunch time and then stopped long enough to eat the lunches Paula and Pamela had fixed for them.

They made it back to the farm late in the afternoon. They came back with quite a load of roots and decided to wait until the next day to process them. They would clean them, cut the roots into two inch lengths, and store them to dry for later use.

Lots and lots of wood was being cut and stockpiled for the cold days ahead. Coal that had been available for bartering in Irvine had all been sold or bartered. They would have to rely entirely on wood for heat.

Because of the extreme devastation in the United States during the war, there were mostly isolated pockets of people throughout the North American continent, with very little communication and transportation between the pockets. Their available resources were all they could count on.

So many things that were taken for granted before were either non-existent or very scarce. Fires were now being lighted with flint and steel. Matches were hoarded for extreme emergencies. Candles and firelight provided most of the light at night.

Drugs were practically non-existent. Some people still had a few aspirin, Ibuprofen, and Acetaminophen stashed away, but most didn't. They made a good item for barter or trade. Heart pills? Thyroid pills? Pain pills? Diabetes shots? All were past history.

With the population badly depleted and the destruction of manufacturing, people were much worse off now, materially, than people were back in the 1500's. There didn't appear to be any hope of ever restoring the material products unless people concentrated their population and pooled their knowledge and resources. With the nation in the state it was in, that wouldn't happen.

On the ninth day of February, the heavens began a series of convolutions that were seen around the world for a period of exactly twenty-four hours. God supernaturally darkened a large part of the sun and moon and stars. It got quite dark. The darkness occurred at the Mercers at about 1:00 p.m.

All the chickens that had been out in the chicken yard went inside, flew up on the roost, and went to bed. Hoot owls came out and hooted. Nocturnal animals came out to do their hunting.

James scratched his head. *I wonder if this is the beginning of the fourth trumpet,* he thought.

The family members in the house came out into the yard and looked. Those in the fields, in the barn, and elsewhere, began to return to the house.

Paula, who had been in the kitchen cooking, took down a candle and lit it from the fire in the cook stove. They did what they could in the way of chores and then went back in the house where it was warm.

As evening fell, some of the stars came out and some didn't. It was as if a large number of them were blanketed from view. The moon came up and shined for a part of the night and then just went out. It didn't go behind the clouds. It wasn't eclipsed. It just went out.

All over the world, humans everywhere got to see the Glory of God as He carried out another one of the things He said He would do.

Why this? Is this just another pause before a more severe judgment falls? Later, the humanity still surviving upon the earth would be the judge of that question.

The following morning, at mid-morning, the skies were back to normal.

Thomas and the sheriff borrowed a horse and buggy, outfitted it, and after loading food, horse feed, bedding and other essentials, began their trip to Elizabethtown to see if they could meet up with the outlaws.

When they arrived in Elizabethtown, they located Bob Parsons, the sheriff, and explained to him what they intended to do. The sheriff wasn't thrilled with the idea.

"Well sheriff," Mike explained. If we can't head the problem off here, and they come to Richmond and start their lawless activities a lot of people will probably get injured badly, or die. I'm surprised you and the people in this area have allowed them to bully and abuse you."

Bob Parsons huffed. "It's our business how we deal with our business. If you don't like it, that's tough. The truth is, we've been putting a lot more pressure on them than you know."

Mike replied, "Sheriff, I don't mean to offend you, but we're living in times where there's not a lot of room for error. If you would rather not get involved in our attempt to solve our problem, just say so. We'll do what we have to do on our own."

The sheriff replied, "I'm not getting involved unless you try something over here that you shouldn't. Then you'll be spending time in my jail."

Following the visit with the sheriff, Mike and Thomas had a discussion and revisited their thinking.

Mike explained his views to Thomas. "I believe it's time for us to completely back away and go back home. From this short visit with Sheriff Parsons, I suppose we could stir up a real hornet's nest. I suspect the sheriff could be in cahoots with the outlaws, or at least, intentionally blind to what they're doing."

Thomas responded. "I arrived at the same conclusion. We understand what we have in and around Richmond. Overall, we have a settlement of mostly dependable, law abiding people. I know there are exceptions, but there aren't a large number of them.

"I'm suspecting that, from a standpoint of security and stability, this settlement here is iffy. I feel sorry for the good folks that live here."

Mike and Thomas traveled back to Richmond and made their report to the Mayor, City Council, and others in the Richmond area.

Frequently, on the afternoon of the Saturday church service, a town hall meeting would be called to update the interested people on the latest news and happenings. The City Council and the sheriff took that opportunity and made their report the following Saturday.

Christmas came and the church celebrated the birth of Jesus Christ by setting up a live manger scene. There were goats, sheep, two donkeys, and a lot of costumed characters depicting the Shepherds, Wise Men, Baby Jesus, Mary, and Joseph.

It was cold outside. However, everybody dressed warm, and inside the church a rare treat of hot chocolate and cookies was available. It was a great time of fellowship.

The service inside the church was a solemn occasion as Christians prayed, meditated, and contemplated their relationship with God and Jesus Christ. Many went outside and knelt for a short time before the manger.

The first day of January was blustery and cold. A snow had fallen the night before, and there was an accumulation of about two inches.

About mid-afternoon, a wagon came into Richmond from the west. It was pulled by a team of two horses. Three men rode in the wagon. Two sat on the seat. One sat behind the seat, all huddled up, and looking backward.

The wagon was loaded with goods for bartering. About half of the load on the wagon was blocks of salt. Each block weighed twenty-five pounds. The wagon pulled up to the South Richmond Market.

The three men went inside and met with the three men working in the store. After introductions, bargaining and bartering began. The South Richmond Market ended up with ten blocks of the desperately needed salt. The price of the salt was high, and a lot of squealing took place before it was all settled.

During the negotiations, one of the three men from the wagon disappeared for a period of time. He walked away rapidly and returned forty-five minutes later, still walking rapidly. He would stop occasionally and take notes.

Fortunately, he was watched. Mike had seen the wagon come into town and immediately sent his deputy to keep an eye on the three men and wagon. Deputy Russell Grose unobtrusively kept him in sight and observed his note-taking. Mike surmised this could very possibly be a spy from the Elizabethtown outlaws.

Following the bartering exchange, the three men got back in the wagon and traveled south and east. They would go south to Irvine and then east to Beattyville. From there, they hoped to go to Booneville, Jackson, and Hazard before heading back to Elizabethtown. This would depend on when they believed they had made a maximum profit from their exchanges.

They retained some of their acquired goods as "must have" and then re-traded or bartered again those items they could exchange and, where possible, gain an advantage.

Wintertime was a good time to trade, even if it was very uncomfortable at times. Most of the people they encountered would allow them to spend the night and feed them. After completing their trading, they traveled back to their headquarters in Elizabethtown.

Alvin started spending more of his time on electrical generation and communication, now that all crops had been gathered and farming work had slowed down. He used Tim quite extensively in doing the work.

They worked with Mike Linden to set up the UHF base station in Mike's office. With help, he found and retrieved a thirty-foot creosote pole and set it at the end of Mike's office where it would be supported by the roof peak. They took two 10 foot joints of 1 ¼ inch galvanized pipe, screwed them together, attached the UHF antenna, then fastened it to the pole, which added another fifteen feet of height to the antenna. This gave them a fairly extensive coverage for the radios.

The UHF system with the six receivers allowed the Mercers to use two of them to communicate between their farms, and also communicate with the base station in Richmond.

Once the UHF system was in place, Alvin, working with Tim, began on the solar system. Back at the cave location, Alvin had stored all the solar panels, batteries, inverter, wiring, etc, to install a 4,000 watt solar system. His intention was to set it up at his farm. In addition to supplying power to his house, he would also be able to charge batteries to take to James' and Tim's houses so they could have electric lights.

A 4,000 watt solar system could power a lot of individual appliances. It wouldn't power an entire house, with refrigerator, air conditioning, lighting, cooking, etc. etc.

It could run a refrigerator. It could run a well pump. It could furnish lighting. It could run a small air conditioning system. Their best use for it would be to keep 12 volt batteries charged for all other uses. Then they could judiciously use it for other things, such as fans.

Air conditioning and refrigerators were probably the most missed, as well as running water and bathroom facilities. The nights without air conditioning became horribly hot during the summer. August was usually the worst month. Fans operated from the solar system would be a real blessing.

The wintertime which they were experiencing, allowed more time for just visiting and talking. Thomas made the church available for community meetings. From the beginning, he made it abundantly clear that all discussions and activities were either pro-God, or at the minimum, neutral subjects such as farming, planting, sewing, etc. etc. If they were there to discuss how to make moonshine, or other alcoholic products, forget it.

By opening these discussions to the general public, there were some opportunities for witnessing. Some of the deeper Biblical and religious discussions took place when the group, at the time, was mostly Christian.

Occasionally, certain individuals would attend, stay for a short period of time, and leave. These were usually more hostile in their attitudes.

One of the favorite forums of the more Christian inclined groups, were to have a list of questions made up by anybody who wanted to pose a question. Once the list was made up, Thomas would act as moderator. He would read the question and then ask someone to hold up their hand as to who would like to answer it. Once the question was answered, it was then open to discussion by the entire group. Thomas was good at controlling the rabbit chasing, and then moving on to the next question.

When there was nobody to volunteer to answer a question, Thomas would answer it.

Thomas spoke up. "I have five questions. I've sorted them out to place them in the order I think would make the most sense. Here is the first question: if these are the end time events, just how far are we from the end?" Thomas asked, "Who would like to answer that question?"

After a period of silence, the mayor spoke up, "Thomas, why don't you answer that one."

Thomas replied, "I'll try to answer that, but if anybody else that wants to add anything, speak up.

"In looking back on all that's happened, the best I can determine the end of the battle of Armageddon will mark the end of the outpouring of the wrath of God and will be followed immediately by the thousand year reign of Jesus Christ. My estimate is, that point in time will happen around eighteen months from now, or a little less. Do any of you have a comment or question?" He asked.

Thomas read the next question. "Will Christians who are living on the earth right now be protected as these other judgments happen?"

Tim held up his hand. "I've really been wondering about that, since we have a new baby. I believe that prayer to God for protection during these times would be honored, according to His will. If God, in His providence, decides to protect us during these times, He will." Tim sat down.

Somebody else asked, "isn't there a verse in the Bible that says the rains fall on the just and the unjust?"

Thomas answered, "Yes, there is. I'll look it up. It's in Matthew, chapter 5, verse 45. Jesus, in pointing out our need to love our enemies as well as loving others, uses the analogy of God pouring out His love on the just and the unjust, good and evil people, and we're to do likewise with our love."

Thomas continued, "I will say this: If Christians who are living right now are killed, we needn't worry, for, in our very next awareness, we would be with the Lord."

Thomas read the next question. "What's going on in other parts of the world? Who would like to take that question?"

Alvin spoke up. "I'll take that one." He continued: "I've been monitoring world news almost on a daily basis. The new world government that rose up following the war gained strength for the first three or four years. However, once the judgments began to fall it seems the nations of the New World Government are taking quite a beating. Tens of millions are dying. All the other nations around the world are being heavily punished also.

"The events in Israel are mixed. Un-Godly Jews are receiving God's wrath while those Jews who're turning to Jesus Christ are being shown mercy.

We get some news from here in the United States, but there's not a lot to tell. The war was so devastating, the country seems to be almost in a state of paralysis. For us, due to the happenings around the world, this is probably a good thing. Do you have any questions?" No questions were asked and Alvin sat down.

Thomas looked at the next question. "What do we know about the outlaws over near Elizabethtown, and what can we expect from them? Are we in danger?"

Thomas looked over at the sheriff. "Mike, would you like to take that question?"

Mike stood up and responded. "Yes. I'll answer it the best I can. We can't be sure at this time what they'll do. We hope for the best and prepare to meet them and do what we have to do. If they do decide to attack, they may wait until early spring while we're busy with farm work. Regardless of when, we intend to be ready." Mike sat down.

Thomas asked if there were any more questions. Most people were ready to call it a day and said nothing.

Thomas closed the meeting with prayer, and the people got up, socialized for a few minutes, and then went home.

Outside of Elizabethtown at the outlaw headquarters preparations were underway for an expedition and a raid. The outlaw leader, Robert Maxwell, met with six of his men who normally helped him with his planning. After everybody got seated, Robert spoke. "We had thought about waiting until around the middle of April to make the raid on Richmond, but we're getting so low on food supplies, we need to do something right away. My thinking is that we need to set the date for the tenth of March. That's in the middle of the week and should be at a time when most people are at home and not in town."

David asked, "What is the guidelines we need to follow when we hit the town? Are we just bullying, shooting to wound, or are we shooting to kill?"

Robert replied, "From what our spy told us about the place, we can expect some armed resistance. Since it's the middle of the week, it should be minimal. Our intention is to go directly to the market area, hit it hard and fast, grab all the foodstuffs we can grab, and then make a run for it. If it's armed resistance, shoot to kill. If the resistance is unarmed, use the clubs to subdue them."

Greg spoke up, "Shooting to kill could be a mistake. Shooting to wound may discourage them to follow us. Shooting to kill may make them angry and determined enough to come after us."

Robert retorted, "Greg, if you aren't tough enough, stay home."

Greg replied, "I'm tough enough. I'll go."

Robert continued, "We can put an assault force together with about forty people if we decide to include the ten women. Since we don't have any children for the women to take care of, I don't see any reason why they shouldn't participate.

"We'll have twenty on horses, two on motorcycles, and the rest driving or riding in the six wagons we'll be taking. We'll be taking six bicycles in the wagons. They can be unloaded and put on the ground about a half mile out of town. Are there any questions?

"Go ahead and set up a meeting with the group tonight at six and we'll explain the plans to them."

Their meeting was held on the first day of March. The raid was set up for March the tenth. Their plan was to set up a forward base at Paint Lick on March 7, about twenty miles south of Richmond, on Highway 52. From there they would make a hit and run raid which they would pull off on the tenth of March.

Once the raid had been made, the wagons would travel south. The raiders on motorcycles and horses would act as a blocking force as the wagons escaped. Their plan was to make it as far as Lancaster, spend the night, and then go on the next day to Elizabethtown.

On the night of March 7, everything was in readiness at Elizabethtown, and the next morning, they would move out to Paint lick.

CHAPTER VIII
FIFTH TRUMPET JUDGMENT (FIRST WOE)

Revelation 8:13 "And I beheld, and heard an angel flying through the midst of heaven, saying with a loud voice, Woe, woe, woe to the inhabiters of the earth by reason of the other voices of the trumpet of the three angels, which are yet to sound!"

Revelation 9:1-12 "And the fifth angel sounded and I saw a star fall from heaven unto the earth; and to him was given the key to the bottomless pit.

And he opened the bottomless pit and there arose a smoke out of the pit, as the smoke of a great furnace; and the sun and the air were darkened by reason of the smoke of the pit.

And there came out of the smoke locusts upon the earth: and unto them was given power, as the scorpions of the earth have power.

And it was commanded that they should not hurt the grass of the earth, neither any green thing, neither any tree;

but only those men who have not the seal of God in their forehead:

And to them it was given that they should not kill them, but that they should be tormented five months: and their torment was as the torment of a scorpion, when he striketh a man.

And in those days shall man seek death, and shall not find it; and shall desire to die, and death shall flee from them.

And the shapes of the locusts were like unto horses prepared unto battle; and on their heads were as it were crowns like gold, and their faces were as the faces of men.

And they had hair as the hair of women, and their teeth were as the teeth of lions.

And they had breast plates of iron; and the sound of their wings was as the sound of chariots of many horses running into battle.

And they had tails like unto scorpions, and there were stings in their tails: and their power was to hurt for five months.

And they had a King over them, which is the angel of the bottomless pit, whose name in the Hebrew tongue is Abbadon, but in the Greek tongue hath his name Apollyon.

One woe is past and behold, there comes two woes more hereafter."

On Sunday night, March the sixth, the outlaws at Elizabethtown were visited with a scourge of pain and torment unlike any that had ever been visited on mankind in the history of the earth. Their plans to move out the following morning were put on an indefinite hold. This torment would continue to punish them, day and night, for five months. During that time, they would wish to die, but could not do so.

Every human on the face of the earth who was not Christian or children suffered the same torment. Absolutely nothing they could take or do would ease the suffering.

The One World Government essentially shut down during this outpouring of God's wrath and judgment. Existing, suffering, and cursing God occupied all their waking hours.

Christians and children throughout the world continued on with their lives. In Richmond, the fear of being raided fell into the background.

In the Richmond area, quite a few people were impacted by the visitation of pain, suffering and torment suffered by non-Christians. A few of the ones afflicted who had been attending the church suddenly quit coming and were later seen, obviously suffering.

On Monday morning, Mike Linden, the sheriff, was visited by a man and a woman named Travis and Mary Lankford. They lived in Richmond about a half mile north of the shopping district. They were suffering horribly and would occasionally cry out with pain. They told Mike of waking up in the middle of the night hurting all over. They also told Mike of seeing some of their friends that morning who were also suffering. Travis and Mary had two children, a girl, eight, and a boy, ten, and they didn't seem to be affected.

As the morning progressed, Mike learned of others who seemed to be suffering from the same symptoms. "I believe I'll try to contact Thomas and see what he thinks about this. I wonder if this could be the Fifth Trumpet Judgment he was talking about?"

Mike got on his bicycle and went to the church. Thomas was there talking to about a dozen people. Apparently, the occurrences were widespread.

"Good morning, Mike," Thomas greeted.

"Good morning, Thomas," Mike returned the greeting. "I see you're hearing what I've been dealing with this morning. Do you believe this is the Fifth Trumpet Judgment you were telling us about?"

"I believe it is," Thomas replied. "From what I've seen so far, this is widespread. As a community, we may have to see if there's anything we can do to help out. Do you think we could call a community meeting about Wednesday or Thursday and get some community input?"

Mike replied, "I'll try to set one up for Wednesday. The sooner we get something going, the better it should be. Could you contact your folks and let them know what's going on? Russell and I will work on notifying everybody else in and around Richmond."

About an hour after Thomas' visitors left, he got on his bike and went home. It was fairly chilly and his heavy coat felt good.

Going in the house, he greeted Rachael. "I'm back, Rachel."

"Why are you back so soon?" she asked.

"Honey, we have a problem. The Fifth Trumpet Judgment is upon us and there's a lot of hurting people here in Richmond, and I'm sure, in other parts of the world."

"Oh my," she responded, "What are we going to do?"

He replied, "I talked to Mike Linden about it, and we're calling a meeting for Wednesday morning at ten. There's a lot of pain and suffering taking place all around, and we need to meet with community leaders and set up a plan to respond to it. I'm getting ready right now to go out to the farm and talk to the rest of the family and tell them about the meeting."

"I'd like to go with you, if possible," she replied.

"Rachael, it's pretty cold outside and it might be better if I made a quick trip out there on a bicycle. I'm sure we can do some visiting when they come in for the meeting on Wednesday," he replied.

"Well, I'm a little disappointed, but what you say makes sense. Would you like something hot to drink before you go?"

He answered. "No thanks. I'll wait until I get out there." Thomas bundled up, kissed Rachael goodbye, and headed on out to Alvin and Rhonda's. They were surprised to see him.

"Come on in and tell me what brings you out here in this time of the week," Alvin greeted."Take off your coat, and I'll see if I can get you something hot to drink."

Rhonda spoke up. "The stove is still warm from this morning. I'll stir up a little fire and have something hot in about ten minutes."

Thomas waited for Rhonda to come back to the living room and then told them what was happening in Richmond. He explained about the meeting on Wednesday.

Alvin replied, "The meeting on Wednesday could get interesting, especially if we have folks attending who are experiencing pain and torment."

Thomas told Alvin and Rhonda, "I'm sure Rachael would enjoy having you visit awhile when you come to Richmond."

Rhonda replied, "You can count on it."

Alvin asked, "Would you like for me to go over and tell James and family what's going on?"

"Yes I would," Thomas replied. "That will save me some

bicycling. By the way, what do you think this might do to our possibility of being raided by the outlaws?"

Alvin answered, "It may slow them down significantly. I would hope it would be permanently, but wouldn't count on it. I suspect that will depend on what else takes place following this happening."

Thomas stood up and put on his coat. "I'll get on back over to Richmond and poke around to see what else I can find out."

Rhonda asked, "Do you think you could haul a couple dozen eggs back with you, or should I just bring them on Wednesday?"

"I can take them now if you have them handy," he replied.

Rhonda got the eggs for him, and he went back to Richmond.

Alvin got on a bicycle and made the trip to the other farm. He met with James, Paula, Tim, and Pamela, in the living room and explained everything that was taking place. "I plan on monitoring the radio tonight and tomorrow night, and I'll let you know Wednesday at the meeting if I learn anything new."

On Monday night, Alvin turned on the short wave radio receiver and tuned in to the station in Switzerland. So far, the Switzerland station had preliminary reports. Some of it, especially for the local areas, was substantive, but the reports from distant places were still very sketchy. However, it was enough to substantiate that the Trumpet Judgment had occurred world- wide. Apparently, the horrible pain and suffering that was being experienced was triggering rioting and confusion.

The areas where significant information was available

indicated that all normal functions had almost ceased. Transportation, essentially, came to a screeching halt. Planes were grounded. Buses and trucks stopped running, and very few cars were on the roads.

About the only people on the earth who were functioning normally were the Christians.

All the World Government leaders, including the anti-Christ and the false prophet, were experiencing the judgment.

The leadership, even in their agony, continued trying to carry out their evil and corrupt work.

Tuesday night, Alvin worked the radios again and got more information on the broader world effects. Apparently, the judgment visited upon the world was very painful, but not deadly.

Wednesday morning the city held a town hall meeting at the church with the Mayor presiding. There was a general consensus in the meeting that the collective city and surrounding population should do something to help the afflicted people, especially their children.

The mayor and city council would work with the local community and come up with a plan. Incidentally, two members of the city council were not in attendance at the meeting, because they were suffering from the woe that had been visited upon them by Almighty God.

Looking around the city, there were other well to do people that were also suffering from the same woe.

After the meeting, Rhonda and Alvin went to spend some time with Rachael and Thomas.

After they got settled in the living room, Alvin stated: "Thomas, I'm curious. We know the suffering that's being endured by all these people is a judgment by God upon His enemies. Therefore, I have a question. If this suffering and torment is God's judgment, are we doing the right thing by helping them?"

Soberly, Thomas replied, "Alvin I've pondered that question and have prayed about it. This almost seems to be a paradox. God is judging them and punishing them because they have rejected Him, and they're His enemies. Jesus Christ said, love your enemies. God loves these sinful people, His enemies.

"However, God hates sin. ALL sin shall be destroyed. Sin is an inextricable part of the people who are God's enemies. Unless they accept Jesus Christ as Savior and Lord and shed their sin through His blood, they shall be destroyed along with their unwashed sin, even though God loves them."

"Wow!" Alvin exclaimed. "I understand for the first time. This has always been a puzzle to me."

Thomas continued, "In our ministrations to these people, I don't believe there's any way we can alleviate their pain and suffering, for it's supernaturally inflicted by Almighty God. If we minister to their physical needs, such as food, clothing, and shelter, or if we help take care of their children, I don't think God will expect any less from us.

Rhonda spoke up. "That makes sense. God's enemies are our enemies. We are to love our enemies. Love is not a passive thing. Love is active, and we can only express that love by doing."

Thomas, I have a question for you," Alvin stated. "I understand that this affliction that non-Christians are going through will last five months. If these people pray to God during this time and sincerely seek salvation, can they be saved? Would that stop their pain and torment?"

Thomas replied, "Alvin, I would think they can be saved. We would have to wait and see whether they would lose the affliction or not. We have a fairly large number of afflicted people here in this area. I'm sure that if that happens, we'll hear about it."

Thomas continued, "There are those who believed the protection against the locust woe only applied to the 144,000 Jews who had the seal of God in their forehead. As we can see, that isn't true.

"The book of John, chapter 6, verse 27, talks about Christians being sealed. The locust woe is the outpouring of God's wrath upon His enemies. The Bible says that Christians will not suffer the wrath of God. It's logical then that non-Christians would experience the woe and Christians would not."

Later in the afternoon, Alvin and Rhonda made their departure and drove their buggy back to the farm.

Alvin, James, and Tim worked together planning and preparing for spring. They made forays throughout the surrounding area looking for farm implements. They were looking specifically for implements that were either horse drawn or could be converted to horse drawn.

They were also looking for horse harness, turning plows, cultivators, corn drills, scissor hay mowers, hay rakes, balers, etc. The needs were endless.

They located a nice blacksmith setup at one of the abandoned farms and hauled it back to their farm. They also found a good stockpile of new horseshoes and horseshoe nails.

Their ideas on long range planning was that they could expect to be an agrarian society for decades to come.

Tim and Pamela had set up a wood shop in their storage building. As some of the days began to warm up, Pamela would take Cathy out there, snugly bundled in her bed. As Pamela worked, she would sing to Cathy when she was awake. Cathy seemed to enjoy the diversion.

While working outside, Pamela noticed Trixie was showing some signs. She seemed to be growing in the abdominal area and her teats were swelling.

"Oh! My!" Pamela exclaimed, "Trixie is going to have puppies."

That night when Tim came home, Pamela told Tim what was going on with Trixie.

Tim was surprised. "I never knew that she even had an opportunity. I'll bet we'll be surprised when we see the pups. Come to think of it, I have seen a light brown dog in the general area a time or two. It's about the same size as Trixie."

February passed, and mid-March came with warmer and sunnier days. The warmer weather made the outside work easier. Some of the March days were still windy, blustery, cold, and sometimes wet. When the weather was suitable the opportunity wasn't lost. The work needs were overwhelming.

Trixie had five pups on March 21, the first day of spring. It was a cool, sunny day; probably around sixty degrees. Two of the pups were male and three were female. There were one brown, and two brown and white females. One male was brown and the other male was white.

Meanwhile, the work went on. The only respite from work was Saturday, when they went to church, and the one day a week when they would go in for Bible study and to do their mid-week shopping and trading.

Alvin kept everybody informed on the happenings in

other parts of the world. The more detailed news came out of the areas ruled by the New World Government. Apparently, the entire world was taking a beating as God continued to punish His enemies with the locust woe.

The Jews in Israel were especially hard hit as God punished the un-repentant Jews who continued to reject Him and his Son, Jesus Christ.

The World Leader (the anti-Christ), and his closest ally, the false prophet, were both suffering horribly along with the rest of the anti-God, anti-Christian world population. They used all their powers and influence to attempt to make their lives more comfortable, but to no avail. The supernatural locust woe would continue to torment and haunt them until the end of the five months duration.

The workers, who were forced to be around them while doing their assigned duties, were made even more miserable, if that was possible.

Fortunately, the Christians who had escaped the concentration camps were able, for the most part, to stay hidden from their anger and retaliation.

The reports that Alvin received from Switzerland indicated also that the entire world had recieved the locust woe judgment. The people of the world, excluding Christians, groaned in agony and torment.

Thomas set up a Bible study for 10:00 a.m. on March 23. He had been working on an outline that would cover about five sessions. These would be held every other week, as they were coming up on spring.

Christians in the community, and a few non-Christians, kept coming to him with questions about past events, present events, and coming future events. Thomas decided he'd try to address as many of them as he could. At the same time, he would be calling upon others of the group for their input.

On March 23rd, about twenty people showed up for the study. Mike Linden and his wife, along with Russell Grose, were there. George Braddock, the mayor, along with his wife, and six of his seven city council members, were also there. One of the council members present, Albert Cantrell, was obviously suffering from the throes of the locust affliction.

Thomas got up before the group and began his presentation. "I've been working on a series of five lessons. I've had numerous questions asked on these subjects, and there seems to be a lot of general interest in them. The title to the first lesson is: Pre-War USA. In hindsight, we'll be able to see some of the mistakes we may have made as a nation and as individuals. There are two verses in the Bible, in Hebrews 10:30-31. The first verse says, "'For we know him that hath said, Vengeance belongeth unto me, I will recompense, saith the Lord. And again, The Lord shall judge his people.' The second verse says, 'It is a fearful thing to fall into the hands of the living God.'

"Without a doubt, we're at that time in history. Even though we know we're Christians, I believe we can all agree, it's a fearful time." Thomas noted.

He continued on, "One of the questions I'm asked the most is, why has the United States been so thoroughly devastated?

"Some of our Old Testament prophets, such as in Isaiah 5:4-6, used a vineyard in comparison, and pointed out that God had done all He could possibly do to make the vineyard (Israel) good and productive, and in return, the vineyard brought forth wild grapes. In verse 5, God explains what He will do to that vineyard. He will take away the hedge thereof, and it shall be eaten up, tramped down, and destroyed.

"Folks, I've heard a lot of our Godly pastors and men say what I'm about to say. I believe that God took away His hedge of protection from our nation, and now we're in the hands of, and at the mercy of, a fearful and angry God.

"Another operative verse in the Bible is found in Luke 12:48. In essence, it says, 'To whom much is given, much is required.' I know it was referring to an individual, but I believe it would also apply to a nation.

"We know that God blessed this nation in a tremendous way. This vineyard, with God's protective hedge around it, produced the wild grapes of rejecting God's Word in the schools and from the town square, trampling the sanctity of life through murdering babies in the womb, forsaking the sanctity of the family through same sex marriage and couples living together out of wedlock, promoting Sodom and Gomorrah life-styles, and promotion of pre-Noah's flood levels of rebellion against Almighty God. If ever a nation was ripe for the plucking, this nation was."

Thomas continued: "Looking back to pre-war United States, we can see how the country had declined in the seven or so decades prior to the war.

"Some would say that World War II was our finest hour. During that war, large numbers of the people of our nation petitioned God for His mercy and His help. Hundreds of thousands of our men and women gave their lives to protect us. Hundreds of thousands more were injured, many of them severely. It was a time of self sacrifice and dependence on God like this nation has never seen, before or since. Public figures and politicians weren't ashamed to petition God for His help.

"Our nation helped other nations rebuild; and our nation as a people, was probably as close to God as it had ever been before or ever was after that time. Satan and his hordes had been beaten back momentarily, but satan and his hordes never rested, even for a minute, in their attempt to deceive and destroy the people of this nation.

"There were too many people with evil in their hearts, and itchy ears, willing to listen to satan and do his bidding, for that level of interest in worshipping God to continue.

"Several attempts at a constitutional amendment were made over the years to declare the United States of America a Christian nation. They all failed.

"In 1962, prayer was taken out of schools. The nation went into a spiritual decline and never recovered. When did God remove His protective hedge from around America? You guess.

"I know we'd like to blame all of our woes on the politicians. Don't get me wrong: They bear a very heavy burden for what has happened to this nation. They, supposedly, are leaders, as well as our elected representatives. They supposedly were elected to look out for the best interest of the citizens.

"Blame? We, the citizens, elected them. We allowed them to stay in office even when we knew they were doing wrong. Ultimately, the responsibility for what happened to this nation belongs to 'We, the people'.

"God will sort it all out at the Great White Throne Judgment and will mete out punishment to the level and intensity that punishment is due. As Jesus said, 'There shall be weeping and gnashing of teeth'.

"During the decades after World War II, and prior to this last war, a spiritual battle had been raging. The battle hadn't been between just Democrats and Republicans, liberals and conservatives, but between God and satan, between the 'principalities and powers of the air' and God.

"The Democrats versus the Republicans, the liberal, progressive, secular forces versus the conservative Christian forces, were merely pawns in this great spiritual battle that was raging prior to the war and still rages around the world, pending the conclusion of the battle of Armageddon. Even then, there will only be a 1,000 year respite until God permanently destroys satan and his cohorts.

"Yes. In a few short months, Jesus Christ will destroy His enemies at the battle of Armageddon. Jesus Christ defeated satan when He died on the cross. Now He will destroy ALL of satan's earthly followers. Satan will be chained and imprisoned in the bottomless pit for 1,000 years. The anti-Christ and false prophet will be cast into the lake of fire.

"Even now, the battle rages for the souls of men. Enemies of God, even at this very moment, can still cast their sins upon Jesus Christ and be saved.

"Even before the war, it wasn't too late for America to turn back to God. In 2 Chronicles 7:14, the Bible says, 'If my people, which are called by my name, shall humble themselves, and pray, and seek my face, and turn from their wicked ways; then will I hear from heaven, and will forgive their sins, and will heal their land.'"

Thomas continued, "Within this very short Scripture lay the solution which would've avoided the awesome and awful destruction of the United States.

"For those of us who may have been listening in on the news and watching television in the time leading up to the war, there was a constant and massive flow of anti-God, anti-Christian, anti-American vitriolic hate spewing out. At the time, I was not a Christian, but I still picked up on the vicious diatribe." Thomas bowed his head a few moments and then looked up, and continued: "Neither were you.

"Thank God that has changed. I don't believe that any of us understood what was happening at the time. Satan had us totally blind.

"Remember the story of the Gadarine man who was possessed by the demons? By the way, that is found in Luke 8:26 and following. He was possessed by legions of devils.

"Have no doubt; before the war, there was a tremendous demonic influence in high places in our government and among the influential people in our land. Keep in mind also that before the war, God continued to welcome all who would, to depart from their sinful ways and come to Him, but they wouldn't.

"I have one more Scripture I wish to read to you. It contains two words which, to me, are profound. We've probably asked ourselves a thousand times why we didn't accept Jesus Christ as our savior before now. Why are billions of people dying and going to hell when there's an alternative?

"In 2 Peter 3:5, the Bible says, 'For this they willingly are ignorant of that by the word of God the heavens were of old, and the earth standing out of the water and in the water.'

"They willingly are ignorant! Most of the people dying and going to hell aren't stupid. Most of them are probably intelligent people. They willingly are ignorant of the truth of the reality of God.

"There are other places in the Bible where it explains that all people, without doubt, know that God is. Those places in the Bible just don't use the words, "Willingly are ignorant." I would like to ask some of these lost people; when you stand before God at the Great White Throne Judgment, are you going to admit to God that you were 'willingly are ignorant'? What an excuse! Well, it's sad and it's so senseless.

Thomas closed his Bible and picked up his notes. "That concludes our study for today and you're dismissed. If there are any of you with any questions, feel free to stay over and ask them. I intend to be here another thirty minutes."

The people began to file out, saying their goodbyes and going on their way.

Albert Cantrell, the Councilman, stayed around and approached Thomas. "Thomas, could you spend a few minutes with me before you go?"

Thomas replied, "Sure thing. I'll stay as long as you like."

Alfred confided in Thomas, "I'm about persuaded to turn my life over to God and Jesus Christ. As you can probably tell, I'm an extremely miserable person with all the pain and suffering I'm going through right now. I need more time to study and pray about this, for I must be absolutely sure I'm making a decision for the right reasons, and not because I'm in so much pain. I've been talking to my wife about this and so far, she isn't inclined to seek God."

Thomas replied, "Albert, you continue to pray and seek God, and I'll keep praying for you. If you have any questions, or wish to talk, come see me at any time."

Thomas had prayer with Albert and they both went on their way.

The first week of March found the Mercer clan gearing up for spring planting. Irish potatoes, mustard greens, turnip greens, onions, and spinach would be planted, hopefully, by the fifteenth of March. The seed potatoes at James' that had been kept in the root cellar this past winter were just beginning to sprout.

Alvin had put the surplus of his potato crop in a "tater hill" which was constructed by layering hay and potatoes with some soil mixed in, to form a mound. Once all the potatoes were in place, hay was laid around the outside and then the mound was covered over with a layer of soil, at least a foot thick to keep them from freezing. Harvesting the potatoes as needed through the winter consisted of digging into the mound at the bottom, rolling out the potatoes needed, and then filling the hole up with the removed straw and dirt.

The potatoes in Paul's potato hill were more advanced in sprouting and ready to plant. The potatoes were cut in thirds or fourths to ensure each piece of potato had enough sprouts and enough potato body to get the plant going. On both farms, the potatoes were one of their cash crops and they each planted about a fifth of an acre.

The tomato and pepper seeds had been planted in trays and were kept in the house in windows where they could get enough sun to sprout and start to grow. As the weather became warmer they were moved out into the sun, either on the porch or out in the yard, until the time to plant them in the garden.

The major planting of gardens and field crops wouldn't begin until after the 5th of May to avoid most of the frosts.

Alvin was still monitoring the radio twice a week. In his relay contact with Elizabethtown, he discovered that the sheriff had undergone the locust judgment. He was finally beginning to perform more of his old duties but so far had no information on the outlaw band. This was a definite matter of concern to Alvin and he mentally made note that he needed to contact Mike and let him know.

World news didn't provide any new insight into what might be happening worldwide. The latest news indicated that the locust judgment brought much of the world to a standstill. This lowered their concern over the New World Government posing a greater threat.

Alvin found some radio stations in Mexico as well as Central and South America. He was able to learn that there were quite a few people south of them. Without being able to understand Spanish he didn't learn a lot. He made another mental note to see if he could find someone in or around Richmond that could speak Spanish. *Knowing more about their southern neighbors could become important as time passed,* he thought.

The Christians in the Richmond area continued on with their lives. They continued their outreach to the non-Christian people and their families. Practically every family in the surrounding area planted and grew a garden. There was a tremendous amount of interaction among the people as those with knowledge of gardening skills helped and trained those who didn't. People were finally beginning to understand that this was their future. They would never revert back to the way things were.

Flower and garden planting, with all the interaction among the people, was creating more community spirit. Flower seeds and flower bulbs were also being saved and replanted. More and more people were learning how to save seeds and how to plant.

Families like the Mercers shared their seeds and plants with those who had not. They also assisted families where assistance was needed. Afflicted families asked for help and received it. A few of the afflicted families were having their hearts changed and were seeking God.

Farming and gardening kept everybody on the farms busy from daylight to dark. The Mercer farms, along with most of the other farms, required extra help to get their work done. There was a stream of people on bicycles leaving Richmond at daylight in the mornings and returning just at dark in the evenings. Many of them showed the debilitating effects of having suffered through the locust judgment.

It was a matter of earning food for survival for the workers from Richmond for many of the people Basic survival with food, clothing and shelter, was about all they could afford.

Early in the spring, Paula and Rhonda would take with them whomever was available to go, and pick greens. There were several edible greens growing wild, such as polk salad, wild asparagus, burdock, cattail, clovers, sheep sorrel, plantain, chickweed, dandelion, etc. These greens were very tasty. Some people liked them with hot bacon grease poured over them. There was also wild onion, but very few people had a taste for them. These greens preceded and then supplemented the lettuce, onions, and greens from the early garden.

For the un-Godly people living on the earth, they essentially marked time for the five months of the plague. Many of the pains they experienced were as painful as scorpion stings. They endured. They waited. Most of them cursed God. They wished to die but God would not allow it. A few of them, worldwide, turned to God in a sincere way and were born again. The vast majority of them doubled down in the evil of their minds and their hatred toward God.

In early July, the pains from the locust judgment ceased. One minute it was there, and the next minute it wasn't. For the settlement in and around Richmond, it was a mixed blessing. It was, no doubt, an untold blessing for those who had been afflicted and suffered. For the community of Richmond, It renewed the possibility of a threat from the outlaws at Elizabethtown.

Alvin, who had re-established contact in Elizabethtown through the relay in Florida, notified his contacts so they could do some extra scouting around the area for outlaw activity.

Alvin made a trip into town and contacted the mayor and the sheriff. Alvin greeted Mike, "Good morning, Mike."

Mike returned the greeting. "Good morning, Alvin. What brings you to town this time of day."

Alvin replied, "I thought that since the locust plague seems to be past, I'd check with you and the mayor about the possibility of our outlaws being a problem."

Alvin, let's walk over to the mayor's office and get his input. We'll see if we need to call another town meeting any time soon."

They visited with the mayor and two of his council members and agreed they would let Alvin stay in touch with Elizabethtown, and Mike would arrange some surveillance around Richmond and see what developed.

Meanwhile, work went on apace in the gardens, on the farms, and in all the other shops and markets in the area.

Over the course of the summer, Thomas had given the people an insight into the events following the nuclear world war. He told them about the world-wide famine as all transportation of goods shut down and how quickly stored foods were consumed. Essentially, a week after transportation shut down, all food had disappeared from the shelves in stores.

Following the famine, came the scourge of disease. With the weakened immune systems from the radiation fallout, people died by the droves. It was probably safe to say that billions died from the war, followed by radiation, famine and pestilences.

As fall approached and the first week of September came around, the harvesting of crops, canning, and gathering of firewood and all these other activities, consumed their time.

On the tenth of September, Alvin got a heads-up from his contact in Elizabethtown. He had been able to ferret out an individual who stayed in touch with the outlaws. The man was a runner for the outlaws and sometimes picked up supplies, delivered messages, passed on information for them, and acted as a general roustabout.

He informed them that the outlaws intended to go ahead with the raid they had planned earlier in the year. Tentatively, the raid was planned for the first week in November. It could be moved to an earlier date, depending on the health and availability of some of their gang. Alvin passed the information on to Mike and the mayor as well as the church people.

Tim and Pamela had done well with their honey bees. During the year, they had increased their bee farm by six hives. By watching carefully, they could tell when a hive was about to swarm. By opening the hive, they could remove the old queen along with a third of the racks out of the brood box, and install them in a new brood box. Care had to be taken in moving the right amount of the unborn bees out of the old hive and into the new.

The downside to making new hives: this cut down on their year's honey crop. However, in the long haul, this would increase their total productivity. Their honey crop was significant and profitable due to the lack of refined sugar.

Other family members would help take care of Cathy while Pamela helped Tim with the bees, as well as their other endeavors.

CHAPTER IX
SIXTH TRUMPET
JUDGMENT (SECOND WOE)

Revelation 9:13-21 "And the sixth angel sounded, and I heard a voice from the four horns of the golden alter which is before God.

Saying to the sixth angel which had the trumpet, Loose the four angels which are bound in the great river Euphrates.

And the four angels were loosed, which were prepared for an hour, and a day, and a month, and a year, for to slay the third part of men.

And the number of the army of the horsemen were two hundred thousand thousand: and I heard the number of them.

And thus I saw the horses in the vision, and them that sat on them, having breastplates of fire, and of jacinth, and brimstone: and the heads of the horses were as the heads of lions; and out of their mouths issued fire and smoke and brimstone.

By these was the third part of men killed, by the fire,

and by the smoke, and by the brimstone, which issued out of their mouths.

For their power is in their mouths, and in their tails: for their tails were like unto serpents, and had heads, and with them they do hurt.

And the rest of the men were not killed by these plagues yet repented not of the works of their hands, that they should not worship devils, and idols of gold, and silver, and brass, and stone, and of wood: which neither can see, nor hear, nor walk:

Neither repented they of their murders, nor of their sorceries, nor of their fornication, nor of their thefts."

In mid October, the world was struck by God's Sixth Trumpet Judgment. As the earth turned on its axis, the second woe visited non-Christians in the middle of the night. When the earth completed the rotation, billions had died.

The earth's population, which had been more than seven billion before the nuclear war, was now significantly less than half that number.

They lost at least a third of the non-Christian population in the Richmond area. Several children were left homeless. The remaining population, Christian and non-Christian, worked together to bury the dead and arrange for a home for the orphaned children.

Although most of the Christians in the area knew what was coming, it was still a great shock.

After about a week, Alvin was able to confirm that most of the outlaw band in Elizabethtown was dead. Six of them survived, including the leader. Practically speaking, the threat of an invasion from that location was gone.

Alvin's source informed him that their sheriff had also

succumbed, much to the relief of some and the consternation of others.

The information Alvin picked up from around the world was the same. Large numbers of people had died.

Most governments, including the ten regional governments of the One World Government, as well as the remaining population of the rest of the world, were very close to paralysis.

The people in Richmond were well assured they would never have to fear threat from any outside sources. Otherwise, their activities continued on pretty much as usual.

Final harvesting, firewood gathering, and preparing for cooler weather occupied much of their time. Hog butchering, rendering of lard, preserving the meat, making soap, etc., would be started in about two more weeks, when it got cooler.

Thomas and Rachael came out from time to time and joined up with the rest of the Mercer clan to help with the harvesting. Once that was complete, Thomas joined up with Alvin, James, and Tim to go hunting, and also to gather wild grapes, hickory nuts, and walnuts.

Trixie made the foraging trips with them and was helpful in finding rabbits and squirrels. She stayed home when serious hunting was underway for game, such as deer. They were hopeful they wouldn't find any bears. There was a possibility some bears could have invaded their area.

James, Paula, Tim, and Pamela went to the woods with the tools needed to harvest sassafras roots. James and Tim had made an exploratory trip during the summer and had located four trees different from the ones they had harvested from the year before.

It took them the better part of the day to get all the roots they needed. They gathered enough for all their families with some left over to barter or sell in Richmond.

Hot beverages required some innovative thinking since coffee was now a rarity. Sassafras tea and dandelion tea were two of the favorites.

While they were back in the woods they also found some black haw bushes and a wild persimmon tree. A few of the persimmons would still cause a little puckering. They needed another hard frost. They also found one butternut tree, which was a rarity.

On November the thirteenth, Pamela and Tim held a birthday party for Cathy. They invited Thomas and Rachael, Herbert and Barbara, as well as all the rest of their families.

The birthday party was a festive event which included a birthday cake with a homemade beeswax candle in the middle of it. Pamela apologized for not having any ice cream to go with the cake.

All the Mercers were together for the first time in a long time, making this a very special occasion. In addition to the celebration of Cathy's birthday, they enjoyed their time of sharing information on their farming and other activities. They agreed to get together again on the 23rd of November to butcher the hogs, and start the lard rendering and soap making.

Alvin shared all the latest information he had on world events and conditions with the clan. Although the One World Government continued in its attempt to dominate, things were becoming much more difficult for them. In the areas where they were still able to exert their dominance, they were brutal. With the shortage of food and the abject poverty of the people, even those who had the mark were becoming more openly rebellious.

Within the United States most activities were localized. There hadn't been any incentive for people to suddenly travel from one part of the US to the other. Most people were focused on the activities related to survival and just being able to have food to eat. Since the last wave of deaths, the isolation had increased throughout the country.

Following the party, everybody went to their respective homes and resumed their normal activities.

Christmas came and was observed and celebrated. A special service was held at the church. It was a time of mostly silence, meditation, and prayer of thanksgiving for God's grace, love, and salvation through Jesus Christ. They also thanked God for His providence in saving and preserving them through these trying and uncertain times.

Rachael whispered in Rhonda's ear and informed her that she would be having a baby in May or June. Rhonda was ecstatic, of course, knowing a second grandchild was on the way.

January and February were cold, with lots of freezing weather, snow, and ice. The Mercers stayed busy keeping the animals fed and watered and the houses warm. Fortunately, nobody got sick during that time, and, except for the inconveniences that winter brought, all went well.

On the first of March the weather began to break with some signs of the approaching spring. They were beginning to see a few Robins walking around the yard as well as a few Blackbirds. So far, they had seen only one Bluebird. It sat for just a few minutes on the Bluebird house.

By Wednesday, it appeared the conditions could be

improved enough that they might be able to go to town on Saturday for church. As Saturday approached, the anticipation grew. When Saturday came, an enthusiastic group set out for Richmond. As the people assembled in the church, it almost resembled a homecoming.

Mayor George Braddock and his wife, Emily, were there. Sheriff Mike Linden and his wife, Stella, were also there. Most of the city council, the deputy sheriff, and many more of the regulars were also in attendance. With all the meeting and greeting, the service was a little late getting started.

Thomas was somewhat sober as he entered the pulpit to begin the service. Following the prayer, and songs of worship, Thomas opened his Bible to the Book of Revelation, chapter 11. "Today, I would like to cover more of the end-time prophecies and tell you where I think we are in the time line toward Armageddon. Chapter 11 tells about the Seventh Trumpet, or the third woe.

"I believe we can expect more events to take place just anytime now. The seventh trumpet judgment is the precursor to the seven vial judgments. If my calculations are correct, we have two months or less before we enter into the thousand-year time period. If this is true, when the seven vial judgments begin, they will probably come thick and fast.

"The first vial judgment will be easy to recognize. The remaining people who aren't Christians will get sores. I'll read it to you. Revelation 16:1,2 'And I heard a great voice out of the temple saying to the seven angels. Go your ways, and pour out the vials of the wrath of God upon the earth.

"'And the first went, and poured out his vial upon the earth; and there fell noisome and grievous sores upon the men which had the mark of the beast, and upon them who worshipped his image.'

"When you begin to see this take place, I advise you to stay home if you can, and stay indoors as much as possible for the next several days. We don't know for sure what all will take place, but being inside would probably be the safest place."

Following the service, a few of the people met at the back of the church, did some socializing, and then left. Alvin met up with Mike and Russell, and they exchanged their latest information.

CHAPTER X
SEVENTH TRUMPET JUDGMENT (THIRD WOE) AND FOUR VIAL JUDGMENTS

Revelation 11:14-19 "The second woe has passed; and, behold, the third woe cometh quickly.

And the seventh angel sounded; and there were great voices in heaven, which said:

"The kingdoms of the world has become the kingdoms of our Lord, and of his Christ; and he shall reign for ever and ever.

And the four and twenty elders, which sat before God on their seats, fell upon their faces, and worshipped God,

Saying, we give thee thanks, o Lord God Almighty, which art, and wast, and art to come; because thou hast taken to thee thy great power, and hast reigned.

And the nations were angry, and thy wrath is come, and the time of the dead, that they should be judged, and that thou shouldest give reward unto thy servants the prophets, and to the saints, and them that fear thy name, small and great; and shouldest destroy them and destroy the earth.

And the temple of God was opened in heaven, and there was seen in his temple the ark of his testament: and there were lightning and voices, and thundering, and an earthquake, and great hail."

Revelation 16:1 "And I heard a great voice out of the temple saying to the seven angels. Go your ways, and pour out the vials of the wrath of God upon the earth.

Revelation 16:2 "And the first went, and poured out his vial upon the earth; and there fell noisome and grievous sores upon the men which had the mark of the beast, and upon them who worshipped his image.

Revelation 16:3 "And the second angel poured out his vial upon the sea; and it became as the blood of a dead man; and every living soul died in the sea.

Revelation 16:4-7 "And the third angel poured out his vial upon the rivers and fountains of waters; and they became blood.

And I heard the angel of the waters say, Thou art righteous, O Lord, which art, and wast, and shall be, because thou hast judged thus.

For they have shed the blood of saints and prophets, and thou hast given them blood to drink; for they are worthy.

And I heard another out of the alter say, Even so, Lord God Almighty, true and righteous are thy judgments."

Revelation 16:8-9 And the fourth angel poured out his vial upon the sun; and power was given unto him to scorch men with fire.

And men were scorched with great heat, and blasphemed

the name of God, which hath power over these plagues: and they repented not to give him glory.

On March 31, people around the world who had not been born again broke out in great sores all over their bodies. Those affected in the Richmond area stayed at home, as they were too miserable, and too disfigured, to go anywhere. Two of the city council members, apparently, were affected, for they didn't show up at the Mayor's office for the next three days.

The second vial judgment came three days after the first one. It wasn't seen or felt in the Richmond area, since it only affected the seas and the oceans. It became as the blood of a dead man, and every living soul in the sea died.

Thomas, who had been studying his Bible almost incessantly, almost panicked. The third vial judgment would affect fresh waters. The fourth vial judgment would cause much of the earth to be scorched by fire. Thomas had no way of knowing if these judgments would affect the local area and just the lost people, or if it would affect everybody.

He went first to the mayor's office to warn him and then to the sheriff's office to let Mike know. Following that, he headed out to the farms.

As a result, the Mercers worked feverishly to protect what fresh water they could and also arranged to get their animals into barns and enclosures to protect them from heat, if it came.

Tim went out to his bee hives and closed them off after dark so they couldn't get out. He planned to go back the next day and let them out so they could get water. Later, after the bees went back in after dusk, he would close them up again.

The chances of anything happening were probably slim, but Tim didn't mind doing a little extra work to make sure.

The Mercers could feel a portent of a climax to the coming events which would greatly affect their lives.

Alvin got on the radio to see what he could hear from the rest of the world. Most of what he heard was meaningless chatter.

Lost people were in charge of world government. The world was under judgment. Lost people weren't faring too well right now, and world government was paralyzed.

Alvin tried to make contact with Florida, but couldn't. From all indications, Alvin's connections to the outside world were all dead.

The night of April the 10th, they were able to see flashes of light on the horizons with an occasional flash across the sky. The colors were a darker red that didn't resemble the Aurora Borealis. From their interpretation of the Scriptures, they assumed this was probably the fourth vial, which caused unusual activities of the sun. They viewed this with some relief, as this would mean their fresh water was safe from that vial, and they wouldn't suffer harm from the fires from heaven.

CHAPTER XI
THREE VIALS OF JUDGMENT AND ARMAGEDDON

Revelation 16:10-11 "And the fifth angel poured out his vial upon the seat of the beast; and his kingdom was full of darkness; and they gnawed their tongues for pain,

And blasphemed the God of heaven because of their pains and their sores, and repented not of their deeds.

Revelation 16:12-16 "And the sixth angel poured out his vial upon the great river Euphrates; and the water thereof was dried up; that the way of the kings of the east might be prepared.

And I saw three unclean spirits like frogs come out of the mouth of the dragon, and out of the mouth of the beast, and out of the mouth of the false prophet.

For they are the spirits of devils, working miracles, which go forth unto the kings of the earth and of the whole world, to gather them to the battle of that great day of God Almighty.

Behold, I come as a thief. Blessed is he that watcheth, and keepeth his garments, lest he walk naked, and they see his shame.

And he gathered them together into a place called in the Hebrew tongue Armageddon.

Revelation 16:17-21"And the seventh angel poured out his vial into the air and there came a great voice out of the temple of heaven, from the throne, saying, it is done.

And there were voices, and thunders, and lightning, and there was a great earthquake, such as was not since men were upon the earth, so mighty an earthquake and so great.

And the great city was divided into three parts, and the cities of the nations fell: and great Babylon came in remembrance before God, to give her the cup of the wine of the fierceness of his wrath.

And every island fled away, and the mountains were not found.

And there fell upon men a great hail out of heaven, every stone about the weight of a talent: and men blasphemed God because of the plague of the hail; for the plague thereof was exceedingly great."

Zechariah: 14:3-4 "Then shall the Lord go forth, and fight against those nations, As when he fought in the day of battle. And his feet shall stand in that day upon the mount of Olives, Which is before Jerusalem on the east, And the mount of Olives shall cleave in the midst thereof toward the east and toward the west, And there shall be a very great valley: And half of the mountain shall remove toward the north, And half of it toward the south."

Revelation 19:17-21 And I saw an angel standing in the sun; and he cried with a loud voice, saying to all the fowls that fly in the midst of heaven, Come and gather yourselves together unto the supper of the great God.

That ye may eat the flesh of kings, and the flesh of captains, and the flesh of mighty men, and the flesh of horses, and of them that sit on them, and the flesh of all men, both free and bond, both small and great.

And I saw the beast, and the kings of the earth, and their armies, gathered together to make war against him that sat on the horse, and against his army.

And the beast was taken, and with him the false prophet that wrought miracles before him, with which he deceived them that had received the mark of the beast, and them that worshipped his image. They both were cast alive into a lake of fire burning with brimstone.

And the remnant were slain with the sword of him that sat on his horse, which sword proceeded out of his mouth and all the fowls were filled with his flesh."

Revelation 20:1-3 "And I saw an angel come down from heaven, having a key to the bottomless pit and a great chain in his hand.

And he laid hold on the dragon, that old serpent, which is the Devil, and Satan, and bound him for a thousand years.

And cast him into the bottomless pit, and shut him up, and set a seal on him, that he should deceive the nations no more, till the thousand years should be fulfilled; and after that, he must be loosed a little season."

As Jesus Christ orchestrated His judgment upon His earthly enemies, the frequency and intensity of the judgments increased exponentially.

The Book of Revelation has much detail, both literal and

symbolic, describing the enemies of Jesus. Revelation also describes the punishments both literal and symbolic.

The bottom line: during The Day of The Lord, which encompassed the time from the opening of the sixth seal through Armageddon, Jesus Christ poured out His wrath, His judgment, His punishment, and His executions upon billions of His enemies, ALL of his enemies.

When God said in the book of Genesis that He wouldn't ever destroy the earth again by water, was that a promise of encouragement or was it a promise of worse things to come?

The sixth angel poured out his vial and dried up the River Euphrates, and the unclean spirits enticed the armies to cross and gather to fight against Jesus Christ.

The enemies of God and Jesus Christ never had the spiritual discernment necessary to understand they were not fighting against flesh and blood, but were fighting against the Word of God, the Sword of the Lord, the supernatural powers of Almighty God and Jesus Christ.

From the beginning, satan never had a chance. The humans who aligned themselves with satan never had a chance. Oh! The tragedy of it all! The billions of humans who would soon be dead and bound for hell! And God was not willing that any should perish, but have eternal life!

As all the armies gathered and prepared themselves to do battle, the seventh angel prepared to pour out the final vial.

The armies from the east, who had crossed the dried-up river Euphrates, armies from the Middle East, from Europe, and from Africa, moved into and across Israel. They completely encircled Jerusalem where all the Israelis were concentrated. Their express purpose was to destroy every remaining Jew, whether Christian or non-Christian.

From the human perspective, the slaughter of every single remaining Jew was imminent.

The seventh angel poured out the final vial.

Horrific earthquakes shook the earth. The entire earth shook as it had never shaken before. In different parts of the ocean, islands moved. In some parts of the world's mountain chains, some mountains simply sank and vanished.

The earthquakes divided the city of Babylon into three sections.

Jerusalem and the surrounding area began to experience a tremendous earthquake. The earth in and around Jerusalem fractured and rose in some places. The Mount of Olives split, from north to south, with part of the mount moving to the west and the other part to the east. A tremendous fissure opened, providing an escape route for the Jews who were trapped in Jerusalem.

As the Jews fled to the south through the newly formed valley, the pursuing forces were supernaturally confused and began attacking each other. God's Jews, who had accepted Jesus Christ as their Messiah, Savior, and King, were miraculously protected. Those Jews who hadn't accepted Jesus Christ died in the ensuing hours as the events of Armageddon unfolded.

Suddenly, great hailstones began to fall, and men continued to blaspheme God. Many of the people in the great armies who were prepared for the battle of Armageddon, perished from the great hailstones.

Jesus Christ, with His army of Saints mounted behind Him, met the great armies arrayed at the battle site of Armageddon.

The anti-Christ and the false prophet led their giant forces against Jesus Christ and His army of Saints.

In the opening event of the battle, Jesus Christ plucked up the anti-Christ and the false prophet and tossed them into the lake of fire. The sword (The Word of God) then came from the mouth of Jesus and destroyed every living enemy in that great army, and, at the same time, destroyed every living enemy of God and Jesus Christ over the entire face of the earth. The army of saints behind Jesus Christ weren't there to do battle. They were His army of occupation who would help Him rule the earth with a rod of iron.

Satan was then chained and cast into the bottomless pit, where he would remain for a thousand years.

Darkness fell over the battlegrounds and killing fields all around the world, as the earth rotated toward the east. The buzzards that had been gorging themselves for hours took to the air and roosted on broken limbs of trees, partial walls of destroyed buildings, burned out vehicles, and other perches, to await the morning. Daylight would find them back at the feast.

Smoke still rose from some locations, obscuring some of the stars as they came out. Flames were still flickering from burning debris.

As the darkness deepened and the night grew older, a deep silence and calm stole across the land.

The Spirit of God hovered over the earth. God's wrath had been expended. A time of healing arrived. Jesus Christ had taken the throne of His world.

PART TWO

THE MILLENNIUM

CHAPTER XIV
SAINT ROBERT RAYBURN

Revelation 20:4-6 "And I saw thrones, and they sat upon them, and judgment was given unto them: and I saw the souls of them that were beheaded for the witness of Jesus, and for the word of God, and which had not worshipped the beast, neither his image, neither had received his mark upon their foreheads, or in their hands; and they lived and reigned with Christ a thousand years."

But the rest of the dead lived not again until the thousand years was finished. This is the first resurrection. Blessed and holy is he that hath part in the first resurrection; on such the second death hath no power; but they shall be priests of God and of Christ and shall reign with him a thousand years."

I Corinthians 6:2 "Do ye not know that the saints shall judge the world? And if the world shall be judged by you, are ye unworthy to judge the smallest matters?"

1 Peter 2:5 "Ye also, as lively stones, are built up a spiritual house, an holy priesthood, to offer up spiritual sacrifices, acceptable to God by Jesus Christ."

Friday, April 20, dawned bright and beautiful. It was a very special day in the life of the Mercers and all their clan. It was the first day of the Millennium, with Jesus Christ, the

Lion of David, as the ruler of the world. He shall rule the world with a rod of iron.

As their lives had progressed through the last five months, Thomas had led them in Bible studies that let them know as the major end-time events unfolded. He had pointed out and predicted that at the end of the battle of Armageddon, the last of the non-Christians all over the world would die.

Thomas and other members of the church had gone to the non-Christians in the area and witnessed to them, explaining they were at the end of the time for gaining salvation. Most of them still refused to believe or change. Some of them were virulent in their hatred toward God.

On April 19, a large number of people in and around Richmond dropped dead in their tracks. From what the Christians knew from the Bible, this signaled the end of Armageddon and the beginning of the millennium. Needless to say, there was a lot of apprehension among those who were left as they entered the uncertainty of the new era. Everybody immediately assembled and quickly searched the entire area for all surviving children. Every remaining household gained at least one child, and some even more. Integrating children from non Christian homes would present a challenge and an opportunity for service and ministry to the orphans.

Following several days of intense activity, life in and around Richmond began to get back to normal. Alvin and Rhonda were on their front porch with a cup of tea. Alvin remarked to Rhonda, "The redbuds and dogwoods are blooming over in the woods. I'm going to miss being able to drive out on Furnace Mountain and on highway 15 between Pine Ridge and Slade. The redbuds are always so beautiful on Slade Mountain and redbuds and dogwood are really pretty going up Furnace Mountain. I'm tempted to hook up the horse and buggy and make the trip anyhow."

Rhonda smiled, "Alvin, there are things like that we miss, but I'll bet there'll come a time when we see places and things that are much more beautiful. I suspect we just need to be patient."

On the first day of May, the mayor, George Braddock, was sitting in his office when he suddenly became startled by a stranger standing in front of him. He stared at him for a few seconds and then asked, "Who're you?"

The man replied, "I'm Saint Robert Rayburn, your new government coordinator. I'm part of the new government installed by Jesus Christ."

Mayor Braddock was absolutely astounded. "From our Bible studies, we figured something would probably happen, but we didn't know what it would be. Robert, I'm at your service. Just let me know what you'd like for me to do."

Saint Robert continued: "There's an overall plan to revitalize the world. I know you have what you call town hall meetings. I would like for you to set up such a meeting, or series of meetings. Each meeting will take two hours. Inform all people that the meeting is mandatory. I shall conduct the meeting and inform everybody at one time what to expect and what will be expected of them. They will be told more as time passes."

They Mayor replied, "When would you like to have the meetings?"

Saint Robert said, "Make it three days from now, on a Wednesday. Make the first one for 10:00 a.m."

Mayor Braddock answered, "Robert, I'll set up the

meetings for three successive days. I believe everybody can attend at least one of the sessions during that time."

Saint Robert agreed. "That'll be fine. I would like to again emphasize, the meeting is mandatory. If anybody misses, I will know."

Mayor Braddock replied, "I'll certainly make it clear. Tomorrow, a lot of people will be in for church and we can start getting out the word. I'll call a meeting of the town council, and we'll work at informing everybody else."

Saint Robert indicated he was leaving and walked through the closed door without opening it. The mayor was left with his mouth open.

The mayor went to the sheriff's office. "Mike, you'll never believe what I had in my office."

Mike replied, "I'll bet it has something to do with what we're about to see in this new world."

"You guessed it," George stated. "I just met a man who calls himself Saint Robert Rayburn. He told me he was from Jesus Christ, and he was our new government coordinator. "I'm to set up meetings, and he'll explain to us what will be happening in our future lives."

Saturday at church there was a lot of excitement as the word got around about the upcoming series of meetings. Saint Robert Rayburn was nowhere to be seen. There was a lot of speculation on what they might expect in the future, but even Thomas couldn't make a good guess.

Wednesday morning at 10:00 a.m., the meeting hall was full. The overflow left and would return at a later time.

Saint Robert introduced himself. "I am Saint Robert Rayburn. In the future, you may address me as Saint Robert or Saint Rayburn. We will use the greeting of a handshake.

"I'm one of the tens of millions of The Lord's Church that was translated into heaven at the time of the rapture. I returned to earth a few days ago when Jesus Christ came down to claim His earth as His kingdom.

"In 1 Peter 2:5, we are mentioned in the Holy Scriptures as being a holy priesthood, and in 1 Corinthians 6:2, it was foretold that we shall judge the world. I am directly responsible to Jesus Christ to enforce His rule over you and over this part of His kingdom.

"You shall not worship me or bow down to me. Neither shall you pray to me. You shall worship God and the Lord, Jesus Christ. You shall pray to God in the name of the Lord Jesus Christ.

"Due to your past experiences in the matter of governance;, you would probably see me in a similar role as a county judge executive." Saint Robert smiled, and continued, "It's similar to that but much more comprehensive.

"Here are His basic rules which shall be posted for all to see.

"His Word is law. The inspired prophecies and Scriptures shall be reproduced in a single format to reflect the accurate rendition of all its content. This shall be the Bible. This then shall reflect His Word.

"The breaking of His law is sin. Sin is punishable by death. There shall be no sanctuary from punishment. Under the authority of Jesus Christ, all punishment shall be meted out by us, the appointed representatives, who are also your judges. Punishment shall be summary. There shall be no appeal.

"The day of worship shall be Sunday, the Lord's Day. It shall be a day of worship, meditation, and rest." Saint Robert looked at Thomas Daley, who sat on the front row. "Pastor Daley, on my next visit, I'll sit down with you and explain how you and I will relate and interact with each other.

Saint Robert continued with his talk to the gathering. "You shall look to Mayor Braddock for information and guidance. I'll be back from time to time to give more detail.

"I will now give you an insight into what the world situation is today and what you can expect in the future as time goes on.

"The world population has been greatly depleted. At present, the only humans living on earth are those who are either Christian or children under the age of accountability. All others have perished.

"Parents, or guardians, have the responsibility to train and educate their children in the way of the Lord. Once a child reaches the age of accountability, they are responsible for themselves before the Lord. However, the parent or guardian is still responsible for their upkeep, training, and nurture until they are grown.

"There shall be higher education. There shall be elementary education for children. Teachers shall be required to teach the truth. Any teacher straying from the truth shall be cut off without remedy.

"Population will increase. Each person will have free will. They can accept Jesus Christ in their heart as Lord, or they can refuse to do so. However, they must accept Jesus Christ as their Lord and Master in their actions or suffer the penalty for disobedience.

"Communities will grow. Cities will grow. Nations will grow. All government entities shall be governed through representatives such as I, who have absolute power and are directly responsible to Jesus Christ.

"Some of the world infrastructure will be rebuilt. However, most of it shall be obliterated and simply disappear. Much of the earth shall be returned to nature.

"There is so much more you will learn as time goes by. I have only told you enough to give you a basic understanding. More will be revealed to you at the proper time. If you have questions, take them to the mayor. He can then ask me. I will reveal what I can as appropriate. May God bless you. You are dismissed."

No question and answer session had been offered, so the people got up and filed out.

The next meeting was scheduled for twelve, and a large number had already gathered outside, waiting to get in.

The mayor asked Saint Robert, "Aren't you going to take a break to rest or to eat?"

Saint Robert smiled, and answered, "I don't need rest, and I don't eat."

The mayor was surprised, and replied, "I had no idea."

Late in the afternoon, Saint Robert reappeared in the mayor's office. "Mayor Braddock, here is a copy of the information I have made available to you and the people in this area. I expect you to take action on the instructions in so far as you are able. I will visit you from time to time to give you more information and guidance."

Mayor Braddock replied, "What authority do I have over the people here to get them to do the things that need to be done?"

Saint Robert replied, "By my authority, which is the authority of Jesus Christ. Ask for their help. Ask for their cooperation. Do not demand, order, or force. If problems arise, refer them to me when I return. Do you have any other questions?"

The mayor replied, "No. That's clear enough. I'll do what I can to get things moving."

"Goodbye, Mayor Braddock."

"Goodbye, Saint Robert."

Saint Robert suddenly disappeared, leaving Mayor Braddock standing alone in his office, his head buzzing, and his mind overwhelmed by the recent events.

Mayor Braddock sat down behind his desk, took the paper that Saint Robert had given him, and began to read it. As he read it, he pored over it, and prayed over it. He began to formulate a plan to approach the daunting, and seemingly overwhelming, task.

The mayor's first step was to call a meeting of his city council. Since two had died during the last event, the council now had five members.

The mayor and council decided the first task would be to take a census of all the people in the Richmond area. The census would include skills, as well as the usual information of names, addresses, ages, etc.

Saint Robert continued the series of meetings for three days. He was aware that a few people didn't come. Following the meeting, the people dispersed and went to their homes.

The Mercers all went to Thomas and Rachael's house for lunch and then sat around and discussed the latest development. Herbert and Barbara had joined them.

Alvin led out in the discussion. "I don't know how the rest of you feel about what's just happened, but I'm feeling so overwhelmed I'm almost speechless. Would somebody else like to say something?"

James spoke up. "I certainly have a lot more questions now than I had before and very few answers. My thinking is, we live in a safer world now than we did before, and our first order of business, until we get other instructions, will be to continue with our lives the way we have been. We'll grow our garden and produce, farm our crops, and take care of our animals. The one big change, so far is, we'll be going to church on Sunday instead of Saturday."

Thomas spoke up. "The one thing we probably need to work on will be setting up an education system. This will have to develop over a period of time. Right now, we have boys and girls who haven't been taught the basics of reading, writing, and arithmetic. Also, I'm pretty sure we won't have a problem with teaching the Bible or having prayer in school."

The last comment got a good laugh from all the others.

Tim joined in the conversation. "I have a lot of questions I'd like to have him answer. For one, since resurrected Christians have come to help rule the world, I wonder where my parents and all the rest of my family are located? I wonder if I'll ever get to see them?"

Paula replied, "Tim, when you get a chance, why don't you give that question to Mayor Braddock and have him ask Saint Robert when he comes again?"

Tim responded, "That's a good idea Paula. I'll do just that. And while I'm at it, I have another question. What would be wrong with going back to the farm and cave in Powell County sometime in the future, since we're now safe from outlaws and those other kinds of dangers,?"

James responded, "I've been thinking of that too, Tim.

Right now, with our transportation the way it is, anybody living there would be quite isolated. Later, it may be something we'd wish to do. In any event, I suspect that before we make any major changes we'd need to run them by Saint Robert."

There was a period of silence as everybody absorbed the implications of what James had just expressed. It was becoming apparent that they were possibly no longer free to do as they pleased, when they pleased.

Following the latest deaths, sixteen children in the area had been left homeless. The mayor and the sheriff, with their wives, and with the help of Thomas and Rachael, had worked from the very beginning to make sure they were housed and fed. James and Paula took in 12-year old Kayla Sherman, and her brother Allen, who was 10; this placed them with Tiffany, 16, and Ron, 12, who were closer to their age. 10 -year old Bradley Stout moved in with Alvin and Rhonda. Thomas and Rachael chose 9-year old Becky Christopher.

All the children were still in shock and grieving from the loss of their parents. It would take time for them to adjust to their foster parents and to their new way of life.

The Mercers went into all-out farming and gardening mode. Since there was still a chance of a late frost, they were mostly plowing and making all the other preparations for planting. They were also collecting the manure from the barns and spreading it over the fields.

Tim and Pamela left Cathy with Paula so she could go work the bees with Tim. Cathy was still too young to have with them as there was some danger related to the bees.

Paula remarked, "Pamela, I have Kayla and Allen here now as well as Tiffany, so I should have plenty of help with

Cathy. I'm interested in seeing how Kayla and Allen relate to a baby. It could be interesting."

Pamela replied, "We're taking our lunch with us so it will probably be late afternoon before we get back."

Tim and Pamela had rigged up carts to pull behind their bicycles. They left, towing the carts, which were loaded with bee-keeping equipment.

The bees had wintered well and were quite active with their collecting of nectar and pollen. In two or three weeks they would probably need to add at least one more super to each bee hive. They might even harvest one rack of fresh honey! Fresh honey in the summertime with the newly made comb was not only delicious, it was exquisite!

James Mercer, with Tiffany, Ron and David helping, finished all the pre-planting preparation in the garden. They checked all the plants they had seeded in the winter time, and they were all mature enough to set out when the time came.

James had been using David in the fields most of the time, plowing and preparing for the corn planting. Their plan was to plant ten acres of corn.

James missed the good old days when he had an electric corn sheller. Now, they would be placing their corn in cribs, in the barns, or loading it up in wagons and take it to town to sell. There was a good market for corn. Some of it would be ground into meal, and some would go to other farmers to feed their livestock. Corn still on the cob was bulkier and took more space, as well as adding extra weight when having to haul it.

In Richmond, the mayor had a meeting with his council, the sheriff and deputy, and Thomas, to discuss planning and executing some of the things they needed to get done.

Work was already underway to get a census of the people in the surrounding area. The information being collected was broader in scope than an ordinary census. It included specifics about the homesteads such as size, structure, condition, and adequacy for the family involved. It also included how much land the property included.

It also asked questions about gardening and farming capabilities, available equipment, products raised, animals, trees, etc. The census was quite nosey. However, the information would be invaluable for future planning.

Resources in the area were minimal. Collectively, the residents in and around Richmond would need to capitalize on all of them.

Mayor George Braddock took charge of the meeting. "I thought we would talk about school first unless there's another topic you would rather cover." The mayor paused, and after several seconds, continued. "We've almost completed the census, and from the looks of things, we'll probably have close to fifty young people who will need to get some education. Do any of you have any ideas?"

After a lengthy pause, Thomas spoke up. "I've been giving this a lot of thought, and I've come up with some ideas. Number one, I don't believe we need school eight hours a day, five days a week. Number two, transportation is going to be a problem. I'm thinking we may have to offer the classes in more than one location. Number three, for the first term, or first few terms, I believe we can restrict the subjects covered to the basics of English, Grammar, Math, Writing, and Bible."

Bert Smith, a member of the council, spoke up. "Bible?

Are you suggesting that we make religion a part of school subjects?"

Thomas responded forcefully. "Yes. Absolutely. You had better believe it. I'm not talking about religion. I'm talking about God's Word, The Holy Bible. We are faced right now with young people growing into maturity, still in a lost and sinful, condition. They, above all people, need to know the saving power of Jesus Christ and the terrible alternative."

Bert rebutted. "I think that's a bad idea. I think we should vote on it."

Thomas responded, "We have just now experienced a time when hundreds of millions have died and will go to hell without Jesus Christ, to pay for their sins. Just in the past few days we saw dozens drop dead right here in Richmond for the same reason. Hopefully, we have learned something."

George Braddock broke in. "Get used to the idea. There is no vote. This is the new way of life." Looking directly at Bert, he continued. "Bert, I'm really surprised at you, and I'm disappointed. I know you're a born again Christian or you wouldn't be here. You need to get your heart right. Weren't you at the meeting with Saint Robert?"

No, Bert answered, and then shut up and remained silent during the rest of the meeting.

By the end of the meeting, they'd come up with a tentative plan for school. Thomas would be the teacher until they could find someone else as well qualified. Hopefully, through the census or in some other way they could locate another, or other, teachers.

Due to the transportation difficulties, school would be held one day per week in five different locations. One location would be at the church in Richmond, one would be at the Mercer farms, and the other three were still to be decided depending on locations of students.

The first day of school was scheduled for Monday, June the fifteenth.

The group disbanded and left. Bert stayed behind to talk to the mayor. Bert went on the offensive just as soon as the others left. "George, we need to get some things straight right now. We're not going to have some outsider come in here and tell us what to do, especially how to run our schools."

Exasperated, the mayor told Bert. "Sit down. Shut up, and listen. Bert, you have no idea the dangerous ground you're treading on. I told you the meeting with Saint Robert was mandatory. Why weren't you there?"

Bert responded, "I know of no good reason why I should jump through hoops when a total stranger tells me to."

The mayor explained, "If you had been at the meeting, you might have a different view, but I doubt it. Saint Robert said the meeting was mandatory, and he would know if anybody failed to attend. He knows you didn't come. I'm sure he knows your heart. Bert, I really and truly believe you're in mortal danger if you don't have a change of heart, and soon. Would you like to talk to Thomas and see if he can help you understand?

"No." Bert replied. "I can figure everything out on my own."

George responded, ""Bert, I'm suspending you as a member of the city council. You may no longer participate in our meetings until you have a change of heart and mind."

Bert responded hotly, "You can't do that. You didn't elect me, and you can't take me off."

George replied, "I just did."

Suddenly, Saint Robert appeared in the room. "Mayor Braddock, I have heard all that's been said."

Turning to Burt, Saint Robert continued: "Bert, for the next thirty days, you shall neither hear, nor speak. If you wish, you may study your Bible, pray, and meditate. At the end of that time I'll determine if you're to continue with us upon the earth."

Saint Robert disappeared just as suddenly as he had appeared.

Bert looked at the mayor and opened his mouth. Nothing came out. He pointed at his mouth. He pointed at his ears. He left.

Mayor Braddock stood there in amazement and just shook his head as Bert walked away.

Later, the mayor met with Thomas and explained the entire episode. "Thomas, I'm really puzzled. If he's a Christian, why in the world would he be acting this way?"

Thomas replied, "George, even though we're Christians, we still have free will. We still have the capacity to sin. If we're a Christian, that sin has already been paid for by the blood of Christ. As Christians, we're to do our utmost to avoid sinning."

George retorted, "I'm surprised that God puts up with that kind of behavior from a Christian."

Thomas explained, "From what you heard Saint Robert tell Bert, I suspect God may not put up with Bert much longer. There are verses in the Bible that speak to this situation. In 1 John 5:16, it talks about the sin unto death. I believe this is the type of sin it's referring to. Acts 1:10 is another example in the story of Ananias and Sapphira, who lied about their giving to the church. However, it states in 1

Corinthians 3:15, that even though a Christian's works may be burned, they will be saved, as if by fire."

George asked, "Can't they just lose their salvation?"

"No." Thomas replied, "Believers in Jesus Christ have the assurance that nothing can ever cause Christians to lose their salvation and separate them from God."

CHAPTER XV
A FAMILY REUNION

Tim and Pamela had been up about an hour and were almost ready to go and work on their bees. They had dressed Cathy who was anticipating going next door and visiting with Paula and her children.

Tim heard a knock on the door, and when he went to answer, he was surprised to see Saint Robert Rayburn. Tim greeted him. "Saint Robert! How very nice and surprising to see you here. Come on into the house."

Tim led the way and Saint Robert followed him into the living room. Tim called Pamela. "Come in here Pamela; we have company."

Pamela came into the living room, with Cathy in her arms.

After a round of greetings, Tim invited Saint Robert to sit down, which he did. Tim looked over at Saint Robert. "Saint Robert, we are honored to have you in our home. I'm curious as to why you have chosen to visit us."

Saint Robert replied, "Tim, I've come in answer to a prayer you prayed a few days ago."

Tim was astounded. "Do you hear and answer my prayers?"

Saint Robert smiled and replied, "No, Tim. I don't hear and answer your prayers. However, I'm in very close touch with the One who does. He is the one who heard your prayer and is working through me to answer it. By the way, do you recall your prayer?" Saint Robert smiled again as he concluded.

Tim replied. "Oh yes. I was praying that God would allow me to see my family. Is there some way you can take me there to see them?"

Saint Robert replied, "Tim, I can't take you there to see them, for you are living in an earthly body and must abide by the natural laws that govern the earth. However, since all your family has transformed bodies, they can travel here." Saint Robert continued, "Tim, another thing I must explain to you. This visit that God has allowed is very unusual. It's a special dispensation from God, and only God knows why."

He continued, "I've come in advance and explained all of that to you before having them come into your presence, for I didn't want it to surprise and shock you. One other thing Tim. This meeting will be relatively short. They have work to do which requires their presence. However, this visit won't be the last.

"Get ready. Don't be surprised when I invite them into your house. Pamela, I would like for you to take Cathy into the other room and close the door. You're not allowed to meet Tim's family at this time, so I will call you when it's over."

Pamela took Cathy into the other room and closed the door. Immediately, Tim's family began to appear in the living room and kitchen. Tim had a blessed meeting with them, and at the end of thirty minutes, they said their goodbyes and left.

Saint Robert explained to Tim and Pamela why Cathy couldn't be in the room with Tim's family. "So many people in the room could be overwhelming and frightening to Cathy. Pamela and Cathy may meet your family when Cathy is older."

Tim turned to Saint Robert. "Wow! That sure was a quick answer to prayer."

Saint Robert laughed. "Tim, it could've happened even sooner than this. God heard your prayer even before you asked it. In Isaiah 65:24, God said through the Prophet, Isaiah, "and it shall come to pass, that before they call, I will answer and while they are yet speaking, I will hear." Saint Robert continued, "Tim, I think you also understand that God's answer to your prayer could have been no."

Tim answered soberly, "I realize that." He continued, "This is absolutely amazing! And, Saint Robert, I want to thank God for bringing you here, and I want to thank you for answering God's call to make it happen."

Saint Robert replied, "Tim, I'm glad you got to see your family. I have one word of instruction concerning this visit: you and Pamela must never mention this to another person."

Tim replied, "We'll certainly make absolutely sure of that."

"Now, I must leave. I'll go outside to depart." Saint Robert walked outside, followed by Tim, who closed the door. Saint Robert said goodbye and simply disappeared.

Pamela let it be known that she was slightly miffed at not getting to see Tim's family.

Tim explained, "Pamela, Saint Robert said you and Cathy can see them when she's older. I think we need to accept things as they come to us and trust God that everything is for the best. However, I'm sure that if we're concerned enough about something, God would accept our questions about it."

Pamela was contrite, "Oh, Tim, I know better, and I apologize. I'm just so thankful you got to see your family."

Pamela and Tim took Cathy next door and met Paula in the kitchen. After dropping off Cathy, they got on their bikes and went to the bee farm to continue their work with the hives and equipment. Trixie went with them, running to keep up. A rabbit, which was sitting in the road, ran off to one side and stopped.

Tim and Pamela stopped their bikes and Tim remarked, "This should be interesting." Trixie, following closely behind, saw the rabbit. Instead of taking off after it running and barking, she skidded to a halt. Trixie walked over, and the two animals sniffed and greeted each other.

Tim almost fell off his bike. "What in the world is going on! Pamela, did you see that? Trixie and the rabbit are making friends with each other!"

Pamela was astounded. "Tim, I can't believe what I'm seeing. I wonder if this is part of the new world we're living in?"

Tim answered, "We'll talk to Thomas about this the next time we see him and see if he has an answer."

They went on to their bee farm and spent the rest of the day there, managing the bees. They added supers, cleared the grass and weeds from in front of the hives, and made sure there weren't any ants trying to invade.

On the fifteenth day of June, M0001(Millennium year 1), Saint Robert Rayburn made another visit to Mayor George Braddock. The mayor wasn't quite as surprised to see him this time as he was the first.

"Good morning, Saint Robert. It's good to see you back

again." Mayor Braddock walked over, grasped his hand and shook it. "What brings you back, and what do you have for us this time?"

Saint Robert replied, "I've come back to exchange information with you. I'm sure you have many questions for me that you have received from the people. I'll try to answer as many as I can. I'll go over some of them with you, and then we'll set up another round of general meetings and pass on as much information as we can to the people. I can tell you right now, life is getting ready to get quite interesting for the people around here, and also for the people around the world."

"Are you ready for some of the questions?" asked Mayor Braddock

"Go ahead," replied Saint Robert.

"One question I got from a lot of people has to do with modern technology, and when would they get it back. They were wondering about automobiles to drive, electricity, running water, air conditioning for houses, Internet, TV, telephone, I Pad and on and on. They miss so many of the conveniences – the supermarkets, etc. etc."

Saint Robert smiled. "I expected a lot of that. I'm going to save time by giving you a short answer now, and I'll go into more detail once we're in the general meetings."

"There are several factors to consider pertaining to technology. I can't give you a general or easy answer. There's one overreaching dynamic in play. Humans made all the former decisions in developing technology, many of which were good. However, others were far from perfect. Now all decisions shall come from God and His Son, Jesus Christ. They shall be perfect decisions, based upon God's will.

"When we get in the general meetings, I'll also explain

other things that are happening in the world which could affect the lives of the people here in Richmond. The world will be an exciting place to live for the next thousand years.

"George, go ahead and set up the meetings for Wednesday, and we'll schedule them just like we did before."

George agreed to set them up, and Saint Robert faded from sight.

George remarked, "I don't know if I'll ever get used to the way Saint Robert comes and goes."

Wednesday morning at 10:00 a.m., Saint Robert went before the first group and spoke to them on all the latest pertinent information. "I'm starting out today by answering a lot of the questions you left with the Mayor. Many of the questions pertained to the return of technology, such as automobiles, air conditioning, electricity, running water, television, telephone, internet, cell phones, etc. etc.

"A short and general answer to that question is that the return to much of the advanced technology may not happen for a long time, if ever. There are four primary reasons for that.

"For the first reason, I'm going to make an analogy. We had over seven billion people on this planet. Many of them were, in essence, parts of an intricate technological machine. Now, more than ninety nine percent of those parts are missing. To reassemble that intricate machine with the parts that are still available is impossible in the short term. It would take decades, if not centuries, to restore it all.

"A second reason is, there are certain parts of technology that are harmful to society. They shall never be restored. Satan used them to great advantage to confuse and mislead people into choosing hell over heaven, evil over good, satan over God and Jesus Christ.

"A third reason is, there are certain technologies that are extremely dangerous to the people of the earth that never should have been developed. Nuclear technology for weaponry and nuclear power generation should never have been developed. Nuclear weaponry, of course, shall never be restored. Nuclear power generation also, shall never be restored. It's too dangerous. There are too many better alternatives that can be used for energy.

"The fourth reason is, the restoration of the earth and the civilization that will occupy it shall be done on a controlled and prioritized basis. With the depleted manpower, it must be done in such a way. Jesus Christ is in control and will use us, His Saints, to carry the plan and execution to all parts of the world. All the work shall be accomplished by earthly means and by people like you, not by supernatural means.

"You, right here in Richmond, will be given the opportunity to volunteer for many of these projects and travel to the four corners of the earth to participate. No person will be forced to do the work, and no person will suffer any retaliation if they decide to stay right here for the rest of their lives.

"I would like to stress the significance of the work that will be done. The world is the Kingdom of Jesus Christ. He purchased it, and all that is upon it, with His life and His blood.

"The work that we do is for Him and His Kingdom. It will be a work showing our love for Him and His great sacrifice for us. Our reward for the work we do is a perpetual thing. We received the down payment when we were born again into eternal life. In addition, we are rewarded continually for our continuing service. I don't believe a one of us will be disappointed.

"Now, to continue about the journey, ships and other forms of transportation are even now being prepared to move people to many parts of the world. Jerusalem and the land of Israel shall be the focus of resources and rebuilding for the first few years. The land between the River of Egypt (Wadi al Arish), and the Euphrates River, shall be the general boundaries of the first selected areas. This is the land that was promised in a covenant God made with Abram in Genesis 15:18. The restoration will quickly expand out from there, as we're directed. If you decide to go there and work you'll meet people from all parts of the world who shall assemble there with you to do the work.

"Some of the questions you asked related to certain types of communication, such as telephones, satellite, cell phones, internet, radio, television, movies, etc. The answer – get used to going without it. When satan walked the earth, the media was his greatest tool. Although satan no longer walks the earth, media as it was then, if re-instituted, would be largely counterproductive. In these early days of earth renewal, communication will be reintroduced selectively and limited. You'll know it when you see it.

"All transportation of humans shall be by earthly means and not supernatural means. For the near future, transportation will continue as it is now. Bicycle use is quite prevalent around the world. Horses, buggies, and wagon use will increase. Railroads, air travel, and some vehicular travel will again develop as the need grows. Because of the depopulation of the world, we lost not only the numbers of people, but also most of those skilled in all of the trades.

"Because of the need for rebuilding in other parts of the world, I would expect to see some faster transportation developing to meet that need.

"I realize that many of you lived a fairly hectic life at one time. Take advantage of these times; enjoy life; enjoy your families; enjoy your neighbors and the other people around you.

"And, incidentally, expect to live a much longer life. You may not have noticed it, but people are no longer falling ill. Don't expect to see a lot of doctors and hospitals. Some medical care will be needed for injuries, etc. but the disease-ridden times are behind us. The book of Isaiah tells us to expect long lives.

"I would ask that you think and pray about what I have said about traveling. When I return, if any of you are so inclined, I will have information on how to make it happen. If you're interested, contact the mayor.

"May the Lord bless and keep you. You're dismissed."

The first group began filing out and, for the most part, left to go on to their homes or other activities. The second group was waiting outside and began filing in and taking their seats.

Tim and Pamela went back behind the church and got in their buggy. Pamela said, "Tim, why don't we go by and see Thomas and Rachael for a few minutes before we go home?"

Tim replied, "Pamela, that's a good idea. We haven't seen them since church on Sunday. Cathy should be ok with Paula a little longer."

At Thomas and Rachael's, Tim told them about Trixie

and the rabbit. "Thomas, what's your opinion or answer for what we saw?"

Thomas answered, "This may have to do with what the Scriptures have to say about the wolf, the lamb, the lion and the bullock all lying down with one another. You can find it in the Book of Isaiah:65:17-25. This may very well be an indication that all animals that may have been hostile will no longer fear or feel hostility toward each other."

Tim commented. "That'll take some getting used to. I wonder if the same thing will apply when it comes to people toward other people?"

Thomas laughed, "That question I cannot answer."

Pamela spoke up and changed the subject. "Rachael, what did you think about what Saint Robert said about traveling to other parts of the world to work?"

Rachael replied, "That sounds quite interesting. It would be an opportunity to visit other countries and meet up with a lot of interesting people. We could also see the Holy Land."

Pamela responded, "The downside to that would be leaving our families and staying away from them for a long time."

Thomas spoke up. "We could ask Saint Robert about that and find out how long we would have to stay."

Tim chimed in. "If it were to be for an extended period of time, then it would be ideal if the entire family went together."

Thomas replied, "That's something to think about. We'll bring up the subject with the rest of the family."

Pamela and Tim left and drove the buggy back to the farm.

For the next two days, different groups went to the assemblies until all the people in the area had attended. Bert

Smith attended the last meeting of the day on Wednesday. Following the meeting, he approached Saint Robert. He immediately regained his speech and hearing. "Saint Robert, I'd like to apologize for behaving so badly. I've asked God to forgive me, and if allowed to do so, I'll apologize to the Mayor and the other people I offended with my rude and unacceptable behavior."

Saint Robert replied, "Bert, you've been heard, and you've been forgiven. Go now and do what the Lord would require of you." Saint Robert immediately faded from sight.

On Saturday Thomas, Rachael, Herbert, and Barbara, went out to Alvin and Rhonda's farm. James and Paula and their family along with Tim, Pamela, and Cathy assembled with them. They met to discuss the possibility of the entire group going to the land of Israel to work. They would have the option of remaining there or, after a period of time, returning to Richmond. Including their four adopted children, there is a headcount of sixteen people. The meeting took up the better part of the day.

By the end of the day, they had come up with a tentative plan. James and Paula would remain in Richmond with their three children, David, Tiffany and Ron. They would also have Allen and Kayla Sherman, their two adopted children. Their job would be to maintain the two farms, as well as Tim and Pamela's bee farm. Considering the age of their children and the two adopted children, James and Paula would have a formidable task.

Their reasoning was that the farms in Richmond would provide a home base. If any of the ones working overseas decided they wanted to come back, they'd have a place to live.

Herbert and Barbara would check with Barbara's parents

to see if they were interested in going overseas, which they doubted. Her brothers, Gary and Robert, might want to come, but that would have to be decided and worked out. Barbara doubted that her parents would readily concede to let either or both of them go.

When Thomas saw the mayor at church the next day, he told him he would come by on Monday morning to talk about the travel plans. This didn't leave the mayor with any good feelings. Thomas' departure could leave a big hole in the community needs.

Monday morning Thomas went to the mayor's office. "Good morning, George. How are you doing today?"

George replied, "As well as could be expected since I talked to you yesterday."

Thomas asked George, "Do we have any good candidates for teachers in this area?"

George replied, "The prospects aren't too good. We have two young ladies who could probably teach some basics, but beyond that, I don't know of any."

Thomas continued, "If I were to leave, I'm not sure who in the area would be ready or willing to take over as pastor of the church. That certainly needs to have continuity, I would think."

George agreed and suggested, "Maybe when Saint Robert comes back, he'll have some ideas."

"When is he due back?" Thomas asked.

"In a week. In fact, it'll probably be this coming Friday. I'll get hold of you just as soon as he comes." George answered.

"Incidentally, how is Bert doing?" Thomas asked.

George replied. "He seems to have done a complete

turnaround. His attitude reflects that he actually is a concerned Christian."

"Well, that's wonderful!" exclaimed Thomas. "We can certainly use all the help we can get."

On Friday, Saint Robert returned to Richmond and contacted the mayor. The first question Saint Robert had concerned the number of people who might have been interested in traveling.

The Mayor explained, "Counting ten from the Mercers, we would have a total of twenty. Of the ten Mercers, there would be a total of four male adults, four female adults, a 10-year old boy, 10-year old girl, and Cathy, the baby. Of the other 10, there would be 3 male adults, 3 female adults, and 4 young teenagers."

The mayor explained the situation on teachers and a pastor. "You know that if Thomas leaves here, that'll leave us short a teacher as well as a pastor."

Saint Robert replied. "I suspected we might come up with a need, and I've been talking to some candidates for both positions. In my duties, I'm in contact with other areas such as this, and when we find out what we have here, I'll work to fill the vacancy."

"That sure takes a load off my mind," the mayor responded. "What would you like to do next?"

"Let's call a meeting of the volunteers and start making plans for a departure. We have a lot of logistics to cover. We'll need to come up with transportation, food during travel, and all those other details."Said Saint Robert.

"I'll set the meeting for tomorrow morning at 9:00 a.m. That should give us plenty of time to do the planning. I'm inviting some other people to the meeting; for we may need their help making everything work out." The mayor replied.

"That's a good idea," Saint Robert responded.

Saturday morning at 9:00 a. m. all the potential candidates for travel were at the church. James Mercer was also there to find out if he might need to be involved in the logistics of the move, such as providing animals, vehicles, feed for animals, food, etc. etc. The mayor, his council, the sheriff, his deputy, and some of their wives, also attended.

Saint Robert met all the people who would be involved and then addressed the group on exactly what they were planning to do. "We intend to move this group of people from right here to a location in Israel which lies on the road between Bethlehem and Jerusalem. In fact, it'll be close to the location of Rachael's tomb. It'll be a temporary city with all that we'll need in the way of living requirements. Our first assignment after we get there and get settled, will be to help in the cleanup, which has already started, preparing for the restoration of Jerusalem and the building of the temple."

"Jerusalem was destroyed several times, and each time it was destroyed, all the rubble was leveled and Jerusalem was rebuilt on top of that. This time, all that rubble will be removed to the ground level, and the new city and temple will be rebuilt on solid ground.

"Our first task, of course, is to move you from here to there as soon as possible, with as little discomfort as possible. Our intention is to travel from here to a seaport at Wilmington, North Carolina, where you'll board a ship and sail to the port of Haifa in Israel. From there, you'll be transported by land to your new homes. Incidentally, your settlement is set up to handle 1,000 people. There'll be other settlements in Israel located where the workers are needed.

"At Wilmington, we'll meet up with one other group of twenty-two people. Once we leave there we'll make a few other port calls and pick up other volunteers before we go on to Israel. We'll visit a port in Fort Lauderdale, Florida; one in Galveston, and one in Corpus Christi, Texas; one in Mexico; two in South America; one in Central America; and possibly, one in Bermuda. Altogether, we should have about 400 people, including children.

"We have about 550 miles to travel from here to Wilmington. We'll be traveling on mostly secondary roads. The interstates and all major highways are blocked in several places and don't make for easy travel. I've already scouted out our path and will lead the caravan. If all goes well, it should be about a two week trip from here to Wilmington.

Saint Robert asked, "Do you have any questions?"

James Mercer asked, "What are your plans in the way of transportation from here to there?"

Saint Robert replied, "Hopefully, we can get enough wagons, horses, and buggies to make the trip. My intention would be that someone from here would accompany us to bring back most of those. It would be good if we could transport some of them to Israel, but I definitely do not wish to deprive you of what you need here."

James replied, "I believe we can come up with enough to leave you with two horses and two buggies to take with you. For this number of people and supplies, I'd like to take four teams pulling wagons, and three buggies with single horses. That should give us enough room for the goods everyone is taking, plus extra room for horse feed. We'll carry some water with us, but hopefully, we can find other water along the way."

Alvin asked, "Saint Robert, what's the chance of us running into radiation contamination?"

Saint Robert answered, "That won't be a concern. We've already scouted this trail and, it should be safe in all respects. Our only potential problem would be for us to get caught in a strong storm. However, at this time of year, it's unlikely."

"What day are we leaving?" asked Tim.

Saint Robert replied, "I hope to leave one week from today. That'll put us into the port in Wilmington on the same day the ship is to arrive. Are there any other questions?"

Everybody was quiet, and after a period of time, Saint Robert dismissed them so they could go home and finish packing, and making any other arrangements that needed to be made.

One week later, the convoy was all loaded up and ready to go. Fortunately, there wasn't much family separation taking place, with the exception of Barbara's family. Her parents certainly hated to see her leave, but stayed upbeat about it. Her two brothers were somewhat nonchalant through it all. This wasn't planned as a permanent separation, as they could be coming back within a few years.

Probably the most difficult parting was Tim having to say goodbye to Trixie. They'd been together now for years. It was understood though from the beginning of the planning, that Trixie would have to remain on the farm.

Practically everybody in the surrounding area came to see them off. As the horses and wagons moved out, there was a lot of hand waving, subdued shouting, and some tears. The passengers in the wagons were feeling somewhat stunned as they ventured out on a journey which they couldn't completely fathom.

Saint Robert rode in the lead wagon with James. David was riding with them and would be helping bring the wagons back to Richmond. They'd also brought Paula, Tiffany and Ron. Although Ron was too young to drive alone, he could ride with David and help out.

Leaving out of Richmond, they headed southeast toward Knoxville, Tennessee. The weather was good. Temperatures were in the mid seventies, which made for pleasant travel. Trees were leafed out; grass was green and plentiful and, hopefully, it'd be an uneventful trip.

At noon, they stopped at a stream to eat lunch. The horses were unharnessed and allowed to drink at the stream, roll in the grass, and then graze while they rested. They built a small fire, made some sassafras tea, ate a cold lunch, and laid back and relaxed. The total time for lunch took about an hour.

The stop for lunch gave some time for the members of the group to get acquainted. Tim and Pamela, with Cathy, singled out another couple who had a boy about Cathy's age. They visited with them for a short time.

Following lunch, they hitched up the horses, loaded up, and headed southeast. So far, the traveling had been relatively easy on them and on the teams. Since the animals had recently been involved in planting crops, they were all in good shape for travel.

That evening, the caravan traveled until almost dusk. They stopped close to another stream, and while the women prepared food, the men and boys collected firewood and started a fire. Although tired, some of them did more visiting and getting acquainted, as they wound down and prepared their bedding. Young men and young women gravitated toward each other and spent time together.

There had been some concern for safety and the possible need for firearms. Saint Robert assured them that none were needed.

The following morning, the travelers got up, prepared breakfast, and did all the usual chores. Within a relatively short time, they were back on the road, heading southeast.

Almost two weeks after leaving Richmond, they arrived in Wilmington, very tired, and ready to see an end to the road trip.

Some of them had never seen a ship or been that close to water before. It was another time of excitement and adventure as they boarded the ship and got settled in. Counting the crew and the other twenty-two people who had joined them, there was quite a bit of meeting, greeting, and getting acquainted to anticipate. Considering all the others they would pick up on the way, and all the different nationalities, it could become quite an adventure.

CHAPTER XIV
THE ISRAEL ADVENTURE

Late that night, the ship left harbor and traveled south toward Fort Lauderdale, Florida, where they would pick up another group. The weather was nice with a light breeze blowing from the west. As they sailed south, many of the passengers went on deck the next morning. Following safety training, they were allowed to stand at the rails and watch the waves, jumping fish, and the distant shoreline.

Tim, Pamela, and Cathy stood at the land-side rail and watched two porpoises as they kept pace with the ship, about twenty feet away. Cathy was ecstatic as she watched them. They were soon joined by Bradley and Margaret Drake and their son, Travis, whom they had gotten acquainted with on their way down from Richmond.

Alvin and Rhonda strolled by, chatted a few minutes, and then went on. Not too long after that, Thomas and Rachael also visited with them. So far, they hadn't seen Herbert and Barbara.

The trip from North Carolina to Fort Lauderdale took the better part of two days. They picked up another group there and then set out for Galveston, Texas, which took another four days. Weather was still holding, which was quite a blessing. They were getting their sea legs, and, hopefully, when rough weather did come, it wouldn't be too hard on them.

Leaving Galveston, they traveled on south to Corpus Christi and picked up two groups. Some of these had come up from Mexico. The passenger population was becoming quite impressive, and they still had four more stops to make.

They continued south and made one stop in Mexico, two in South America, and then turned northeast from Rio de Janeiro toward Gibraltar and the Mediterranean Sea. The pickup in Bermuda had been cancelled, possibly because of the lack of space for more passengers.

As they traveled north along the coast of South America, they moved farther out to sea. The third day out, the weather got rough. It was so rough, all the windows from structure to decks were closed and all the doors going out to the decks were sealed. It was far too dangerous for passengers to be on deck.

Sea legs or not, it wasn't long until many passengers were glad to be able to lie flat and not move. Barf bags were very much in demand.

Tim and Pamela were both hard hit by the nausea. Cathy played in the floor and had a ball. She had a toy car and let it run up and down the floor of their cabin as the ship rolled. The bad weather continued for another twelve hours and then eased up.

The following day the sun was out, the weather calm, and the passengers were back out taking advantage of the better conditions. However, the passenger load at this point was quite crowded and most of the people remained below deck in their cabins.

Very few of the passengers wanted the cruise to continue on and on. Most of them were ready to see some dry land.

It took twenty-two days to travel to Gibraltar, where they went through the straits and entered the Mediterranean Sea. The sea was much calmer, and there was quite a bit more for the passengers to see. 10 days later, they arrived at the port of Haifa, Israel.

Saint Robert and about 20 others were available to assist them in disembarking and moving all their possessions to vehicles that were there waiting on them. There was a variety of buses and trucks.

Saint Robert helped the group from Richmond get in two vehicles which would keep them together. At the village, assignment to dwellings had already been made, which would make it much simpler when they got there.

It took a little over two hours to travel from Haifa to the village just outside Bethlehem. When they arrived, their escorts took them in hand and began leading them to their new homes in this, a faraway land.

Following several hectic minutes, Tim, Pamela, and Cathy, stood inside their new home. They were alone for the first time in several days. They had received instructions that in two hours, they were to meet at the assembly hall, which was about a city block away.

With Tim carrying Cathy, and holding Pamela's hand, the three of them began the exploration of their new home. It had a small living room, kitchen/dining room, bathroom with tub and shower, and two bedrooms. It was about 700 square feet overall. Just outside the back door was a small porch with a table and four chairs. Steps went down from the porch to a small yard, which was fenced in. Two fig trees were planted in the opposite far corners.

Pamela exclaimed, "Tim, this house is brand new, and it's so lovely! It's completely furnished, including dishes, pots and pans. All we need now is food."

Pamela walked over to the refrigerator and opened it. It was completely stocked with food! She then looked in the pantry. It was also stocked. Even the foods and supplies needed for Cathy had been provided! Wow! Nothing had been missed.

"Tim, I just can't believe this! I'm so excited!" Pamela gushed.

Tim laughed, "Slow down Pamela. Wait about a month and see if you're still as excited. Everything is so nice. I suspect we're really going to like it."

They continued their exploration and checked out the bedrooms. The bed in the second bedroom was small and could be moved from there to their bedroom, if needed.

The beds were unmade, but all the sheets, pillows, pillow cases, and blankets, were on the beds, still folded.

"Pamela, we need to rest a few minutes before we go to the meeting. Why don't we make the beds and lie down?" Tim suggested.

"That's a good idea, Tim. You make our bed and I'll do Cathy's." Pamela replied.

As the time came for the meeting, they got up and prepared to go down the block. As they left their home, they blended in with several others walking down toward the assembly area. There were no sidewalks, just sandy walkways down the sides of the streets.

The assembly area would only hold 100 hundred people,

and they discovered different groups had been scheduled at different times. They went in and found their group and took their seats.

After everybody had settled down, their speaker went to the podium and introduced himself. "My name is Saint Chaim Rosenbloom. I wish to welcome all of you to the land of Israel. I thank all of you for caring enough to volunteer for the restoration of this country, which is the birthplace of our Lord and Savior, Jesus Christ.

"I know you have many questions. This week is orientation week for all of you. During this week, I hope that most of your questions will be answered and you'll understand exactly what's happening in this part of the world, during this, the millennial reign of Jesus Christ.

"In the weeks and months ahead, our first task is to rebuild Jerusalem and clean up the land of Israel, which extends from the River of Egypt to the Euphrates River. The next task will be the restoration of the land, building villages and homes, and making the land of Israel a lovely place to live. It'll also be a place to praise and worship God and our Lord Jesus Christ.

"Each of you will be interviewed and assigned to teams which, hopefully, will take advantage of your skills. However, much of the work is manual labor, which we shall all be asked to do. When you leave this meeting, you'll be given a set of instructions with your team assignment, assembly point, and time to assemble. If you're late, you'll be left behind. The instructions will explain most of what you'll need to know. If you have questions, ask your team leader.

"We have children who need to be taught. Some of you who are qualified may be asked to be teachers. We shall also

213

have some classes which adults will be required to attend. For example, we shall all be taught a universal language which will be used by all people around the world. The Bible shall be taught to adults and children alike. The new language is in the developmental stage and will be available soon. The Bible is even now being transcribed into an accurate format. It shall also be out shortly.

"Now, I would like to explain our hierarchy and our command structure.

"Jesus Christ, our Lord, Savior, and King, is the ruler of this Kingdom which God gave to Him at the price of His life and His blood. Jesus Christ shall rule the earth and all that is upon it for a thousand years. I shall not go into any explanation beyond that.

"Jesus Christ has the twenty-four elders, on their thrones, ruling with Him.

"We, the Saints who were transformed and caught up into heaven at the rapture, answer to the elders. We shall rule with them over the people of the earth and oversee the individual tasks that are to be done. In a sense, we will be your supervisors.

"Each of us has supernatural powers. I will give you just a few examples. We can heal injuries or illnesses, if they ever occur. We can communicate without speech. We can move from place to place instantaneously. We can know what is going on and what is being said without being at the location.

"Most of you are born again Christians. Although you have been spiritually regenerated and are indwelled with the Holy Spirit, you have never been transformed and have never been to heaven. Your bodies are earthly bodies, subject to injury and all the other natural rules that govern fleshly beings.

"A few of you have already reached the age of accountability and have not yet turned your hearts and lives over to God and Jesus Christ. You do have that opportunity, even now. Each of you will be held accountable for your actions and will be held to high standards of conduct even though you are not yet a Christian.

"Jesus Christ has made it clear through the Scriptures that He shall rule with a rod of iron. I won't try to translate that, except to say that Jesus means exactly what He said."

Following the assembly, Tim and Pamela went back to their home. Rhonda had kept Cathy while they were at the assembly. Rhonda chatted for a few minutes and then left.

Tim and Pamela took their separate set of instructions and spent the next several minutes reading them. Pamela finished first but kept silent until Tim finished reading his.

"Well, Tim, tell me what your instructions say," Pamela asked.

Tim replied. "For one thing, I've never seen a set of instructions that is more detailed and thorough. This is the first week's schedule. It tells me where to be and at what time. Tomorrow, I have orientation, and I'll be issued some work clothing and items such as gloves, goggles, etc. The next day, I meet my team at 6:00 a.m. and go off to work. I'm scheduled to get back here at 6:00 p.m."

Pamela replied, "I also have orientation tomorrow. I get an issue of clothing and some items. The next day, I report to the nursery and pre-school. I start out there but have no idea how long that will last."

The next morning, Tim and Pamela dropped Cathy

off at the nursery, which was on the way to the orientation hall. During the orientation they learned that they would be working six days a week every other week. The extra day off every other week would be for recreation, sightseeing, resting, or whatever the person desired.

Sunday each week would include church, worship, meditation, resting, visiting, and family time.

During the work week, 6:00 a.m. was assembly time and 6:00 p.m. was return time. With travel time to and from the job site, plus lunch time and rest breaks, the actual work time was about nine or ten hours per day.

Tim's initial job site would be in Jerusalem where work was already underway to clean up and restore the city.

Tim and Pamela finally unwound and settled down. After their evening ritual of kneeling at Cathy's bedside and hearing her bedtime prayers, they went to bed.

Wednesday morning, they were up at 4:30 with the help of an alarm clock which had been issued to them. Nervous energy helped them through the first morning of getting dressed, shaving, eating, and getting Cathy dressed.

As Tim prepared to leave, he approached Pamela. "Well, my sweet little wife, I'm off to the races. I love you and I'll miss you." He kissed her.

Pamela replied, "I love you and I'll miss you, too. Be careful."

"I will," he responded, and then left to go to his assembly point.

Tim went to his assembly point which was two blocks from where he lived. There were thirty stations at the location which were filling up rapidly as people approached from all directions. At every station, there was a bus with the door open, and everybody entered their designated bus as soon as they arrived. By ten minutes after six, Tim's bus was loaded. The door closed and the driver pulled out into the road. As they began their journey, Tim looked at the person sitting next to him and introduced himself. "Good morning. I'm Tim Bailey. I traveled here from the state of Kentucky in the United States, and this is my first day on the job."

The man seated next to him responded, "My name is Jacob Everson. I'm from Germany. I've been working here for about two weeks."

Different ones around the bus began introducing themselves, and there was an atmosphere of goodwill within the group.

A man stood up front next to the driver. Tim assumed he must be their leader, or foreman. When they arrived in Jerusalem, the bus stopped but the door remained closed. It was still not quite daylight. Their leader took a position a third of the way down the bus and introduced himself. "I'm Saint Lemuel. I'll be your team leader as we do our work. Since some of you are new, I caution you to work moderately for a few days until you become accustomed. There's much to do here in Israel. It will take years.

"The work here in Jerusalem is threefold. The new part of Jerusalem spreads over a very large area. It was built using modern technology. Much of it was destroyed during the great world war about ten years ago. Much more of it was destroyed after that, during the small battles that took place leading up to Armageddon.

"Most of the newer city will not be rebuilt for many years, if ever. We will clean up the land and restore it. The landscape will resemble a large park-like garden with flowers, fruit trees, shrubbery, landscaping, and other work, to make it a pleasant place to visit and enjoy.

"The old city was mostly destroyed. In past centuries, it was destroyed multiple times, and much of the rubble was leveled out, and new buildings were built on top of it. We'll clear out all of the destroyed buildings and remove the rubble down to the bare soil or rock upon which it rests. The city, if it is to be rebuilt, will be rebuilt at some future time and in such a way that has not as yet been revealed to us.

"We've been instructed that we're to leave any of the structures that are still recognizable, such as the old wall and the old entrance gates. We're to protect and preserve such things as the Pool of Bethsaida and the pool of Siloam.

"In the area of the temple mount, the Dome of the Rock and the Al Aqusa Mosque were completely destroyed. The western wall, sometimes called the Wailing Wall, is still standing and shall be preserved. We will clean away all the debris and rubble in that entire area. In the areas outside the old city, we shall also thoroughly clear and cleanse the area of all inappropriate structures or disfigurements. In your work, if you have any questions on whether you should or should not do something, check with me.

"There's a depressed area outside the perimeter of the newer city. All the debris that can't be burned will be moved to that location. Once the debris removal is complete, that area will be covered with soil and then planted with trees and grass. It won't be used for human or animal use due to possible contaminants.

"Do you have any questions or comments before you go to work?"

No questions were asked, so they all got off the bus and commenced their work.

Shortly after Tim left for work, Pamela took Cathy and walked down to her work station. She was greeted at the door by Saint Eliana. "Good morning Pamela. Good morning Cathy. It is so good to see you."

Saint Eliana then took Pamela to the pre-school area, introduced her to the teacher, and helped get Cathy enrolled.

Saint Eliana then took Pamela into the third-grade classroom and introduced her to Talia. "Talia, this is Pamela. She recently arrived here from the United States. She'll work as your assistant and will also work as your substitute when you aren't here."

Talia replied. "I'm certainly glad to see you. I'm sure that I'll enjoy working with you. Since you're new here, if you have any questions, be sure to ask. I certainly asked a lot of questions when I got here." She laughed.

Pamela replied, "I certainly won't be bashful about asking questions."

Saint Eliana left, and Talia got a list of the students and showed it to Pamela. "I'll introduce you to the class, and then I'll take you to each student and introduce them to you by name. They're on this chart the way they are seated, which should help you learn their names faster."

The class had eleven girls and nine boys.

Talia wrote a reading assignment on the blackboard and had the students study that as she introduced Pamela to the individual students. None of them were from the same location or knew each other when they came there. They all had to start at the beginning, getting acquainted.

The languages were all quite diverse. Since Talia was

from Israel, she was fluent in English but was at a loss when it came to Spanish. Since a new, universal, language was being introduced, her task, along with Pamela, was to help the Spanish-speaking students develop enough English skills to get by until the universal language was in place.

During the morning recess, Talia sat down with Pamela at the front of the classroom. "Pamela, do you have any questions or comments?"

Pamela replied, "I'm almost overwhelmed! I'm sure that I will adjust to everything just fine as I learn more and become accustomed to the work. And the answer is yes. I do have a million questions, not just about the school, but about many things. I'm not going to burden you with them just yet, but as I get settled in, I'll be asking you about a lot of things."

Talia replied, "Pamela, don't hesitate to ask me questions. If I can't answer them, we'll ask Saint Elania."

Pamela and Tim returned home from their respective job sites and had quite a bit to tell each other about their day's experiences. Having experienced their first day at work in a strange environment, they were both exhausted. They took showers, prepared and ate their supper, spent some time with Cathy, and went to bed early.

The second day at work went better for both of them as they were more relaxed and began to settle into a routine. Pamela had prepared a list of questions she wanted to ask Elania or Talia, and she wasted no time getting started when the first break came. "Talia, my first question is, will we get to see Jesus Christ while we're here?"

Talia replied. "Pamela, I'm not sure. So far, none of us that lived through the Tribulation have seen Him. Unless we learn otherwise, I suspect that will be reserved for the resurrected Christians."

"Talia, my next question is this: how do I know a resurrected Christian from a Christian like us?"

Talia smiled as she replied, "Pamela, most of the time, they will have identified themselves to you. However, If you're in the presence of someone you wonder about, think a question to them. If they answer, then you know."

Pamela replied, "Oh my!"

The third day was a day of orientation. The weather was calm and the day was sunny and beautiful. Tim and Pamela took Cathy to the pre-school and then went on to the assembly hall. There they met up with their family. A lot of hugging and hand shaking went on as they greeted Rhonda, Alvin, Rachael, Thomas, Herbert and Barbara.

They were directed into a room where the orientation would take place. Looking around, they noticed that all the rest of their group from Richmond was in the room. They milled around, greeting and handshaking, until the door opened and Saint Robert Rayburn walked in!

Another round of happy greetings ensued. Finally, they settled down and took their seats. Saint Robert went to the podium and began to speak. "Greetings. I realize that you've all been through some busy and hectic times the past few days, and I know you have many questions. I can sense and know your questions and during this orientation period, I'll try to enlighten you as much as I can.

"As you know, Jesus Christ is now ruling over the world. He is ruling with the twenty-four elders and the saints. He is here in Jerusalem. You shall not see Him. Only those who have been resurrected can see Him, only when He desires to make Himself visible.

"Another question I perceive concerns the number of people who have died, and how many are still alive in the world. Over seven billion people have died in the past ten years, beginning with the worldwide nuclear war, which was followed by the famines and pestilence. Multitudes more died from persecution and atrocities. Hundreds of millions died just after the rapture, which was followed by the heavens and earth upheavals during the sixth seal judgment. Also, as you know, many more died during the trumpet and vial judgments, and at the time of Armageddon.

"The other question pertains to the number of people who are still living on the earth. That number shall not be given.

"One other question on the minds of many of you has to do with the status of those who died without the salvation of Jesus Christ. Are they in hell? The answer to that is no. They will remain in their graves here upon the earth until the resurrection of the dead at the end of the millennium, at the Great White throne Judgment.

"Another question I get has to do with levels of punishment and levels of reward. For those who chose hell over heaven; and, by the way, they did choose; the greater the offense, the greater the punishment.

"For those who chose heaven over hell; and yes, they did choose; the greater the service, the greater the reward.

"Hell is a terrible place. The least punished is in a terrible place. Heaven is a wonderful place. The least rewarded is in a wonderful place.

"The one question that is uppermost in the mind of most

Christians, from the time they were born again until now, has to do with their future relationship with God and Jesus Christ. Exactly what does their future hold?

"The resurrected Christians have had this revealed to them. The Christians living here on earth at this time will not learn their eternal future until they are resurrected. I can only say this, it will be glorious!

"Looking to the future decades and centuries here upon the earth, I will tell you enough to give you a glimpse of some things to expect.

"As you know, the only humans who lived past Armageddon were Christians who were born again after the rapture and those young people who had not reached the age of accountability. At this moment in time here on this earth, we have Jesus Christ and His resurrected saints, born again Christians who have not been resurrected, those who have just reached the age of accountability, those who have not reached the age of accountability, and of course, the small children and babies.

"It is imperative that our top priority shall be to teach all young people about God and about Jesus Christ. Sadly, regardless of how hard we try, there will be many who will reject God and Jesus Christ and end up in hell. Although satan is bound for the next thousand years, and will have no influence over the people in the coming centuries, the sin nature is imbedded in mankind and will have its sway.

"Some of you have traveled here from other countries. You will have the opportunity to remain here, travel to other parts of the world and work, or go back to where you came from.

"One of our main tasks is to restore the earth to a place

of beauty and a garden-like state. Although you're limited in travel by your earthly bodies, this is not so for us who are now residents of the heavenly realm. We have the ability to soar over the Alps, the Himalayas, the Rockies, Mount Fuji, North Pole, South Pole, or wherever our hearts desire. Your loved ones who are now saints are able to see and experience the entire realm of God's Glory, including all of His creations. Once you are resurrected, you'll be able to see and experience the wonders of the world as you have never experienced them before, in addition to all God's creations."

Saint Robert continued, "Some of you may live for centuries. Some of you may die, but will be resurrected and transformed at the end of the thousand years."

Orientation was over by 2:00 p.m. and the Mercers decided to assemble at Pamela and Tim's house for a family get together. Pamela and Rachael went to the nursery and pre-school and picked up Cathy and Tyler.

There was quite a buzz as they all started discussing and commenting on the latest information they had been given at the orientation.

Alvin spoke up, ""Well, Thomas, what do think about the orientation?"

Thomas replied, "I believe we're getting another glimpse into God's plan for humans as part of His creation. We were given a pretty clear picture in the Bible, but we haven't quite absorbed all that God was trying to tell us."

Alvin responded, "Thomas, how do you perceive us as fitting in to God's plan?"

Thomas replied, "Alvin, think of God's creation as a big piece of machinery where each part is needed to make it work properly. Think of humanity as one of the parts of that piece of machinery. Then consider a flawed part in a piece of machinery. That part would then need to be replaced or repaired to make the machine work properly.

"If this analogy were to hold true, then God's redemption of mankind through the sacrifice of the life and blood of Jesus Christ would be equivalent to the repair of a flawed part, versus replacing it."

"Wow!" exclaimed Alvin, "That's a stretch!"

"Not really," Thomas responded. "If you recall, God stated in the book of Genesis that He considered destroying all of humanity versus saving mankind through Noah and his family."

All the rest of the Mercer family listened avidly to the discussion. It gave them all something to ponder and consider.

Rhonda changed the subject. "Saturday is a day off for all of us. I've been looking at some of the things available to us in the way of recreation or education, and the one that really catches my eye is a tour which would take us to Bethany, the Garden of Gesthemene, Mount of Olives, Jericho, the Jordan River and the Dead Sea. What do the rest of you think?"

Barbara answered, "I think that's a great idea. In the Bible, we read about all those different places and I certainly would like to see them."

Tim spoke up. "There are so many things to see in this country. Many of them aren't accessible due to road conditions and other hazards. When tours are offered, they must be accessible and relatively safe, so we should take advantage of it."

The family agreed, and it was settled they would all

meet at the tour assembly point, which was the same location where they went for orientation.

At 7:30 a.m., their bus pulled in, and their tour guide stepped out, introduced himself, and gave them an orientation speech for the trip

Following the orientation, they boarded and then went toward Jerusalem, which was about seven miles away. They drove past Jerusalem, across the Brook Kidron, and then to the city of Bethany, about a mile and a half from Jerusalem and on the side of the Mount of Olives. They stopped at Bethany and their guide pointed out the traditional site for the tomb of Lazarus.

Their next stop was the Garden of Gesthimene where their guide pointed out some old and gnarled Olive trees. One of the passengers asked, "Are these the same trees that were here at the time of Jesus?"

The guide replied, "No. These trees are probably not more than a thousand years old. I don't think they live to be much older than this."

The guide went on to detail the visit of Jesus and His disciples when they came there to pray, and then he went on to point out an area which tradition said was where Jesus and His disciples came to rest and pray from time to time.

Leaving the garden, they drove on up to the top of the Mount of Olives and the tour guide pointed out the location that tradition said Jesus stood when He arose and went to heaven. At that point, they were about 250 feet higher than the old city of Jerusalem, and could look down on that part of the city.

Tim pointed to Jerusalem and told Pamela, "Look where I'm pointing. That's the place we're working and loading debris. The area there is pretty well flattened. There are some large chunks of walls, but it's easily broken up. Sometimes, it takes two of us to lift and load a chunk."

The top of the Mount of Olives showed signs that it had recently been occupied by a large number of people, but was totally vacant. The dwellings were all mostly flattened.

"This looks like another area that will require some cleaning," Pamela noted.

The guide got their attention and explained, "Due to the earthquake, the Mount of Olives was split right down the middle. During our trip down the mountain, there will be times we'll be on a temporary road. We will also be crossing over two temporary bridges. When we come to the bridges, you will be asked to get out and wait until the bus crosses over. After that, you will walk across the bridge and get back on the bus."

The guide motioned to the driver and soon they were going mostly downhill around some winding roads. They came to a location where there was a flat area hollowed back into the side of a hill. There were at least a dozen tents of various sizes, and they were all covered with animal skins. It looked as if a small community may have lived there.

Their guide explained, "There was a tribe of Bedouins living here when the end time came. The bodies that were here have all been removed. For a time, there were several sheep and goats with two watch dogs. They have either wandered off or have been taken." Just beyond that location, they began their detour and soon crossed their first bridge.

The bus continued on down the mountain until it came to a wide place that was fairly flat on one side, and there it stopped. The guide explained, "This is the traditional site of the Inn where the Good Samaritan helped the poor man that had been robbed. You can still see some of the foundation stones of the building."

The bus then continued on down, and they could tell by the popping of their ears that they were changing altitude.

They finally arrived at the site of the old city of Jericho and stopped again. The guide then related a short version of the history and pointed out the location of the excavated walls of the old city of Jericho where Rahab sheltered the Israeli spies. He also explained that the Israelites marched around the city seven times, blowing trumpets, until the walls fell. The guide also pointed out the traditional site where the bad waters in the spring were healed by a miracle performed by Elisha.

The guide explained that Jericho was a prominent place in the story of Jesus, who, along with his disciples and followers, always passed through there on their way to Jerusalem.

He related the story of Jesus and Zacchaeus, the tax collector, who was very short and climbed a tree in order to see Jesus. Zacchaeus renounced his riches and turned his heart and life over to Jesus.

They continued downhill past Jericho and came to the Jordan River. There, a place had been made available so tourists could dip their hands in the water. The guide advised them to stay behind the barriers and not try to wade out in the river. The banks dropped off sharply, and a person could drown. "We'll stay here twenty minutes and then we'll move on," he advised.

They all got back on the bus following their time at the Jordan. Shortly after, they pulled into a parking area on the side of the Dead Sea. The guide explained to them, "You are now at the lowest point on earth where there is dry land. We're at 1410 feet below sea level. We were at 846 feet below sea level at Jericho. Since Jerusalem is 2474 feet above sea level, it means we're 3900 feet lower than Jerusalem. Most of you probably noticed your ears adjusting their pressure as we came down the mountain.

"And, incidentally, you may not realize it, but the Sea of Galilee and all of the Jordan River from there to the Dead Sea is also below sea level. For those of you from the United States, your Death Valley is only 282 feet below sea level.

"If you would like, you may dip your finger in the Dead Sea and then stick it to your tongue. You may find that it stings a little. The Dead Sea water is more than 30 percent salinity, and much of it is magnesium, which stings your tongue."

Most of the tourists dipped their finger in the water and stuck it to their tongue.

The guide went on to explain, "If you took a hen egg and placed it in a glass of the Dead Sea water, the egg would float. Also, in this water, a person would tend to float, versus sinking.

"Many plans were made in the past to harvest the minerals from the Dead Sea, but, so far, it hasn't happened except in a small way."

The trip back to their homes was mostly uphill and boring. They had seen many sights during the day, but now they were tired, hot, and ready to get home and rest. Cathy's face and arms were reddish, indicating she had gotten quite a bit of sun. After her bath, Pamela put some lotion on the reddish areas, and she could tell that Cathy felt more comfortable.

Pamela, who was now five months pregnant with their second child, was worn out from the day's activities. Tim hovered over her like a mother hen, and helped her get Cathy settled in for the night.

"Tim, I have no doubt that this baby I'm carrying is a boy. He's been stretching and pushing like nothing I ever saw with Cathy," Pamela exclaimed.

Tim replied, "Oh boy! I hope you're right! However, I'll be happy if it's another girl."

CHAPTER XV
BEULAH LAND

Isaiah 62:4 "Thou shalt no more be termed Forsaken, Neither shall thy land any more be termed Desolate: But thou shall be called Hephzi-bah, And thy land Beulah.

For the Lord delighteth in thee, And thy land shall be married."

Sunday morning found all the Mercer clan in church. The worship service was conducted by a Christian Jew by the name of Simon Bar Joseph. He would serve as pastor to the Mercers for the remainder of their time in Israel.

Multiple services were being held with different pastors, or worship leaders, for each group, due to the large number of worshippers in their settlement,

Simon Bar Joseph opened the service with prayer, reading of the Scriptures, and another prayer. He asked a young lady by the name of Lavona to come up and lead the music. Although Lavona had a heavy accent, her English was well understood by all. The song books were mostly in English, and a few were in Spanish.

Following the worship in music, Pastor Simon got up and delivered a message, telling of the love of God and Jesus Christ for man. He also stressed the love a man should have for his neighbor and the love a man should have for God and Jesus Christ. Following the message, Pastor Simon encouraged any that wanted more information to stay after the service, and he would talk to them.

Following the service, Thomas approached Simon and invited him to come home and have lunch with him, Rachael, Tyler, and Becky Christopher, their adopted daughter. Simon accepted the invitation and accompanied them to their home after the services.

They finished the meal and returned to the living room. Thomas asked Simon, "Would you mind answering some questions I have concerning Jews?"

Simon replied, "I'd be happy to I may not be able to answer them all but I'll do what I can."

Thomas continued, "Since arriving here in Israel, I haven't seen very many Jews. I wonder why not. In the years leading up to the nuclear war and the end time events, there was a lot of teaching and speculation that Israel and the Jews were somehow sacred to God and would be given a special dispensation and miraculously preserved and protected by God."

Simon replied. "The questions you have raised are quite complicated and many faceted. I don't have a clear understanding or a clear answer. I'll explain as much as I can the way I see it. Also, I'm sure if you asked the same questions to others, you would get entirely different answers. Some of the actual events seem paradoxical.

"However, let me be clear. No Jew, since the coming of Jesus Christ, has entered heaven or shall enter heaven, except by the blood and sacrifice of Jesus Christ. Jesus Christ said, I am the way, the truth and the life, no one comes to the father except by me.

"Concerning the 144,000 Jews who were called out of the twelve tribes and supernaturally protected; each and every one of them accepted Jesus Christ as their savior and became born again Christians. They aren't in heaven. Even now, they're walking the earth, witnessing and testifying for Jesus Christ. In fact, I'm one of the 144,000. I'm a Christian of Jewish descent, no more and no less. I was supernaturally protected by God during a special time for a special reason.

"The nation of Israel was reborn on May 14, 1948 as prophesied in the Bible. Millions of Jews from around the world flocked back to the fledgling nation and rebuilt it. The nation has since been supernaturally protected and preserved by God. However, every individual Jew, including the 144,000, was given the opportunity to accept Jesus Christ as their Lord and savior, or reject Him. Those who accepted Him shall go to heaven. Those who rejected Him are dead and shall go to hell. To the best of my knowledge and belief, that's the total dispensation where salvation of individual Jews is concerned.

"Now, where the nation of Israel is concerned, at the present time there are Christian Jews living here in Israel. All the lost Jews who rejected Jesus Christ are dead. There are Jewish children who will have the opportunity to accept or reject Jesus Christ as their Lord and Savior when they reach accountability. Some will, and some won't.

"Where the nation of Israel is concerned the land is still here, from the River of Egypt to the Euphrates. It's occupied by Christian Jews who have been saved since the rapture. It's occupied by Jesus Christ and resurrected Saints He brought down from heaven with him. This condition shall remain until the end of the thousand years.

"The rest of the world is occupied by Christians and their children, plus all the resurrected Saints who are watching over them and guiding them. Their condition will remain until the end of the thousand years.

"People from all over the world will move from continent to continent, restoring the damage that humans have inflicted on the planet for the past six thousand years.

"At the end of the thousand years, satan will be loosed for a season to wreak havoc on the world for a time, and entice many to revolt against God and Jesus Christ, thereby losing their lives and losing their souls to hell.

"At the end of the thousand years, there will be another harvest of the saved, who will be resurrected and transformed and gain their place in eternity and in heaven.

"Some of you will live to see the end of this thousand year age. You will see the New Jerusalem in all its glory as it descends from heaven and hovers over the earth. Beyond that, I'm like you and don't know, for I haven't yet been resurrected and translated into my new body."

"Wow!" Thomas exclaimed. "I've never heard it explained like that. This makes a lot of sense. Looking at humanity as a whole and their interaction with God, it would seem that from humanity, God has gleaned a total harvest of millions of people who will worship and serve Him from now through eternity.

"It would seem that early on, Enoch went to be with Him, and then Elijah. We have the Old Testament Saints, plus the Lord's Church, and then we'll have all those saved through the tribulation and the thousand year reign of Christ.

"The sad part is the billions and billions who rejected God and Jesus Christ and will spend eternity in hell. Many of them were deceived by satan. Most were willingly ignorant of the truth. Most of them rebelled against the very idea of subjecting themselves to God.

"The big question now in everybody's mind; what does the future, and eternity, hold in store for us?"

Simon responded, "Much of it we can't know at this time. However, we know enough already to know it's good."

Rachael had a question, "Simon, can you tell us where Beulah Land is located? There's the song about Beulah Land, and the best I can tell, it must be talking about heaven."

Simon smiled. "The reference to Beulah is found in Isaiah 62:4. If you look at the entire chapter of Isaiah 62, you see a prophecy which is only now being fulfilled.

"Have no doubt, the Land of Israel, from the River of Egypt to the Euphrates River, has a special place in the heart of God. It's a chosen land to hold His chosen people.

"The Land of Israel, as well as the entire world for that matter, has been cleansed of ALL of God's enemies. Twelve years ago the Land Of Israel was populated by hundreds of millions of people. It now contains only thousands. As the decades and centuries come and go, this Land of Israel shall be populated by kings, and priests, and saints, and servants of Jesus Christ, who all serve and worship Jesus Christ, the Lion of Judah, and God, the Father.

"This land, which has a special place in the heart of God, is being transformed even now into the Land of Beulah, the place where God dwells with His people. To sum it up, The Land is Beulah. It's the equivalent of being married. That's the measure of the relationship of God to the land and the people who shall occupy it."

Rachael laughed. "I'm glad I asked the question. This Beulah Land may not exactly be heaven, but it apparently will be very close."

Weeks turned into years as the members of the Mercer family continued to work at the different chores related to the cleansing of the land. They were briefed occasionally by their contacts on the progress of the cleanup in other parts of Israel. Several other settlements had been established similar to theirs, which put those workers in closer proximity to their work sites.

Some of the more significant areas that were being cleaned up had to do with Syria, Iraq, Jordan, and Iran. Following Jerusalem and the surrounding areas of Bethlehem, Mt. of Olives, Golan Heights, etc, the next highest priority was Iraq, with the ruins of Babylon as the first target.

Ancient Babylon and the surrounding nations had worked hard in centuries past to make themselves the number one enemy of God.

Babylon, with its highways, buildings, and traces of mankind, would simply disappear from the face of the earth. There would not be enough left of Babylon to even identify the location. As time went on, other cities, such as Baghdad, Tehran, and Damascus, would also disappear.

Where climate condition permitted, trees and plants would be planted and allowed to spread, reclaiming the earth.

Tim prayed that God would allow him to visit with his family. Cathy was now five years old and, hopefully, would be old enough to meet his family and understand who they were.

The following day, Saint Robert approached Tim at his job site. "Good morning, Tim."

A surprised Tim replied, "Good morning, Saint Robert."

Saint Robert continued, "Tim, God heard your prayer, and I'm here to set up a meeting with your family. I'm arranging a meeting place where you, Pamela, Judah, and Cathy can meet with your entire family in private. This meeting is to be kept secret from everybody, including her family and all your friends. It will be in a location on the side of the Mount of Olives, not far from the Garden of Gethsemane. The meeting will take place this Saturday, on your day off."

Tim replied, "I thank you, Saint Robert. I've been feeling somewhat lonesome for them and I'm looking forward to seeing them again."

"Tim, this time, you'll see more than your mother and your father. You'll also see your brothers, sisters in law, nieces, and nephews. You'll have the entire day to visit with them. You should take food and drinks for you, Pamela, Cathy and Judah. However, don't take anything for your visitors, for they won't need it."

When Saturday morning came, a vehicle came to their door, picked them up, and transported them to the meeting site.

Following the traditional hugging, handshaking, kissing, and greeting, it was quite a reunion as they all visited, talked and exchanged information. John got Tim and Pamela's attention and reminded them, "Keep in mind, we can all read your thoughts. However, to avoid any confusion, ask all of your questions, and make all of your comments and answers out loud. Following that, we will answer your questions."

John laughed, "If reading your minds is an embarrassment to you, we just can't help it."

Tim replied. "Don't worry. I have no problem with that."

Pamela responded, "That's fine with me, also."

Ellen spoke up, "Tim, at first we were sorry that you weren't taken up when we were, but we almost immediately knew you were alright."

Tim replied. "I'm not sorry; for I would have missed marrying my wonderful wife, Pamela, and having two beautiful children like Cathy and Judah." Tim continued, "Somehow, you all look different. There's a radiance, calmness, and peace emanating from you that you never had before. It leaves me with a feeling of comfort and peace as well."

Mark replied, "Tim, since I'm closer to your age, I may be able to explain it better. We had cares and concerns, worries, nagging feelings, and all those sensations associated with our own minds. They aren't there anymore. All cares, concerns, and worries are past."

Tim replied, "I can see how that would make a difference." Tim asked, "Where do you stay all the time?"

Bob answered, "Tim, that question has an answer that is hard to understand unless you're in our shoes. The answer is, we stay where we are at any given time. We think our way to where we wish to be. For example, I thought of myself being here, and I'm here. I can think of myself in heaven, and I'll be in heaven. I can think of myself in China at my job site, and I'm there. When my job is over for the day, I may remain right there until the next day, unless there's something else I wish to see or do. I could go back and spend the night in heaven if I wanted to." Bob continued, "I hope I haven't confused you."

"No," Tim replied, "I think I understand. As humans on earth, we're connected by sight and sound. In your state, you're connected by spirit, mind and thought. To be together here on earth, our bodies must assemble. To be together in your state, your spirit thoughts and minds assemble."

Bob answered, "I think you have a good understanding of it. We're perpetually assembled as a family, although I'm working in China and dad is working in South America."

Pamela asked Kathy, "Kathy, what do you do in your role as a Saint?"

Kathy replied, "I sometime work with Mark, and I sometime work alone. I may work with others, depending on the need. This business of being one of God's Saints is unbelievably rewarding. In addition to the work I do, I've been able to visit the moon, Mars, and so many other places on earth and in the universe."

Kathy continued, "There's much I'm not allowed to tell you. You'll just have to wait and experience it yourself."

Tim spoke up. "There are times I wonder and worry about Trixie."

Jesse laughed and responded. "Don't worry about Trixie. She's being fed and pampered and she, also, just had another litter of pups."

Tim replied, "I figured Trixie would be too old to be having pups by now."

Jesse replied, "In the world you're living in now, I'm not too sure how much Trixie might be aging. She may continue having pups for a long time."

John spoke up. "Tim, we recently looked in on the

Mercers in Richmond. They're all doing quite well. You'll be surprised at all the progress that has taken place in that area. Also, don't be surprised if you see a population growth at the Mercer farms."

"Can you tell us who?" asked Pamela.

"I'm afraid not." John laughed and replied, "That would be cheating on my part."

When mid-afternoon came, the vehicle arrived to take Tim and his family back to their home. They all said their goodbyes. Tim's family stayed in place until the vehicle went out of sight. John, Ellen, and their gathering, faded from sight.

CHAPTER XVI
RETURN TO RICHMOND

16 of the 22 people who traveled from Richmond to Israel packed up their few belongings and prepared to return to the United States and Richmond, Kentucky. In addition, they were taking back a few extra babies.

Two young men and two young women who were single at the time they went to Israel, decided to marry Jewish Christians and stay in Israel with their spouses. They didn't have any close family in Richmond to draw them back. The four had already left the settlement and moved to a permanent location where they would live, work, and serve the Lord.

Tim and Pamela now had the two children. Cathy was five and Judah just had his second birthday. Rachael and Thomas had two children also, a four year old boy and a two year old girl. Barbara and Herbert had two children, a three year old boy and a one year old girl.

In their original group from Richmond, there had also been four other children born. With all their children, the number of their group was now 26.

All the adults had some misgivings about leaving. Although they hadn't been paid wages while they were there, every need had been provided for. Everything had been plentiful in the way of food, clothing and shelter. Transportation to recreation, sightseeing, and other events were also provided. There were no needs that were't met. Clothing was plentiful, although simply made.

If there were wants that people desired and didn't have, they weren't voiced. Although they had led lives with much work, they had led peaceful and pleasant lives.

As Tim and Pamela packed and prepared for their departure, they reminisced.

Pamela remarked, "Tim, in a way, I'm really going to miss this place. We haven't had a worry or a care in the world about what we would eat, or what we would wear, or illness, or anything else. I really hadn't given much thought to it until I started thinking about what we'll be facing back in Richmond."

Tim replied, "That reminds me of what Jesus had to say about our worries and our cares. In Matthew, chapter 10:29-31, Jesus told about how valueless the sparrows are, but God even knows when one of them falls to the ground. Jesus said that if God cared that much for the sparrows, how much more He cared for us. We certainly haven't wanted for anything."

Pamela continued, "I've made a lot of friends here in the settlement and in the school. I'm really going to miss their fellowship. Also, working with the children was such a blessing. When we get back to Richmond, I'm going to see If I can get a job in the school."

Tim replied, "Pamela, I'm sure that God will watch over us even when we're back in Richmond." He continued. "I met a lot of interesting people here in the settlement and also on the job. I can remember when I was a teen in school. Overall, the people I'm meeting and working with now, seem to be much nicer and easier to like and trust."

The next morning, they loaded up in the buses and went back to Haifa where they boarded the ship.

The trip back to Richmond was uneventful, except for three rough days as they were crossing the ocean. During the voyage, they could tell by observation that there was more ocean traffic now than when they came over. However, it was still quite sparse compared to the past.

They didn't see any aircraft the entire trip. They could assume that if there was any air travel, it couldn't be much.

When they got to the port in Charlotte, North Carolina, they disembarked and were met by an entourage of wagons, horses, and buggies that were driven by many of their families and friends. There was quite a reunion right there on the docks.

Saint Robert and James led the group that was there to welcome them home and transport them to Richmond.

James brought David, Tiffany, and Ron, as well as Kayla and Allen Sherman, to help with the driving, cooking, and camping chores. He actually had to bring an extra vehicle in order to bring them all. However, this was a rare opportunity for him to reward them all for their help and diligence back on the farms.

Bradley Stout, the adopted son of Alvin and Rhonda, and Becky Christopher, the adopted daughter of Thomas and Rachael, were absolutely thrilled when they met up with Tiffany, Ron, Kayla and Allen. In the four years they had been gone, quite a bit of growing had taken place. Several were now very close to adulthood. For the older members of their group, watching the interaction between the younger generation gave them mixed feelings of pleasure and trepidation.

Seeing this take place, James was doubly glad that he had brought all their group with him.

Unloading their belongings from the ship and getting them loaded for travel took about an hour and a half. Before leaving, James made all the assignments for drivers, assistant drivers, wood gatherers for cooking, and all the other chores anticipated along the way.

James walked down the line of wagons and buggies checking to make sure nothing was being overlooked. He then went back to the front, climbed into the lead buggy, and headed down the road, which ran northeast. The young people had been spread out somewhat throughout the caravan, but still were able to make quite a bit of noise as they left out. The exuberance was catching, and all the adults were in high spirits. The horses didn't seem to mind.

James remarked to Saint Robert, "Wait until about seven or eight days from now and see how it goes. Hopefully, we'll still have the same enthusiasm."

"We'll see," replied Saint Robert.

Following two thunderstorms, a broken wheel, for which they had a spare, and other minor events, the caravan arrived in Richmond. All the people in the entire area turned out to greet them. It became quite a celebration.

The greeters had prepared food and drinks, and the event turned into a glorified picnic. The mayor and his council were there. The sheriff and his deputy were there. The new pastor was there.

Paula hadn't come. She was occupied with keeping things

together at the farms. They had one mare that was ready to foal and didn't need to be left alone.

Following an official greeting from the mayor, which included giving Alvin the keys to the city, the caravan disbanded, and everybody headed for their respective homes.

Tim and Pamela, with Cathy and Judah, rode out to the farm in the buggy with James. They pulled up in front of their former home, and before they even had a chance to get out of the buggy, Trixie came bounding toward them, barking and whining. Tim jumped down and gave Trixie a big hug. Amazed, he exclaimed. "Trixie hasn't changed a bit. I was expecting to see an old dog but she doesn't look a day older!"

James replied, "We've noticed that about other animals. They don't seem to be getting any older. We've noticed the same thing about people as well. Children seem to be maturing normally, but once they're grown, the aging seems to slow down."

"What about our honeybee farm?" Pamela asked.

James replied, "The bees are doing great. We've been able to increase the number of hives. We've sold or bartered off a few, and we moved some over on the farm with Barbara's parents. We still have twelve hives here."

Paula had come out of the house and greeted Tim, Pamela, and their two children.

James asked her about the mare.

Paula replied, "She foaled about two hours ago, and it seems we have a healthy baby mare."

Tim asked, "Where are Tiffany and Ron?"

Paula replied, "Tiffany and Ron are still in town and should be back soon. Tiffany has a boy friend who has been courting her quite steady. They may have already told you that David got married a year ago to a girl by the name of Brenda Cutterfield. Her parents live on a farm close to where Barbara's parents live. He met her in church. They're living in a house they built on her parent's farm."

It took several days for everybody to settle back into some semblance of a routine. There was quite a bit of interest among the people in Richmond about the adventures their missionaries had encountered. A community meeting was held a week after they returned so all the travelers who were willing could get up and relate some of their work, their adventures, their sightseeing, and their overall perspective of the entire episode.

Rhonda got up and related the Mercer's adventurous trip to Bethany, Mount of Olives, Gesthemene, Jericho, Jordan River and the Dead Sea. The place got very quiet as she spoke.

Pamela followed Rhonda with a tale of her experiences in the pre-school, working with her friends and associates. Some of them were Israeli born, and getting to interact with people from other lands and learn about their culture was fascinating. She also told about the work with children in the pre-school, and with themselves, in converting over to the new language.

Saint Robert followed up with information on the work in Lebanon where they were re-foresting with seedlings of the original cedars of Lebanon. In addition to the restoration of the cedar forests, he told them of the cleanup work in places such as Jerusalem, Beirut, Damascus, Tehran, Baghdad, and Babylon. He indicated that once these locations were cleansed and cleared to the bare rock and earth, they would be seared with intense flame and heat for further cleansing and sterilizing.

Saint Robert went on to say as an afterthought, "Much of the world has been greatly abused over the past 6,000 years. It will take centuries to cleanse, heal, and restore the earth."

As a result of the individual testimonies of the travelers, quite a few people showed interest in making a pilgrimage to some foreign country to work for a few years. Saint Robert spoke to them and let them know he would begin working on it, and hopefully, they could send out another group very soon.

Saint Robert went to Mayor Braddock and arranged for a general meeting of all the people in the area. The meeting would be used to bring everybody up to date on all the changes that were taking place and the progress that had been made up to now. Since their people from Israel were now back in the area, this would be a good time for everybody to be brought up to date. They would soon be coming up on the sixth anniversary of the first day of the millennium.

Three days later, the meeting was held. Saint Robert addressed the assembly and informed them of what had taken place and would be taking place in their community as well as around the world. At the end of the meeting, they would be given a copy of a bulletin which listed the major topics and a brief explanation. They could give this to any of their friends or neighbors who missed the meeting.

Saint Robert told them, "We're close to six years into the millennium, and here are some of the major changes and accomplishments.

"The corrected Bible has been introduced and is now

in every settlement and community in the world. This was completed almost four years ago.

"The new language has been introduced and is being used almost exclusively here in the Richmond area as well as in all the other settlements and communities around the world. Although there's still some use of other languages, it's being discouraged and will disappear within one generation." He smiled. "I have been asked the name of the language. The answer is it doesn't have one.

"Schools have been established in every community and settlement in the world. Teachers are teaching the truth. The love of God and salvation through Jesus Christ is being taught in every school. The teacher prays to God at the beginning of each class.

"A form of civics is being taught in every school. The universal form of government worldwide is very simple. Jesus Christ is King of Kings and Lord of Lords. He rules with the twenty-four elders and His multitude of Saints. A Saint judges and rules each community or settlement. Local leaders, such as mayor and sheriff, are recommended through election by the people. The Saint endorses the election or asks for another recommendation from the community.

"The form of government will change as time passes. When population increases require it, nations will be formed. This will not occur for decades or centuries. The rules shall not change. Although there will be some resistance to the government that has been established, Jesus Christ shall rule His world with love and with a rod of iron.

"There shall be no poverty. There shall be no rich. All people will have ample necessities of life. All who are capable of work shall work. The words "rich" and "poor" are no longer needed in the vocabulary.

"There are those who will be satisfied with the minimum necessities and will produce at a minimum level. They shall be rewarded at the minimum level. If they have assumed the responsibilities of a family, they shall be required to support that family responsibility at an adequate level. To those who would think otherwise, take heed. Any person who does not intend to perform at the level to provide adequately for a family, mustn't take a spouse. It could cause you great grief.

"There are those with more initiative who will produce at a much higher level and accept greater responsibilities. They shall be rewarded at a higher level.

"This work ethic applies to Christians and non-Christians equally. Christians, who are resurrected and spend eternity with God, and Jesus Christ, shall be rewarded eternally for their work."

At the end, Saint Thomas delivered an ominous warning, "There shall be those who resist the rule and authority of Jesus Christ. I caution you now, do so at your own peril. Take heed. You shall not prevail."

Saint Thomas concluded: "Activities will increase as population increases allow. The earth is being reclaimed and shall be returned closer to the purity it was when created. Though it will take centuries, it shall be done."

Saint Robert completed his speech and faded from sight.

The people left the auditorium, picking up copies of the bulletin on the way out. Another group started in as they left.

The Mercer clan quickly settled back into their homes in the Richmond area and into some semblance of a routine. In the time they had been gone, there had been some changes made in the social and organizational structure. Saint Robert Rayburn had been spending more time at Richmond working with the mayor and his council.

In the old way of life on earth, every individual could essentially do as they pleased as long as they didn't get caught breaking the laws. This was no longer true. Indirectly, every living soul in the Richmond area came under the rule and oversight of Saint Robert Rayburn.

The oversight structure was loose-knit and flexible. However, every person in the entire area was accountable to someone, who indirectly was accountable to Saint Robert Rayburn.

The Mayor still had his council, whose duties had evolved from making rules and establishing guidelines for the people, to co-ordination of communications.

All authority lay in the hands of Saint Robert. This was communicated to twenty-four others, who were, in turn, overseeing others, who were, in turn, overseeing others. Much of it extended down family lines. The rest of it was an intricate weaving of oversight to make it solid and complete.

For example, Alvin Mercer and James Mercer were two who were responsible to Saint Robert through the Mayor. Each of their extended families, including spouses and children, came under their jurisdiction. In addition, each of them was responsible for other families and other individuals in the area. This didn't mean they had to know the whereabouts and conduct of each person, but would follow up on individuals if incidents occurred.

The sheriff reported to the Mayor. He and his deputies were primarily responsible for looking into accidents, incidents, disagreements, etc. that needed to be dealt with.

They still had the jail which would be used for temporary restraint when needed, but the arbitration and settlement went immediately to the individual's overseer who either resolved the problem, or sent it up through the Mayor to Saint Robert for final resolution. Resolution would seldom include jail time and never include prison time. There were no prisons.

Saint Robert Rayburn called a special meeting for his leadership team which included the Mayor, the Sheriff, the pastor, and the twelve men he had selected as overseers. This included James and Alvin Mercer, and Thomas Daley.

Saint Robert spoke, "I'm giving this group an insight into what you may expect in the years and decades ahead. I'll reveal much of this to the general population as events and circumstances evolve.

"Much of what shall be done and much of what shall be allowed is predicated on the specific length of time remaining, which is one thousand years. Following that, there shall be no more time as you know it. At that time there shall be a major shift in circumstances which I'm not allowed to divulge, except what has already been divulged in the Scriptures.

"On day one of this present age, the only people remaining were Christians who were born again after the rapture, and children who were too young to be held accountable. All other living people died at the time of Armageddon. At the present time now, six years later, we have that same group of survivors plus children who have been born since then.

"Many of the children are now adults and accountable to God for their actions, their sins, and their decisions. Some have been born again and are now Christians, but many of them are not. As the years pass, many more children will be born. They will mature into adults, and they will also be faced with the choice of becoming a Christian or not becoming a Christian.

"At the present time, the population of the earth is still in the survive and maintain mode. Meanwhile, Jesus Christ and His saints are working toward the cleanup and restoration of the earth, beginning with Jerusalem and the land of Israel. In the decades which follow, this work will accelerate and expand to other parts of the world as the population increases.

"Many shall be given the opportunity to travel to other parts of the world and work. Those who wish may stay in their own areas and do the work there.

"During the thousand years, modern technology shall never return to its former state. The only technology to be restored will be that which facilitates the restoration of the earth.

"For example, some forms of motorized transportation, heavy equipment for earth work, and equipment of that nature, will be restored. Fuel to operate them will also be produced. Some communication shall be restored to facilitate the work effort. Other communication will be allowed to inform and educate the people around the world. Uncontrolled communication for entertainment and personal indulgence shall not be allowed.

"Life upon the earth is a serious matter. Living that life in a responsible way can be pleasurable and satisfying. Reasonable activities for entertainment and pleasure will be allowed. Unreasonable and extreme activities for self gratification, which is harmful to the mind and soul, shall not be allowed.

"God offers a safe, secure, and rewarding life here on earth, with an unimaginable future in eternity for those who would seek after Him and obey Him. However, each person still has the free will to accept Him or reject Him. There's a multitude that will still reject God's offer of grace.

"At this time, I shall give a word of warning to those who would reject His offer. In the 1,000 year reign of Jesus Christ upon the earth, you do not have free will to do as you please in all other matters. Jesus Christ said He would rule with a rod of iron, and He shall do so. Disobey His rule at your own risk."

Saint Robert continued, "As you are well aware, manpower in the world is extremely limited. This is especially true here in the United States. The bulk of the work to be done will have to wait for population growth.

"Within the United States, there are pockets of people scattered from one end to the other. They are small pockets. None, by themselves, are able to produce an effective work force except for local use.

"One of the more immediate goals, in parts of this continent as well as in other parts of the world, is to establish rail travel. It will be the most effective, the most economical, and the most easily achieved in the short term. This will facilitate the work that is being done by transporting equipment, fuel and other needed supplies.

"There will be some forms of gasoline transportation made available as well. They will be primarily used for local business. Automobiles for recreational use shall not be allowed in the first few decades or centuries, if ever. Fuel use shall be rationed and closely monitored. Inter connecting and interstate roadways are a low priority. Many of them shall never be reopened.

"Keep in mind, the population of the earth is less than one percent of what it was before the nuclear world war. That doesn't leave many people for the size of this planet. As you can see, it may take up to 200 years to establish an effective rail system worldwide.

"Now, I would like to address you on the most critical matter you will encounter in the years ahead. As the leadership in this area, it will be your responsibility to deal with and manage rebellion at the human level. Beyond a certain point, we, the Saints, shall intervene and resolve the problem.

"Children are growing and maturing. Marriages are taking place and families are being established. The population is increasing.

"Even now, at this early date, there are Christians and non-Christians who are feeling resentful toward the restrictions placed upon their freedoms. As the years and decades go by, this resentment will grow and break out from time to time in open rebellion, which shall be immediately judged and punished. Open rebellion shall not be allowed again until satan is loosed for a season at the end of the thousand years.

"Although satan is no longer able to whisper in your ear to tempt and cause trouble, human nature and free will are still factors that will help create unacceptable behavior. This will lead to action by some that will have to be judged and punished."

Saint Robert smiled. "You have all laid aside your

firearms, and rightfully so. Don't take them up again to meet the challenge. You shall be supernaturally protected as you serve, and obey the Lord.

"Beloved brethren in Christ, I leave you now. I will be back from time to time as our work for the Lord continues."

Saint Robert faded from sight.

EPILOGUE

Not one enemy of God was left alive. Every accountable human being on earth, who hadn't accepted Jesus Christ and worshipped God, was dead.

They died at the time of Armageddon. They died a supernatural death delivered by Almighty God and his Son, Jesus Christ.

The anti-Christ and the false prophet are in the lake of fire, where they will burn forever. Satan is bound and imprisoned in the bottomless pit where he will remain for a thousand years.

Jesus Christ is on the earth with His church Saints, Godly people of Old Testament times, and the restored Christians who were martyred during the tribulation. They will rule with Him as He rules the people and nations of the earth with a rod of iron.

Millions of the Tribulation Saints are also on earth, having accepted Jesus Christ as savior after the rapture, and before Armageddon. Christians and their children, who passed through the time of Armageddon and entered the millennium, will re-populate the earth, re-form into nations, and do the bidding of Jesus Christ as they live out their lives.

Life on earth for humans, Christian and non-Christian, shall be significantly less than a Utopia. Humans, Christian and non-Christian, with their inherited sinful nature, will resist the restraints upon their free will.

Before the millennium, man's laws and man's justice attempted to restrain the lawless. During the millennium, God's law and God's justice shall restrain the lawless, as Jesus Christ rules with a rod of iron.

Another harvest will be garnered for God's Kingdom. Hundreds of millions will accept Jesus Christ as savior, be born again, and serve and worship God and Jesus Christ here on earth. They will later be resurrected and will perform services in the hereafter that our finite minds can't even imagine. It will be a wonderful and glorious experience!

Another harvest shall be wasted. Hundreds of millions will reject Jesus Christ as savior. They will die, and lie in the grave until they are resurrected, judged, and thrown into hell.

Scars upon the earth will heal. Radiation will abate. Seeds from trees will sprout next to highways and their roots and growth will break up the asphalt and concrete.

Will the satellites again be launched? Will the internet with Facebook, e-mail, twitter, blogs, web pages, etc. etc. be reborn? Will the airwaves be filled again with television signals with all its mind and soul-deadening clamor? Will we have automobiles humming up and down the highways again? Will the trains run as before? Will the airplanes leave their contrails across the skies, as before? Will Hollywood be reborn or remain a deep hole in the ground? **GUESS!**

What does the future hold in store for Tim and Pamela Bailey, and their children?

Printed in the United States
By Bookmasters